CW00858934

Best Wishes
Matildawren x

WHEN RAVENS FALL

By Matilda Wren

authorHOUSE®

AuthorHouse™
1663 Liberty Drive
Bloomington, IN 47403
www.authorhouse.com
Phone: 1-800-839-8640

Published by AuthorHouse 7/18/2012

ISBN: 978-1-4685-8577-3 (sc)
ISBN: 978-1-4685-8576-6 (e)

The Initiation
The Beginning of the End

"Now this is not the end. It is not even the beginning of the end. But it is, perhaps, the end of the beginning."

Sir Winston Churchill 1942

In the morning
of the day
BeeGees

Chapter 1

December 1997

Peeing on a stick is not as easy as it sounds. Women cannot aim, so it requires skill and one cannot rely on the fact that the body will release a gentle stream. In fact, when the act of peeing on a stick is required, inevitably, your body will let you down and the gentle stream becomes a gushing waterfall.

Not only do you completely miss the object you are trying to pee on, but also you manage to pee on everything else but. Without doubt, your hand will get drenched along with the toilet seat, the floor and anything else in the immediate vicinity.

You then need to start the process all over again, after of course, consuming large amounts of liquid so you can pee again.

If by miraculous chance (*and most of it will be by sheer luck*) you do actually manage to hit the target so to speak, the three minutes it takes to get the result will be the longest three minutes of your life. It will feel more like three hours than the hundred and eighty seconds it actually takes.

Waiting for that blue line to appear was probably one of the most terrifying three minutes of Rachel Marsden's life. This was not something she had expected to undertake four months after her eighteenth birthday.

Three days previously, she did not have a care in the world; her main concern being she had enough weed to smoke that week and she had obtained enough amphetamines to take with her to whatever rave she would be attending with her boyfriend, James Porter.

Pregnancy, babies and responsibility had not been at the forefront of her mind, but here she was seventy-two hours later sitting in her boyfriend's parent's bathroom, with her knickers round her knees, on the toilet, peeing on a stick and silently praying to god that the blue line that was going to appear was a vertical one and not a horizontal one.

Even then, she was striking. Dark flaxen corkscrew curls fell around her face; the mismatched lengths framing her curved profile, finally resting in a bouncy mound on her shoulders, home-coloured highlights dazzling under the spectacular lighting of the bathroom.

A parted fringe plunged like disused springs over her teardrop shaped eyes that were the deepest darkest brown, swirling like melted chocolate and encased with long black eyelashes that only required the bare minimum of make-up to accentuate their natural beauty.

Her creamy, light complexion exposed the youth she bore, presenting a false innocence, but it was those huge gemstone eyes that told anyone that looked into them that they held a veil of concealed secrets.

The same unconscious defences were portrayed through her style as well, preferring to mask her hour-glass figure in baggy jeans and sweatshirts, giving her a curvier outline than that which she really possessed.

The bathroom was one of three, which had always amazed her. Having three bathrooms in one house was just ridiculous. James' house presented a huge four bedroom, double garage, detached property in Blackmore.

The Porter's believed they were a middle class nuclear family; living in an idealic world where their son didn't take drugs, talked to them about what was going on in his life and their only major concern was where they would holiday that summer or winter.

If they knew what was happening at this very second in their plush bathroom they would have died of absolute pure shame. Rachel, not particularly welcomed by either Mr or Mrs Porter, smirked slightly at the metal image of them slowly melting into the floor, much like the wicked witch in the film The Wizard of Oz, as the disgrace and disrepute engulfed them.

James' parents had money; lots of it. She had never really been friends with anybody that had money before. They were a different sort of people. They had atypical thought processes and carried a persona about them that would make Rachel feel inadequate and not up to standard.

It's not that they had ever said anything out right as such; it was little things like his mother prompting her to use a coaster with her drink or suggesting she may like to get changed for dinner. That and the fact they were both religious nut jobs who were devoted followers of the Evangelical Church.

Being in the lavish bathroom with its large, oval, roll top bath that had old fashioned gold taps with the heads of cherubs as knobs; which took pride of place in the middle of the floor, made her feel paltry and incompetent. The separate shower that stood over in one corner had no surround but a plug hole in the black tiled floor. She stared at it, almost wishing herself to be sucked down it. Anything to prevent her from having to deal with what was happening.

The whole place seemed to be mocking her; jeering at her flaws. The tiny gold and silver mosaic tiles that covered the entire bathroom walls gave an air of superiority over her. She didn't belong here.

Rachel looked at James. He looked just as scared and apprehensive as she did. He was only a year older than her and was at the beginning of a three year apprenticeship four hundred miles away. This was not something he had expected to have to deal with on his first break home and in the midst of a comedown too.

James was what Rachel called a 'pretty boy'. He had the model appearance about him and a wardrobe to match; his chiselled features and brooding scowl were the epitome of every teenage girl's desire. All but hers it would seem.

The soulful blue eyes and sandy blonde hair that was chopped and spiked gave away the young skateboarder he had not fully let go of; the underdog kid, from the right side of the tracks that had crossed over to the bad and popular.

Caught between being charming and a nerd, a hermit and confident but more happy playing the role of an introvert; an observer who likes to watch people and try to figure out who they really are, as opposed to who they think they are.

The subdued, calm presence he characterised made him seem meagre and feeble, obscuring the hostility and antagonism that built up inside of him daily.

They had only been together for a short while, about nine months and the last three of those nine months, he had been in Liverpool, living away from home for the first time.

This was not where he wanted to be and he too was

secretly praying. Numerous thoughts were running through his head.

How could this have happened? Rachel was on the pill. Her mood swings were volatile, which was a side effect of this particular contraception, so James knew she had been taking it. Whether or not she had been taking it properly was a different matter of course.

There were bound to have been times she had forgotten to take it, but would the occasional lapse result in a baby? *Surely not?* Couples have to try for months to have a baby after coming off the pill, sometimes years. His brother and his girlfriend had been trying for a couple of years and still nothing had happened, so why was he now sitting in the bathroom with his future being determined by a thin blue line?

Rachel herself was thinking other thoughts. She knew she had not exactly been taking the pill correctly. She knew that it was probably more than just an occasional lapse and adding the narcotic use into the mix, the pill was no doubt completely ineffective. These thoughts, of course, she was going to keep to herself.

Having recently been sacked from her job because she constantly turned up late or was completely useless due to self inflicted sickness and moving out of yet another foster home because her foster mum was more worried about the effect her behaviour was having on the younger children than the fact she was a frequent drug user, meant that she did not have an exactly stable life. She never had.

The damp bedsit in Shenfield that reeked of stale fish and chips and vinegar, which social services had dumped her in, was probably the size of James entire bathroom. Although she was eighteen, she was still a subject of a care order which meant that, until a judge said otherwise, social services were responsible for her well being.

She had been signing on the dole once a week since she lost her job. This enabled her to receive £80 once a fortnight, as well as what she received from being attached to the care order and if she was completely honest, this way of life suited her down to the ground.

As long as she could afford her daily fix of weed, nothing else concerned her. She would quite happily go without necessities such as food, electric and heating; so long as she could smoke a joint, she could face the world, or so she thought.

She would frequently turn up at her grandparent's house for a hot meal and a shower, so the necessities that most people could not live without were not as important to Rachel.

The very fact that she was over two weeks late with her period had not concerned her. This was not out of the ordinary. She did not eat properly, participated in drug use and did not take the pill correctly, so her periods were often messed up. It had always arrived at some point.

James had bought the pregnancy kit. He insisted that they find out one way or another. He had wanted to do it before they had gone raving three days previously but Rachel refused point blank; she would not even entertain the idea. That would have meant it could interfere with her going out, getting completely off her head and dancing the night away.

If it were not for James insisting, Rachel probably would have left it for several more days, even weeks before finding out.

So here they were, intently staring at the white stick with two little windows in the middle, waiting to see which one would decide their fate. Sure enough a hundred and eighty seconds later a watery, pale blue, horizontal line appeared in the pregnant window. Rachel felt her world crumble down around her.

The panic started in the pit of her stomach. It begun with a dull ache and very quickly rose to her heart. She felt like she could not breathe. Something was pressing down heavily on her chest and everything suddenly intensified.

She could hear her heart beat. It was so loud that she began to think James' parents, who were sitting downstairs watching television, would be able to hear it. Her eyes did not move away from the stick.

That awful white stick that was the bearer of such terrible, terrible news. She threw it onto the floor in front of her. Leaping off the toilet and pulling her knickers back up haphazardly, she walked into the bedroom.

Compared to the rest of the house, his bedroom was actually quite small. The walls and ceiling were a brilliant white which gave the room a false sense of it being bigger than it really was. To the right of the doorway a fitted wardrobe extended along the side of the wall, where his clothes hung neatly in coordinating colours, starched and ironed; seamed nylons perfectly straight.

The whole room was obsessively neat and organised, matching the rest of the house. James' mum was a cleaning freak who polished and vacuumed the entire house every day. It was only her and James' dad there now; how they could possibly make the house that dirty Rachel did not understand.

She felt cramped and confined. The clinical and unemotional decor of the room suddenly felt alien to her and the translucent emptiness that resided in the rest of the house was forcing its way in. A Chelsea Football Club rug, which lay in the small space available between the wardrobes and his bed, was the only thing that gave a hint that the room did indeed belong to a nineteen year old lad.

Rachel held onto the desk in front of her for support. She thought that her legs were going to give way on her. Then the tears came; huge salty tears that ran down her face.

James followed her into the room. He hesitated behind her, wanting to put his arms around her and hold her but scared of her reaction if he did. Sometimes, she looked at him like she really hated him; it wasn't just looks either.

There would be the snide comments, the put downs, the emotional blackmail and then just to confuse and baffle him she would switch to loving and clingy. This would be the time she wanted sex constantly.

It was never affectionate tender sex; it would be frenzied possessed sex that *she* was in complete control of. She totally wore him out both physically and mentally. Sometimes he felt like she was punishing him for something.

Her mood swings could be so volatile that he never knew where he was with her. She had been his first everything. First love, first proper kiss, first sexual experience, and the girl he lost his virginity to. To *her,* he was nothing but the rebound guy. He knew that, he knew it as soon as she befriended him.

Essex was a pond but Brentwood was a puddle. He also knew he was playing with fire just by being with her, considering who the guy was that he was replacing, but he couldn't resist her. She was slightly dangerous and unhinged. She was too alluring, even when she rebuked him for not being what she really wanted

But the resentment of being made to feel guilty for having a good life, a decent childhood and parents that made sure every opportunity was open to him, fed the hostility and antagonism he was already harbouring. Turning away from her he slumped down onto his bed.

The sobs were violent and painful. They caught in her throat. The reaction took her completely by surprise. The result took her completely by surprise. The decision she made in the next twenty seconds took her completely by surprise.

Rachel truly believed James did not want the baby. That actually did not bother her at all. He was never going to be the love of her life. He was the 'time being' guy; the one that just happened to be there, when she had walked away from Sean.

James was supposed to make her forget him. He hadn't. But a baby just might be what she needed to get over him. A baby was time consuming and life changing. It would occupy her mind and her heart and she very desperately needed that.

It had only been a short while since she had ended things with Sean. She knew it would take time to make her heart stop missing him. James had been a distraction but he wasn't the cure. It had been fun over the last year but there hadn't been a day when Sean hadn't entered her head.

James had not stopped that, the drugs had not stopped that and her life had to change. She had to sort herself out.

She looked over at James; he wore a face of sheer terror. His head was in his hands. She realised that she felt no empathy for him. In fact she didn't really care about him at all. Rachel wiped her face with her hands.

He hadn't come to her when she was sobbing. He just sat on the end of his bed. He was a weak person and this annoyed her more than anything.

He had no backbone. No spirit about him. He was just sitting there, saying nothing. She felt a sudden urge to punch him straight in the face. She suppressed this of course, making a conscious effort to relax.

Instead, she got her coat and scarf that were hanging on the bedroom door. She put them on and turned to face him once more.

"It's ok, I'll sort it."

"What does that mean?" He sounded so pathetic and pitiable.

The urge to slap him rose again. She felt guilty and lifeless at the same time. The sigh was louder and implied more impatience than she had intended.

"I mean I will deal with it. You don't need to do anything James. I don't need you. I can sort this out myself." Closing her eyes she tried to regain some lenience and forbearance towards the boy sitting on the bed.

It wasn't really his fault that he had not lived up to her expectations; that he had not managed to accomplish the unaccomplishable. She knew he had tried but he was never going to succeed. James was never going to be *him* for her.

"What are you going to do? I… I don't…" He looked disorientated; his voice low and bewildered.

Chewing her bottom lip, she smiled at him sadly. He was quite good looking; even in his dishevelled state. She briefly thought about the utter shame of it all. If James was someone else she secretly would be over the moon. But he wasn't and she needed to stop pretending he could be.

"I am going to get rid James. I am eighteen. I don't need or want any of this."

James half nodded and watched her walk out. He heard the front door close a few seconds later. Then he cried. He knew she was letting him go. He had served a purpose and now it was over; or more accurately, he hadn't served the purpose.

Rachel walked along James' road. It was more of a lane than a road and coordinated adeptly with the house she had just walked out of. On one side, it was lined with big detached properties all sporting long or wide driveways, double garages and a couple of brand spanking new Range Rovers.

The other side of the lane gave view to a far reaching lowland landscape. Fields that stretched out further than the eye could see. The tessellated parallelograms separated by hedgerow and trees.

Making her way slowly down the neat cared-for lane, towards the busy A414 that it led out onto and the petrol station that was situated on the junction to call a taxi, it dawned on her that she would probably never walk this path again.

She had no intentions of ever having to see James Porter or his parents once more, if ever. The calmness she felt stunned her. She had experienced such a range of emotions in the space of about an hour. In that hour she had also made a decision that was going to affect the rest of her life; all because she couldn't get over a boy.

James went back to Liverpool believing that Rachel had an abortion and expecting to never see her again. For Rachel, the consequences of her decision to keep her baby would come much sooner and in a way she could never have imagined. She had no idea that by trying to protect her heart, her actions and decisions would result in what was to come.

Chapter 2

February 2001

The old dilapidated warehouse had a distinctive odour of rats and rusty nails. It filled the room as soon as you stepped in, its barrenness held an eerie feeling of despair. Once used as a slaughterhouse, until the Foot and Mouth epidemic swept across the country, environmental health officers had made a spot check inspection in Barking and closed it down due the unsanitary conditions the animals were being slaughtered in.

A drainage system criss-crossed the uneven concrete surface leading to the centre point of the warehouse. Above this, a hose pipe on the ceiling, that was formerly used to wash away the blood and guts from the butchery hung from a conduit.

Sean Fergus looked down at the man that was crumpled on the dented floor. Both his legs were broken, as were his arms. His face was a bloody mess and at some point during his beating he had soiled himself. Sean felt disgust and anger, nothing else. The two emotions were what he experienced daily.

It felt completely normal to him and in Sean's eyes the man lying before him deserved it; he had mugged him off. Translated, this meant that the man had used the services of one of Sean's girls and thought he didn't need to pay. This had offended Sean greatly.

He was shocked that someone felt brave enough to take the piss out of him like that; as if he was nobody. The handsome face was screwed up like a twisted wolf, as he let the anger and sheer annoyance loose. His near six foot frame, significantly well-built, yet defined and toned, expressed the power and dominance he held.

At twenty-one, Sean believed he had accomplished a great deal. He was known to some of the larger faces of Essex and London, due to his sheer enjoyment of violence. He was useful to them as an enforcer and from time to time, Sean would take on the more nasty jobs for them. The sort of jobs that they themselves didn't want to do yet had to be done.

He would dish out the beatings to people who owed money and didn't pay up when he arrived to collect. He would find those who went into hiding to avoid the people who hired his services. It was a lucrative job for Sean and it put his name on the map. That is, it put his name on the criminal underworld map.

He had come a long way in a very short space of time, starting off as a 'runner' for a small time drug dealer. He would pick up drugs from one address, pass them onto another address, collect the money and take it back to his dealer. It was easy money, and at seventeen it suited Sean down to the ground.

The longer he did it the more he realised just how much money his man was making and he wanted a slice of that pie. He resented handing over a big wad of cash only to receive a small portion back himself, especially when he was the one taking the risks. By the time he turned nineteen, he had pushed his dealer out of the game.

He went to all the guys' customers and undercut his prices. This enabled him to take all the customers away from the original dealer.

Obviously this wasn't appreciated by his old boss, but Sean fronted him out and took over his patch. He would chop somebody in half just for a reputation and that is what he did to the dealer, not literately but close enough. Sean was after the money, drugs and power and was not about to let anybody stand in the way of him getting them.

He became feared, as people were aware of what he would do to them. His main clients were the crack whores, they were always regular customers. From this, Sean had turned his hand to managing prostitutes. This is what he called it. What he really was, was a pimp. He had a large number of girls working for him all over Essex.

All the girls were one of two kinds of prostitutes. They were either drug addicts who worked the streets or prostitutes who worked his houses. The girls who worked the houses were not crack whores though, not like his customers. Sean ran these women with an iron rod.

They weren't allowed to take drugs and if he found out they did, then he would beat them to within an inch of their life and they would never work for him again. He made sure they were clean and disease free, ensuring that they took regular STI checks at the local GUM clinic and that they never, ever rode bareback.

No matter how much they were offered, Sean had a fast rule of condoms to be used every single time. Never having sex with the girls was another rule, not wanting to blur lines or appear to have favourites. He preferred the junkies anyway, as they were more disposed to be used and abused.

He collected the money from them daily and paid them their cut. He had found out about the man trying to rip him off just twenty minutes after he had left the working house.

That man had been found within the hour, he was now lying on the floor in a warehouse in Barking and Sean Fergus looked like he was going to kill him. Sean prided himself on his ability to find people who were running from him. Like a werewolf can sniff out the vampires. He had learnt from the best.

The broken man on the floor had no idea who Sean was. He was just a regular bloke, who drank too much and thought he would try to get away with a free fuck. He had a wife and three kids at home and now they were going to be left without him. He felt another kick in the head and the room went black for a few seconds.

He could smell the fear inside of himself. For a brief moment, he wondered if his family would be better off without him. His wife wouldn't have to put up with his philandering ways. His children wouldn't have to be subjected to his broken promises.

"You think you can fuck me over do you?" The words were spat out in venom.

Sean was jumping around the warehouse, like a demented kangaroo with rabies.

"You think you can fuck my girls for free?" His eyes, normally a seducing blue that could occupy and dominate the smallest of attention spans, had adopted a chameleon effect and taken on a demented grey stance.

"I am s…s…sorry." The punter tried to crawl up onto his knees.

He wanted to talk himself out of this situation. He

needed to be able to walk away from this alive. Or at least crawl away, as his legs were pretty broken. "I didn't know."

"Keep pissing me off and I will shove your teeth so far down your throat; you will have to shove your fingers up your arse to bite your fucking nails." The manic words were spat out by Sean.

The man didn't give up. He tried to reason with him. "I mean, I didn't ..."

Sean's foot caught the man's chin, just as he had managed to steady himself onto his knees, the sound of the blow reverberated around the empty warehouse; echoing into the vacant twilight.

His light brown hair glistened with droplets of sweat, as he soared with the exhilaration. As much as he made a show of being pissed off at such disrespect, he secretly wished for it to happen. The retribution he pelted out was just as good as any illegal high.

The man struggled to speak. He had swallowed a lot of blood, from the numerous punches that Sean had rained on his face. He didn't want to die. It may have been a little late to have such an epiphany but it was a realisation all the same.

Death was something that one needed to prepare for and he was not prepared; not at all. He didn't know what was on the other side. Was there a heaven? Or would he be going to the other place.

Would his soul burn forever, in a nothingness void that spun around the earth? He slowly closed his eyes to pray to any higher being to end this for him. Just make him survive this, please.

As his eyes closed to embrace the darkness he saw the glint of the shiny iron crowbar just before Sean embedded it into his skull.

Sean hadn't killed him, but he had made sure the man

would be in hospital for the next six months and that he would never forget who Sean Fergus was. This was what had pissed him off more. The stupid ponce had never even heard of him; had absolutely no idea who he was or what he owned.

This galled Sean. He had worked hard over the last three years, to get where he was. He was not about to let some no mark disrespect him like that. He was young. At twenty-one, he had achieved what some men spend their whole lives trying to accomplish.

It wasn't an easy job managing girls. You had to be on their backs constantly and have your eyes and ears open. He had enjoyed giving out the beating. It was like having a workout for him. He really did enjoy the violence of his job, almost as much as finding new blood, to add to the vast network of girls he had.

That part he really did like. He went for the runaways and homeless mainly, they were easy to break. He would befriend them; give them a place to stay, food and money. Then he would introduce the drugs, if they weren't already on something. Usually it was crack or heroin.

After a few hits they were hooked and willing to do anything he wanted. He was always fascinated by how easy it was. They never resisted. He was too good at it.

A pimp needs charm and Sean had it abundance. It seeped out of him. He had a special knack of tuning into people's insecurities. It was almost as if he could read their inner most thoughts. He could do it with men too. A whore once told him he could charm the pants off the straightest bloke. It was why he had got to where he had.

It was why the faces trusted him and it was what the girl's fell for. It was such a waste of life. These women had almost no self respect or dignity. If there was any, Sean stripped it away quite quickly.

He was pissed that he had to put his plans for the evening on hold to sort out a whore's punter. He had a lovely new tart ready to be groomed. She was just ripe and he was about to do the picking.

He was also pissed that his name obviously wasn't as known as it should be, otherwise he wouldn't have had to sort out the punter. He was running late and now he had to stop off at home in Brentwood first for a shower; the punter had bled all over him as he had helped to put him in the car, so his henchmen could drop him off at the hospital.

And he would be dropped off, literally out of the car door and left on the pavement outside Queen's Hospital Accident and Emergency department, in Romford.

It was hard enough for Sean to make sure all his girls toed the line, without having to ensure the punters played by the rules too. The fact that he had some major trust issues with just about everybody he came across meant it virtually impossible for him to find hired help. He had a few heavies that would help him out from time to time but no permanent crew.

It was one of the reasons why he appealed to the faces of Essex; the solitary way he chose to live. If one man could cause such destruction, then that one man was worth having on your side. That was just common sense and for a face to be a face; common sense and nous was what would keep you alive and your status and reputation intact.

Sean wasn't that interested in being a face. He enjoyed the notoriety it bought and the money, but the power over turf control held no concern for him. He enjoyed working with different people, taking on different jobs. He loved the diversity but above all he longed for the precipitous carnage he could cause; holding that supremacy over another person. It ate away at him if it had been too long.

As much as he had shown the man, who thought he

could shag his girls and not pay for the privilege, just how pissed off and offended he was, he secretly buzzed on the fact it had happened. It had been too long and now he had a slight taste of it again he wanted more.

Sean Fergus wanted a hell of a lot more; his whole body craving to feel that rush of pre-eminence and domination again.

Chapter 3

Ginnie was waiting outside the children's home she was presently staying at and Sean was two hours late in picking her up. She looked what she was; another homeless teenager who had been in and out of care homes all their life.

Her clothes, although in good condition, were hand-me-downs from previous unwanted kids. The flowery chiffon blouse was slightly too big for her slight, not yet fully matured body and the short denim skirt hung from her developing hips.

She wore far too much make up for her age, her pretty childlike face revealing the innocence and naivety she held, disguising the fact she had just become an adult. The only feature that set her apart from the rest of the duplicate 'care-home kids' was the fire-cracking red of her hair.

The home itself was made up of two houses, originally built as private properties; its facade was classically Georgian, dating back to 1750. The characteristic and distinctive square and symmetrical shape revealed the precipitous beauty and size of the building. The pillars in the front of the house, which gave the building an air of importance and officialness, were added much later, when it was converted into one.

A panelled front door took centre place and the sash window frames gleamed in the twilight haze. The driveway was still scattered with dead leaves. They were piled high on both edges, all the way along to the twin iron gates, which were guarded by two gigantic oak trees on either side. The overhanging branches provided privacy from the busy main road and the vast girth of the trunks made ideal hiding places, as Ginnie had discovered.

They were perfect to stand behind and not be seen by the house or by the road and, as she was way past her curfew, being able to hide was unquestionably a benefit. The house was comprised of a library, a lounge, a games room, kitchen and dining areas. There were five single bedrooms and three shared ones.

She had a single bedroom, due to her age. There were eight of them in the home, aged between four and eighteen. Some children were there for a short time, while others stayed longer.

She moved around a lot but had been at this one for about three months, which was a record. Normally she only lasted a few weeks before she was moved on somewhere else. In between homes she would be placed with temporary foster parents but they never lasted very long either.

She was just about to be given her freedom. She had been in care all her life and knew the system well. She had just turned eighteen, social services were going to set her up in a nice little flat and she would start college.

She would never have to deal with foster parents or

social workers again. She would be completely independent and have nobody else to answer to. Life was looking good for Ginnie; she had a new boyfriend and was enjoying life for once. Although, considering how late he was in meeting her, she was beginning to doubt her current status.

Her slim, scantily dressed, body shivered in the night air and she jumped up and down in a bid to warm up. Finally, seeing Sean's car turn round the corner and pull up to her, she loosened the tense stance that had taken hold of her as every minute he was late ticked by. He leant over, opening the passenger car door and she jumped in. The relief swept through her that she hadn't been stood up.

She had only been seeing him for a week and the longer she was waiting, the more paranoia set in. She took one look at his face and her smile dropped away. He looked really pissed off. Something told her she should be quiet and not antagonise him further. She decided not to say anything about him being late. She just reached for her seatbelt and strapped herself in.

Sean though, had other ideas. He grabbed her legs and shoved his hand between them. She felt his fingers, roughly trying to get inside her knickers. She tried to push him away but he was too strong.

"Don't fight me!" He shouted at her, as he pushed his face into hers. "I am not in the mood tonight."

His eyes flared wide open and Ginnie could see he was speeding out of his head. She stopped struggling, as he wanted and allowed herself to relax a little.

"What are you doing?" She heard how meek it sounded.

She suddenly looked very young and this excited Sean. The anger he was feeling earlier was beginning to slowly subside. The two grams of coke he snorted, not ten minutes ago, was also helping. Now, this girl sitting in his car was going to help him further. He needed her to unleash the frustration of his day and he was determined to make that happen.

"…sshhh… just relax… you will enjoy it more if you keep still and relax."

His fingers were still forcefully trying to get underneath her knickers. Ginnie was scared. She silently scolded herself for wearing the short denim skirt.

"Please… don't… oh god… please" She whimpered. She knew she couldn't fight him. He was huge, compared to her small size 8 frame.

What had happened to make him behave like this? He was certainly not the guy that had charmed her a few days ago.

That guy had taken her out for a proper dinner, in a proper restaurant. He had ordered a bottle of wine and poured it into a wine glass for her. He treated her like an adult. He made her feel special and exclusive. He had walked her home and held her hand. He had been nothing but respectful. They hadn't even kissed.

She had fought off young boys her age, with their fumbling advances towards her, but nothing to this degree. Normally, she only had to push them away but that wasn't going to work here. Sean wasn't a teenage boy. He was a man, who obviously had needs and she was going to fulfil them, even if she didn't want to.

He was also on something because his eyes were rolling about in the back of his head. Ginnie instinctively knew that she wouldn't be able to reason with him. She screamed out loud when four of his fingers found their way inside her. She had never felt anything like it.

It was a fierce, sheering burn, deep between her legs. As he forcefully penetrated her, she felt a warm trickle of fluid run down her legs. She thought she had wet herself. She was scared enough to do so. Sean had felt it too because it caused him to stop and look at his hands.

She was bleeding. He knew he had been a bit rough but surely he hadn't been that rough. Had he? Then he realised. He smiled and stroked her face.

"You're a virgin?" His voice was husky.

Ginnie nodded while a tear rolled down her cheek. Before she knew what was happening, Sean had lay the seat back and was on top of her. He tore off her knickers and ripped open the flimsy blouse she was wearing. He pulled her bra above her breasts and grabbed at her nipples with his teeth.

He brutally bit and sucked at them, ignoring her screams and pleas of wanting to go home. She had never experienced anything like this before. Although she had spent most of her life in and out of care, she had been one of the rare lucky ones that had managed to survive relatively unscarred.

She had heard of and known other girls that had fallen prey to 'the system' and had been abused by their social workers or foster parents but it had never happened to her. She now almost wished that it had. Then, maybe she would know how to handle this situation.

The pain was almost unbearable. How did people do this for fun? She wondered. Terror was mounting up by the second. She couldn't understand why he was doing this to her. She had no idea that he was rushing from the exhilaration of half killing a man, just before picking her up. She also had no idea that this would have happened sooner or later anyway, it just so happened to be tonight.

Sean was fascinated by her body. It suddenly occurred to him just how young she was. Her breasts were budding. They sat pert and static. She felt different inside too he decided. She was tight and clenched. It was different to the other women he had shagged, especially the working girls.

This one was a rarity. You didn't often come across them untouched. They were all slags in the end though. They all ended up on their backs, with their legs open, beckoning him. He had a strange power over women. Some, like Ginnie, did it out of fear; some because they found him dangerous and exciting; others did it because they wanted their next fix.

As he shoved himself into her and begun to ride her, she looked out of the car window; she could see her children's home. All the lights were still on. They would all be gathered in the large lounge, watching TV or playing on the PS2, all unaware of what was happening to her outside.

She thought she had found a lovely new boyfriend; she had in fact, attracted a complete nutter. She tried to think of something, anything to stop her brain from registering what was happening. He was raping her. Thousands of alarm bells were going off in her head; the ringing was so loud in her ears. The comprehension of the situation imploded her mind. It hurt. It really hurt. Her lower body was on fire.

When he had finished the torrid abuse, he rolled off from on top of her and lay beside her. Her body was exposed. He had taken off her skirt and bra and was gently tracing his finger around her breasts and down to her stomach. It was a very different touch to the one she had just encountered.

It was soft and tender, unlike the animal attack that had just occurred. One thing Ginnie knew she could definitely rely on was that Sean Fergus was very weird and that he flipped from Mr Nice to Mr Terrifying within seconds.

"Did you enjoy that?"

Not sure if he wanted an answer, Ginnie nodded her head slowly. She had not enjoyed it. In fact she was absolutely disgusted. She had had to physically stop herself from heaving when he came inside her. When he lay on top

of her afterwards, suckling at her nipple, she had to stop
herself from shrinking away from him.

The more she had begged him to stop, the more he had
shoved himself into her. She wanted to run from the car as
fast as she could but something told her that if she wanted
to survive, she would have to ride this out and play the long
game.

"I said you would."

He purred in her ear. His fingers stroked the hair
between her legs. "You were a virgin? No fucker had ever
touched you?"

"No." Ginnie said "Can I go home now... please?"

She tried to sound as polite and humble as she could. She
sounded like a little girl. And she was. She was a frightened
little girl, who was in way over her head.

She was ecstatic when he had turned his attentions to
her. She had known of him, heard of his reputation and
rather fancied some of the notoriety. She thought she was
so lucky, when he started chatting to her in the park a few
days ago.

He had singled her out and had been so sweet. He had
known her name and that impressed her no end. But now
she had changed her mind. She was terrified and he knew
it. It suddenly occurred to Ginnie that he didn't just know
she was scared; he actually got off on it.

"Not yet." He was smiling. He watched his hand stroke
her hair. He slipped his finger down slightly further, to her
clitoris and watched her face crumple up with revulsion.
He had had plans for this one. She was going to be one of
his new girls.

She was young and the punters would like that. They
would pay a fortune for her. She was slim and very pretty,
which meant he could use her for his more prestigious

clients, the judges and alike. But now he knew that she was a virgin, it changed things slightly.

He wanted her to himself for a while. She was untouched goods. He had been the only man that had been there and it made him feel invincible. It was actually the vast amount of cocaine that he had consumed that was giving him this invincible feeling but for now he was happy to believe in the myth that it was her.

He let his fingers play with her at their own free will. He liked the control he had over her, the fear he had already instilled in her. Ginnie would do as she was told, he knew that. She was innocent and reminded him of someone he used to know and love and for a while he was going to pretend he had *her* back.

"I want you to be a very good little girl and do something for me." He kissed her then; his tongue deep in the back of her throat. Ginnie couldn't help but gag this time.

"I want to you to pretend to be someone." He slipped a single finger inside her, much gentler than before. Then he whispered. "Rachel."

* * *

Four days later, she found herself standing in a small bathroom, in a flat in Harold Wood, wondering what the hell was happening to her. The building itself was rat infested, with water leaking from pipes along the skirting boards. Needles and burnt tin foil lay in the passages outside, the domineering smell of urine clung to every wall.

The bathroom was in no better state. The walls, that may have once been a creamy yellow, now bore a murky grey soot that layered everything. The toilet and sink sustained mass rust erosion and what was left of the white paint work was melting into an abyss of reddish brown.

The bath was filthy and covered in a black scum. She turned on the shower and it made a chugging noise that travelled along the pipes on the ceiling and down the walls, there was a gurgling before water spurted out the mouldy head.

She undressed and stepped into the bath. Every bone ached and throbbed. She looked down at her battered body. Her legs were a mass of black and purple. He had hurt her pretty badly. She couldn't do what he had wanted. How could she? She had never so much as kissed a boy with tongues, let alone done the things he had asked of her.

He had punished her when she couldn't perform to his commands. Then he tortured and raped her, over and over. He had to carry her from the car to the flat because she couldn't walk. He laid her on the bed and stroked her hair, while whispering soothing words into her ear, until she fell asleep.

He switched from nice to terrifying and back to nice so many times throughout the first night, but all the time he called her Rachel. It was only days later, when he helped her to the bathroom so she could shower, that he called her by her name.

As the warm water washed away the blood and semen that was stuck to her body, she wondered who Rachel was. She hoped he never found her because the girl was in for a much worse time than she had suffered, Ginnie was sure of that. He loved and hated her so much; it was frightening to see how much it consumed him.

As much as he had let rip on her, Ginnie was also sure he had held back. He had known she wasn't this Rachel girl but he needed to pretend she was. The more coke he snorted, the quicker the switches happened. It got to the point that Ginnie didn't know which one he was going to be at any given second.

She had never felt so relieved as when he finally fell asleep and stopped pawing at her for a while, Although, even then, he still held her very close to him, in a vice like grip. Before he fell asleep each time, he told her that she was now his. He said he now owned her and if she tried to escape he would kill her and set fire to the children's home, with everybody inside it.

This was enough to make sure that she did as she was told. She wasn't particularly fond of the home but it had small children in there. They were innocent, but then so was she. He said that, if she was a good girl, then he would let her go when he had finished with her. She wasn't entirely sure he meant it. She had a feeling this dingy flat would be the last place she ever saw.

She kept that thought to herself though and only allowed herself to think it once.

Chapter 4

October 2005

Walking through to the bar, Rachel gave a huge sigh of relief the lunchtime rush was over. She hated that part of her shift. It was too fast and stressed. The various ovens, microwaves, fryers and grills bleeped and beeped for two hours solid; the orders flying out of a ticket machine that sat on the gantry. Little notes of paper, with the orders printed in a feint black ink.

Whoever was on that particular station had to be quick to catch them, otherwise the order was lost and forty five minutes later, an irate waitress would be standing in front of you shouting obscenities, waving her arms, going red in the face and almost imploding.

There were constantly members of the kitchen team running in and out of fridges and freezers, shouting out orders to other stations. It was a very noisy place to be and Rachel's head was thumping.

All she wanted was a coffee, a cigarette and fifteen

minutes peace. The bistro was lively at all times of the day and night but the lunchtime was the worst. The advantage of being situated in Brentwood's busy high street was that the place was never empty. The benefit of this to Rachel was that there was always plenty of waitressing shifts on offer for her.

The bistro was laid out around a long counter that housed five high-yield espresso machines and several glass display cases, containing pastries and savoury items such as sandwiches. It had an unrefined feel to it; retaining that permanent sense of "just came in from the rain".

The interior was slightly dingy; dark colours, low light. Bizarre, raw artwork lined the walls and the muted couch pillows on the leather sofas were perpetually warmed by the sitting locale.

A slight musty scent was partially covered by the smell of roasted coffee that hung in the air; aromatic and alluring. An odd assortment of tables and chairs were staggered across the wooden floor in front of the bar, each honoring a chic, red lace table cloth. Dried flowers, in miniature glass vases, sat in the middle.

Among the throng of Wi-Fi sipping laptops, sat people reading the dog-eared pages of books or newspapers. There were mothers with babies and prams clogging up the avenues for the waitresses. A small group of college students had taken over the black leathers sofas that lined the walls. The cornucopia of sounds became a mishmash of noise; Rachel always found it surprisingly invigorating.

She put her cup under the coffee machine that sat at the end of the bar and pressed the button. Then she heard him.

"Coffee mate"

Rachel's whole body jolted, as if she had just had an electric shock. Her fingers trembled, as she removed her cup and reached for a spoon. She took a deep breath and turned round to face the voice.

He didn't see her at first. He was concentrating on the barman serving him; dressed in a dark blue pair of fitted jeans, a charcoal grey T-shirt and white loafers.

God he looked good! The thought overwhelmed her. He was supposed to have gained weight, grown a beard, looked older. The years were supposed to have been unkind.

"Latte, Cappuccino, Macchiato, Mocha, Espresso?" The barman asked.

"Fucking Hell! I just want a coffee". He snapped back

He started sorting out his change. Rachel smiled to herself. He hadn't changed. He was still just as arrogant. It surprised her, that the thought made her smile. It is hardly a personality trait that should be found attractive, but she did. She always had; in him anyway.

Those seducing blue eyes still catapulted her heart out of her chest. For a split second, Rachel considered walking away, before he saw her, before she opened that door again. The door that had stayed closed for a long time.

"You're not causing trouble are you, Mr Fergus?"

The words were out before her brain had even registered what was happening. It was too late now. Walking away was not an option anymore. She had made that initial contact. She had crossed the line. Rachel knew that.

She knew she should have walked away, before he had seen her, before he could enchant her with that smile; the smile that was enchanting her right now.

Why, out of all the bistros, had he walked into hers? After eight years, why today? Why did he look so damn good? Rachel's head was full of why's.

"Not anymore. Can I get you a drink?"

That smile was still there. It transported Rachel, back to a time where she was young and free, when she first met him, when he had swept her off her feet, when he had managed to take a piece of her heart that would never be owned by another person ever again.

"I don't finish for another two hours. If you are still here, you can buy me a drink." With that, Rachel turned around and walked out, to the back of the bar.

He watched her leave and smiled. His day just got a whole lot better. He picked up his coffee and went over to a table that was near the kitchen entrance. He would see her come out when she had finished her shift. He wouldn't miss her. No way. He had only just found her again.

Rachel sat down outside, on the step at the back of the Bistro. She lit herself a cigarette, dragging deeply and exhaling loudly. The small car park was full, which was surprising for a midweek lunchtime.

She thought it had been more busy than usual. The steps in front of her were littered with cigarette ends and half drunk coffee cups. She cursed the kitchen boys and made a mental note to remind them to clear up after themselves.

She stared out across the industrial sized bins that were lined up against the wall of the bistro; flattened cardboard boxes lay in metal cages to the side of the steps. It was a beautiful day, considering it was still late winter. The sun was high and the air was so still against her skin, she was assailed by the memory of him once more.

Then she realised that, as cool as she had thought she had just handled the situation, it was all undone by the fact she was wearing the bistro's strict white blouse, black skirt, black low heeled shoe dress code, a very unflattering hairnet and an incredibly dirty apron.

Oh she had it going on all right. She groaned inwardly. She looked a mess. As if he was going to still be there in two hours. What was there to wait for? She hardly oozed style. She finished her coffee and smoked another cigarette.

Walking back through to the kitchen, her mind wandered back to the day she realised she could not be with him; not ever. They were seventeen and completely smitten.

Actually, infatuation was probably the better term to use; it bordered on fanatical and obsessed. It only lasted a few months. Rachel put a stop to 'them' on January 24th 1997. The date she will remember forever. It was the day she made either the best decision or the biggest mistake of her life.

Even now, nine years later, she did not know which one it was. She knew that there had not been a day gone by when she had not thought about him, dreamt about him, fantasised even. Sean Fergus.

She had fought against her every instinct every day. He was the love of her life. That she was certain of. But they were self destructive together. That she was certain of too.

Although nothing had ever happened between them when they were together that had caused her to think this, the amount of sheer physical emotion she felt for this boy terrified her.

At seventeen, the brain is not mature enough to cope with that magnitude of passion. She genuinely believed, what she felt for him would be what destroyed them in the end.

So, she had chosen to stop it before it got to that point and in doing so had spent the rest of her life trying to get over him. She had jumped from one serious relationship into another, searching for someone that would give her back the part that he had taken; stolen. One child and a few relationships later, time had still not ameliorated the constant ache that consumed her daily.

She had never let anyone in fully after him. She had fallen pregnant during her first relationship after they split up. She thought that would make her move on, but it hadn't. She still thought about him constantly. That particular relationship had fallen apart and the second one finished because Rachel wasn't in love, pure and simple.

Now the third relationship, her current relationship, was different. She was in some kind of love; the comfortable kind. She had built a family, and convinced herself it was enough this time. Contentment had a lot going for it.

It wasn't a perfect relationship and it had been through its fair share of trauma but it had lasted and it was for this reason alone that she pursued it. Even so, he was still there, in the background, in her thoughts, just as frequently.

Rachel sometimes wondered if it was because they had never had sex. That it was all built up sexual frustration. If they hadn't refrained, then maybe the intense feelings would have fizzled out, the relationship would have run its course and she would have moved on, then able to give herself completely to another.

Was it all just about that raw, penetrating desire that is full of enticement, temptation and allure? It had always fascinated her, how a basic emotion could control a whole lifetime; that desire could be dangerous and destructive. The physiological power it holds is robust and pungent with domination. It engulfs the environment in which it resides, much like a parasite.

It hadn't diminished in strength or presence and there was nothing that could eradicate it; for she had tried. She had tried and tried again, to dispel the feelings that captivated her psyche. She had found love and as much as she was in love and she was, she knew that for certain, she had not, could not, give herself over completely.

She had always held something back and that something was the part that would always belong to the man that was sitting in the bar waiting for her. He had staked his claim on her all those years ago and his hold was as fervent as it had always been.

Now he was here; in person. She always imagined what would happen and how it would happen, when she saw him again; for she knew she would. Essex was too small for them not to cross paths at some point.

The next two hours dragged slowly by and she found herself thinking more and more about Sean. She couldn't concentrate on anything else and was almost certain she was more of a hindrance than a help for the remainder of her shift.

Applying the finishing touches to her make-up, Rachel stepped back to get a full view in the mirror. He was still in the bar, waiting for her, had been the whole time. The look he gave her when she walked out of the staff room was full of unspoken sentiment.

Had he thought about her, just as much as she had thought about him? Had she affected every single one of his relationships, like he had hers? Her head was spinning with questions. It had been so much easier to believe that all this was one sided. That she had not meant to him what he had meant to her.

Men didn't form emotional attachments like women did, especially not at seventeen. He had never said those words, 'I love you'. He had never disagreed with her decision to end things, hadn't tried to fight for her. Even when she jumped straight into another relationship, he hadn't expressed any sort of opinion.

But that look he was giving her right now made everything stand still. Her heart was thumping so loud she thought everybody in the bar would hear it. It was a look that provoked an electrifying sensation way down in the pit of her stomach and she suddenly realised she was physically aching for him.

He held her gaze as he walked towards her, still looking at her like he was undressing her with his eyes. It was like she could read what he was thinking and her interpretation of his thoughts made her blush. This wasn't real. This amount of sheer physical wanting could not possibly exist. Could it?

Was it not just a whimsical flight of the imagination that Hollywood had projected onto the world? That millions of lovelorn women had bought into because the fantasy was always going to exceed the reality. By the time he had reached her, Rachel's breathing was somewhat erratic and she could feel herself shaking.

Her desperate attempt to control her reaction to him failed and he was only too aware of what he was causing. She looked around the bar. Nobody seemed to have been alerted to them. They were inconspicuous to the rest of the world. He was standing too close now, just inches away.

His imperious presence was very quickly eating into the very little composure she held on to. He smelled really good, he looked really good and if he touched her now she knew she would lose control completely.

"You want to go?" It was more of a request than a question. Its meaning was solicited. He still wanted her.

Was this fate seeing him again? She didn't know. What she did know, was that Sean was asking her to leave with him and go somewhere to be alone. No small talk, no flirting, no romanticised build up. He was asking her to be with him.

It was his way of being honest. Showing her the real him. Not the loud, brash bad boy he made himself out to be. She was the only girl he ever showed this side too. She was the only girl he had ever met that he genuinely respected. She was the only girl he had ever loved. She made him feel good.

It was not a feeling that he experienced often and when

he did, Rachel generally had something to do with it. Sean was a bad boy, who had done bad things. He knew what he was. He was a pimp and a drug dealer. He was an enforcer and he associated with some very dangerous people.

He believed it was his destiny. He was living his life just the way he thought he should be. Rachel could never be part of that world. She held too much goodness inside her. She was pure and untouched by the grime and stench that his way of life put on you. He knew she was right, in leaving all those years ago.

He knew he may have hurt her terribly in some way. He knew that she knew it and that ripped him up inside. She was a good girl. That was what his dad said about her and he was right. She shouldn't give him the time of day, yet she was here, right in front of him, looking just the same as she did at seventeen.

Sean could hardly contain the craving he had, to touch her, to feel her body next to him. He had been searching for years for that fix, like an addict, someone to quench that craving; someone to fight against the evil inside him.

Hundreds of women had crossed his threshold and not one of them had come close to stopping the yearning he had for her. Not one had impacted the desire he held for her. There had been so many faceless women. If he came across one of them again, he wouldn't have known.

He wouldn't remember if he had already had sex with them. They had not even entered his orbit. Faceless women, which were there to replace what he had lost. To make him forget for a while at least, with a shimmer of hope that maybe this one, this time, would take her place. But it never happened. The faceless women didn't help. Only she could stop the ache he felt for her.

It had been a very long nine years, to constantly think about one person and here he was, laying it all out on the line, praying to some higher being that she would say yes and go with him. He looked into her eyes, as if he could somehow penetrate just what he was feeling into them, so she would know just how much she took of him, when she left. That she took him completely and the women, the faceless women; some of them had paid the price.

Some had paid the price emotionally. If their encounter had happened more than once, which was rare, Sean would emotionally abuse them. He would grind them down until they were vulnerable and defenceless and then he would dispose of them and move onto the next. The weak ones just plain annoyed him. There was no empathy with Sean, no compassion.

He punished the girls because they let him do it. They were needy and requested constant affirmation. They were not Rachel, they didn't behave like Rachel and they weren't strong like Rachel. They didn't know when to walk away. They were insignificant.

Some paid the price physically. Sex was all he was after and it was self gratifying sex at that. Sometimes it was consensual, other times it wasn't. But it was always rough and commanding and sometimes violent. They were irrelevant faceless women.

Sean knew he was bad. He believed he was born evil and that was the way it was. He couldn't change it, it was the hand he had been dealt. He had accepted his fate. He was first aware of it when he was about seven years old. His sister had been given a kitten for her birthday.

One day, for no reason at all, just because the idea sprung into his mind, he took the kitten out into his dads shed at the bottom of their garden and spent several hours torturing it.

The more he tortured it, the more he enjoyed it. It had caused a stirring sensation in his groin. The more the kitten squeaked, the more intense the sensation. They were his first intimate feelings. Although at the time he didn't know what they were. That knowledge came much later.

It was after Rachel had walked away and the torrent of faceless women that he made his way through did those particular feelings surface again. He enjoyed stripping away their dignity and dehumanising them. He became aroused when they begged him to stop; their pleas goading him on. He took pleasure in their pain, like with the kitten.

Only, women were better than kittens. They begged, which made him feel powerful. He was in control. They would leave when *he* was done; when *he* was ready for them to leave. But every now and then, he secretly hoped that one of them, just one of them, would make him feel like she did, like he could be normal and good inside.

But of course they never did. But then, they were lost faceless women, with no real connections to anywhere or anyone. That is why he chose them to begin with. They wouldn't tell anyone the things he had done to them because they had no one to tell. Some had been prostitutes, some were crack addicts and some were nice good girls that had fallen prey to Sean Fergus.

Whatever they were or became, they had never told. They had never stopped him. It was only when he was around her, did he question his immoralities and malevolence. He would never intentionally hurt her in any way. He would die protecting her. The faceless women never received the same courtesy. He was so glad that she didn't know about some of the things he had done over the years.

He looked at her now. To him, she was his angel. The devil had been living inside of him for so long and right now the other side started fighting back. After what seemed to Sean as an eternity, Rachel nodded. It was all she could do. Speaking was not an option.

Before she knew what was happening, he had led her out of the bistro and into the car park. There was a wintry feel to the air now and Rachel welcomed the chill. It seemed to steady her a little. Sean took a small bunch of keys from his pocket and pressed the button on one of them. The lights of a black BMW bleeped on and he directed her round to the passenger door.

He leant across her, as if to open the door but instead grabbed hold of her and pushed her up against the car. As much as he forcibly held her, he could feel she hadn't struggled, she hadn't even gasped when he grabbed her. She just looked at him, waiting to see what he was going to do next.

"Do you know how many times I have thought about this? Being this close to you?" His hand moved up into her hair.

She could feel his finger, gently tracing the outline of her ear. His thumb brushed along her chin and over her lips. Rachel instinctively opened her mouth a little and lightly kissed his thumb. The action was the most natural response she had ever made towards another person.

There was no forward planning, no thinking. It was like her body was taking over her mind. His lips were so close she could almost feel them. Any second now he would kiss her… she was certain of it, until his hand wavered. He was hesitating. Rachel pulled him even closer to her.

"Please, don't stop…" She whispered

"Not here" He murmured.

He slid his hand behind her and opened the door, gently moving her aside so he could open it fully. He smiled at her then and his fingers entwined with hers.

"Can I take you to mine?"

* * *

The house was not what she was expecting. A five-bedroom detached house, on the Essex-Suffolk border; Sudbury was a tiny, archaic market town on the River Stour. Rachel had never been to this part of East Anglia before and the sheer sense of tranquillity that lay siege to the rich mosaic landscape enchanted her.

It was definitely different to the council house he had lived in with his mum, dad and sisters, nine years ago. It was a typical example of Suffolk vernacular architecture, constructed from a timber frame with wattle and daub in-fill. It really was quite stunning, Rachel thought as she stood in the entrance hall. This was so big you could have fit the whole of her flat in it.

The stone walls were painted a brilliant white, giving an air of vastness to it; a magnificent marble staircase with classical columns faced her and led to the upper floors. The staircase hall was lit by a central dome and the fan-shaped plasterwork matched the wrought iron baluster. The rooms off to either side of the hall each possessed a solid oak door, with black iron handles and, somewhat in contrast to the house, the walls were adorned with various pieces of modern art.

Standing a little way away, watching her, he was pleased with her reaction. It looked like he had done well for himself. It was certainly true that crime pays. She was impressed and that was what he wanted. She turned to face him.

They hadn't spoken for what must have been an hour journey in the car. The tension was rising. Rachel could feel it. Sean could feel it. One of them had to say something soon. Sean could feel the impatience rise inside of him. He was trying so hard not to let it show, to not reveal the evilness that lived there. He was totally out of his comfort zone.

He didn't know how to respond to the sexual chemistry that was so evident. It wasn't anything that he had experienced before. All he knew was how to degrade a woman into doing what he wanted. But this was her; Rachel. She was entirely out of his league, yet she had implored him not to stop.

"Come here." Finally he spoke; although it was more ordered than requested; silently his infuriation rose. He had not meant that tone.

Rachel bit her bottom lip.

"Why am I here Sean? Why have you brought me here?" She waved her arms to exaggerate what she meant. "What...? You think if you bring me here and show me how well you have done, that I would realise what I could have had and just fall to my knees?"

"I had you falling to your knees in the car park." Sean interrupted, walking towards her. "Remember?"

Rachel smiled then. "Who just made who come to whom?"

As he reached her, he realised what she had just done. He saw the glint in her eye.

Her hands grabbed his belt, she ferociously pulled him towards her and brushed her lips against his.

"Sean, don't ever underestimate me."

He looked into her eyes. They told him in no uncertain terms that she was not one of those faceless women who would participate in his demands. He told her to come to him and she had instantly made the opposite happen. God he loved this women.

He loved the feel of her hands on his belt, pulling him to her. He loved her soft lips, teasingly tracing his and he loved it when she pressed them onto his, with such ferocity that he could have taken her there and then. But he didn't. He wanted to explore every inch of her. Her tongue slowly wrapped itself around his and her lips moved around his, in perfect motion.

He hadn't let himself remember her kiss. It was too painful. He had blocked it out and now, here she was, kissing him. Her hands dug deeper inside his belt. He felt her urgency. He ripped off her coat and she lifted her arms for him to take off her dress. He managed successfully to do this in one swift movement, as she took off his t shirt and undid his belt and jeans.

Within seconds, they were both standing naked. He ran his hands up her back and over her shoulders. She shuddered at his touch when his fingers slipped inside her. He thrust them in and out, making her involuntarily moan. She felt as if she was going to explode if he didn't stop. The sensation was nothing she had experienced before. Her head spun frenziedly and she could feel every part of her body shaking.

She had experienced orgasms before, but nothing like this, nothing quite so extreme; nothing so fast. As she felt it release from her, she suddenly became aware of him watching her so intently.

"I never knew I could make someone respond like that." He breathed heavily as he found her mouth with his.

Sean was as completely taken away as she was. He had never been interested in pleasing the faceless women. It was all about his fulfilment with them. Rachel made him want to kiss and stroke every inch of her, to entirely take her in.

He lifted her up; instinctively she wrapped her legs around him, still kissing her he walked across the porcelain tiled floor to one of the large oak doors.

It opened onto a large, round reception room, equally as spectacular as the hall, although in a more lived-in, used, way. A colossal TV screen stood in front of the extensive bay windows and to the right a magnificently crafted Portland stone and black fossil-filled limestone fireplace displayed old and recent photographs, in heavy silver frames.

Slim-line, black, shiny speakers stood in solitude in their prestigiously placed positions around the circular room, all enfolding to an enormous sofa in the middle. A deep red, soft leather frame that was abundant with giant soft chenille cushions. The darkness of the red reflected in the paleness of her milky white skin.

He lowered her down gently but she kept her legs wrapped round him; as her head hit the cushions she arched her hips slightly making Sean enter her. He wasn't ready yet, he wanted more time to observe her and touch her but she felt so damn good and she wanted him.

That much he definitely knew. She really wanted him. If he wasn't careful he could lose control, he could feel himself losing control. He wanted to grab her hips and ride her so fucking hard. He wanted to pull at her nipples with his teeth. He wanted to sink his face into her and taste her.

He didn't want to hurt her, he really didn't, but he just had all these feelings and drives on overload. Every sense was heightened and he couldn't stop himself. He lifted her arms above her head, pinning her to the sofa. He thrust himself roughly inside her, again and again.

She took him each time without fail. She didn't cry out in pain, she didn't beg him to stop. She cried out in pleasure; more than once. She cried out his name and she groaned in rapture. She lifted her legs a little higher so he could move in deeper. He was unaware he was about to come, right up until he did.

Neither of them moved. They both lay as they were, panting and listening to the drumming of their heartbeats. Sean still had Rachel's arms pinned above her head, although his grip was looser now. He was still inside her and she wasn't recoiling from him, which felt a little unusual.

She didn't have a look of fear and hatred in her eyes either. What was it about this girl? Why did she make him feel like she did? He couldn't believe it when she got in the car. He really thought she would suddenly come to her senses and walk away from him. Any minute now, he kept thinking.

He knew she was with someone. He knew him. They had been in the same year, at the same school. That was the thing about Essex. Everybody knew everybody. They weren't friends but Sean knew who he was. He was a decent bloke, with a decent job. He was a decent bloke, who got to take this girl, his girl; and she was his girl, always had been, to bed every night. The image of him touching her suddenly drove him madly insane.

"Does he make you feel like that?" He had to ask. He couldn't help himself. The words were out before he realised.

"Sean… don't…"

"Does he? Does he make you come within seconds?" As he spoke the words, Sean felt himself get hard inside her again.

So did Rachel. She felt him move in and out incredibly slowly. It felt amazing, the less he moved the more intense it felt.

"No…" It was a whisper. "He doesn't make me feel like you do. No one ever has. It has always only been you."

He smiled slightly. He needed to hear that. He needed to know she was still his, always his. But he was still preoccupied. He had to know. He had to ask.

"Then, why did you finish it?"

Rachel looked at him, she could barely speak. He was slowly bringing her to ecstasy and now he wanted to talk. He needed answers though. She accepted that.

She clenched herself tightly around him and felt his reaction. He breathed in huskily.

"You feel that? Me and you together… that intense wanting… the hunger that's there between us?"

Sean couldn't answer. The euphoric provocation she was instrumentally creating was too much for him.

"That is why I left. We can't handle it now, let alone when we were seventeen. I had to stop it Sean, before it got too much to control."

"What do you mean, we can't handle it now?" The obscurity in his voice was evident.

"You're trembling like anything… so am I."

He realised then, the effect they had on each other. He didn't know what it was; scientists would explain it as a series of chemical reactions, caused by neurons firing in the synapse. All he knew was that she felt like electric. She made him buzz all over and he hadn't snorted a line in hours.

This was a completely natural high and it was all reciprocated. She wanted him as much as he wanted her. He was so used to taking women as and when he pleased, he forgot what it was like for one to actually want him back. To be lying on her back for him because she enjoyed him touching her and kissing her; to have her body physically shake in pleasure. It all came back. Those feelings he felt when they were together.

He thought his heart would burst with the amount of love he had for her. It was almost suffocating. There was a pull around his lungs, which made it hard to breathe. He could feel himself thrusting into her more. It became harder and faster, he tried to slow it down but he couldn't stop. He didn't want to hurt her.

He was terrified of doing just that but she felt so unbelievably good. He never imagined in all his fantasies that it would feel like this. Just when he thought he really was going to lose control, she rolled him over, so she was on top of him. Grabbing his wrists above his head, she rode him with as much ferocity as he had her.

Sean was in complete awe. He had never had a women take charge when it came to sex. The faceless women would lay still waiting for it all to be over. Rachel was delightfully different in so many ways.

She arched backwards, so she could take more of him in. He felt mind-blowing. She had fantasised about this so many times and the reality definitely outweighed the fantasy. She had missed him so much. She now knew what it felt to be complete. He had filled the hole inside her heart, which had been gapping wide open.

She had never given herself to anyone fully before. Not with her mind and not with her body, but Sean got it all. She felt so abundant with him, self assured and confident. Nobody had ever made her feel like this. As they came together, she realised she was totally and entirely his.

There was never any going back.

Chapter 5

Kenny Maltrowitz was an incredibly charming Jewish man. He had arrived in England during World War II, when he was a small boy, with his family. He was as cockney as they came but every now and then, when it suited or benefited him, he would revert to his former ethnicity.

He owned a number of back street pawn shops all over Essex and played an active role in the running of each one. He was an incredibly shrewd man, especially when it came to money. He knew where every penny he made was. His school teacher used to say, "Take care of the pennies and the pounds will take care of themselves." It had stayed with him all his life. It was what had made him his fortune and given him the ability to take care of his family.

When they arrived in London in 1942, they had the clothes on their back and nothing else. Kenny's father worked hard all his life, to provide for his family and made sure his children received an education.

He had worked in all kinds of jobs to ensure this. It had completely devastated Kenny when he died. He was only fourteen and it was suddenly his responsibility to take care of his mother and his two younger sisters.

Kenny would take on as many jobs as he could, before and after school. He would knock on doors and offer his services for all sorts of work. Shoe shinning and chopping firewood were normally the ones chosen, by many of his customers. It was during his time doing this that he came across a man named Vince Paddock, who seemed to take a shine to him and took him under his wing for a while.

Vince Paddock was an associate of the notorious criminal family, the O'Leary's. Kenny was never fully informed of the relationship between Vince and the O'Leary Brothers and he never met them face to face, he just knew of the stories that Vince and his friends would tell. He paid Kenny to be his eyes and ears, out on the street.

Vince saw him as a bright kid, plus he was impressed with the business that Kenny had managed to conjure up for himself. If anybody in the east end of London wanted anything doing, Kenny would be the one they called on. He was quick and reliable.

He was especially good with fixing broken things; furniture, clocks, musical instruments. But above all, he was quiet. He didn't ask questions and he did as he was told. This attracted certain types of people, who trusted him to be around their home or workplace.

This was post war Britain and ordinary folk did not have the money to pay someone to fix their broken clock, or shine their shoes or chop their wood. Most of his customers were members of society that like to keep a private life; either people in authority such as Judges, M.P's, Policemen or people that were more likely to follow the same path as Vince or the O'Leary Brothers.

To Vince, both were equally important. It was Kenny's job to listen and report back. He very quickly learnt that by saying nothing, people would reveal a whole lot more than they intended to, especially if they thought you weren't listening. Vince taught Kenny that information was the most valuable asset a man could own. If they had the right information, they could name their price.

He had taught him the benefits of working in a small team, keeping a low profile and only dealing with people that come recommended. But the most important lesson Kenny learnt, was always pay your suppliers promptly and in full. That way, they will use you again.

Unfortunately, what Vince had failed to realise was that, if you were going to sell information, you had to decide on which side of the fence you sat. You couldn't sell to both sides.

If you were going to transact with the police, then you had to take the status of a paid informant; though that of course came with its own risks. Or you sold within the criminal infrastructure, between the different crime families that ran the width and breadth of the country.

Vince got greedy and made the mistake of trying to sell to both, which only ended in having a price on his own head from both. It was never really established which side got him, but it happened all the same. He washed up on the embankment, next to the building site of the Thameside Restaurant. It was in the process of being turned into, what is now, the National Film Theatre.

Kenny however wasn't that bothered. Vince had taught him all he needed to know, directly and indirectly. He had also left him quite a large sum of money in his will, which had enabled Kenny to start his legal enterprises.

Kenny still traded and sold information. Sixty nine years old and he was still at the top of his game. He was admired and feared simultaneously, by most people he had met in his lifetime and was now able to live on his reputation alone.

His silver grey hair retained shards of ebony, revealing the blackness it once held. Beady, pallid irises, almost colourless, blended into the whites that lay underneath. Old kind eyes that could be replaced with a fear-provoking stare, by the mere dilation of dark furtive pupils.

The lines around his jaw gave him more of a distinguished and illustrious style, rather than the old and ripened age it should show, assisted by the fine-cut tailored suits; his trademark attire. The opened top buttons of his crisp white shirt revealed skin that was not grey and saggy but toned and with an olive complexion. His total physical presence commanded utter attention.

Over the years, he had expanded his little profitable business of intelligence laundering and branched out into information gathering. This meant that if anybody wanted to find someone or dirt on someone, he was the person to go to.

He took full advantage of all technological advances that had occurred over his life time and there wasn't any security he couldn't work his way around. The boom of the internet in the 90's helped his business no end. Nobody could really hide then.

He had the pawn shops for legitimate reasons. He had children and grandchildren and wanted to leave them something that was honest and clean. The money from his other business was dirty. Kenny was as bent as they came but his family was everything to him and he never involved them in his other dealings. Not even his wife knew about his other life and the incredibly dangerous and violent men he dealt with on a daily basis.

It's funny but a lot of wives and girlfriends of the

criminal fraternity do not know what their man is really involved with. They frolic in the fantasy of being married to a bad boy, a face, they enjoy the money and the big houses and flash cars and the expensive clothes but they generally have no idea of the extent of their partner's ventures.

Kenny believed this was a good thing. He never let on to his old woman, when she was alive, although she was probably turning, make that spinning, in her grave; god rest her soul. Kenny had done some bad things in his life. Things he wasn't particularly proud of. He justified those parts in his life that were deemed unholy, by telling himself that he did what had to be done.

He ran a risky business and dealt with some low lives of the world. Sometimes people would try to pay him retribution and he would manage that, as and when it happened. Kenny's gift was always being one step ahead. He knew to expect the unexpected. It had served him well and more importantly, kept him alive.

Even now, he could still handle himself, although his reputation alone these days provided him in good stead and he rarely had to exercise any physical assurances to protect himself. He hoped those days were over. He didn't like violence, couldn't condone it. Especially when it was directed at people who were weak and had no way of protecting themselves.

But mainly it was the blood. The sight of it made him feel ill. The colour, the thickness of it. It was glupey and warm. Sometimes it gushed, other times it trickled but it freaked him out every time. He learnt to control his physical reaction to it, to suppress the automatic gag reflexes.

The only time violence should ever be used is in self defence. That was how he defended his actions. He took them out, before they took him out. It was the way of life for people like him. That was why he was so intent on building up his legit businesses; so his family would not have to walk down the path that he did.

He made sure they had the opportunities that he never had. His children had attended the best private schools, as his grandchildren also did now. He made sure his sister's families were provided for. Family was important to Kenny.

His parents instilled that into him at an early age and it was probably why he took the death of his father badly. He also thought it was why he had accepted Vince's attentions so hurriedly but he had learnt a lot from the older man and realised what a commodity he was to Vinnie.

So he applied some of the techniques he had acquired to his own businesses, such as keeping a small crew of young wannabes around him. If you got them young enough, they remained loyal. He ensured they dressed well, as they were representing him. A uniform commands respect; it's important to look good.

Kenny knew he was being watched all the time, by the authorities, new emerging crews and by normal folk, so his boys would be suited and booted at all times.

Imprisonment is an occupational hazard, although Kenny had never had a capture, he made sure that if it was ever going to happen, his businesses would be protected. Having a steady turnover of young associates ensured his place at the top was secured.

The shop he owned in Romford stood in the middle of Victoria Road. The front had two huge glass windows with bars on them, exhibiting second hand televisions, stereos and other electrical equipment such as games consoles, irons and hair dryers. There was neon yellow cardboard stars with various promotions written in black marker pen, stuck down either side of the large glass area.

The signage above bore the signature '*Maltrowitz*

Lendings' in white calligraphy on a black background and was painted by Kenny's own hand, as were the signs on all of his shops. Between the tasteless florescent advertising, the windows bore a description of the place of business, declaring Kenny a jewellery specialist.

He didn't just pawn jewellery. He would take anything he thought he could sell on. He was fair and always made sure he traded within current regulations when it came to money borrowing. That was why people came back to him again and again.

As long as you don't take the piss, your customers will remain loyal. He would give them a fair price for what they wanted to pawn and also adequate time to buy it back from him, before he put it out in the shop for sale.

Kenny had trained up his two grandsons and four of his nephews, to take over when he died. They basically ran the shops now but he wasn't quite ready to hand over the reins just yet. His illegal enterprises wouldn't be handed down though, he already knew who would inherit the many hidden stakes he held in nightclubs, pubs and brothels across England. His protégé was ready now, but Kenny wanted the reins for a while longer.

He was mighty proud of his legal business. It made him feel less uncomfortable about his other business. Maybe that was why he spent so much of his time in his shops.

He particularly liked the Romford one though. It was one of his bigger premises, which meant he had the room for bulkier stock; furniture and appliances such as fridges and ovens.

It was a real money spinner too. He had gained new customers who didn't want to pawn their belongings but had stuff they no longer required. He bought them and sold them on. People lapped up second hand items. He had turned the Romford shop into a little showroom, with separate areas for kitchen appliances, sofas and dining room sets.

The windows gave a good view of the busy street and the road that separated the two long sides of terraced shops. He saw the car pull up outside and the driver get out. He smiled to himself. It was going to be another prosperous day, he thought.

Sean swung open the door with a force and bounded in.

"Fuck me old man... Y'take some pissing finding y'know."

Kenny just grinned and settled himself on his stool, behind the counter. He picked up his glasses and perched them on the end of his nose. He didn't need them. There was nothing wrong with his eyesight. He liked to use them as a prop; he thought it made him look important.

"I have been all over the fucking show looking for you this morning. I found your eegit of a nephew, screwing some sort out the back, up against the bins. Real classy that Ken."

Kenny chuckled and shook his head. He knew who Sean was referring to straight away.

"You been up Barking then?" he asked

"Yeah...Fucking Barking, Ilford, Dagenham and now here... I was just about to fuck it off altogether."

Sean was pacing the floor. He looked slightly agitated

"You alright there Fergus? Something you wanna talk about?" Kenny enquired, interested. There was always a drama with Sean.

"Do you not like phones or something? Where's that mobile I got you?"

Kenny could feel the antagonism from Sean pervade into the room. He grinned, showing a full set of perfectly white veneers.

"Why do I want my ear'ole to be permanently connected to an electronic device that ends up ruling my life?" Kenny imitated a telephone attached to his ear with his thumb and finger. "Besides, I'm always around." Why are you so restless anyway?"

"I want you to find someone for me Ken."

"Sure. No Problem. Got a name?"

Sean hesitated for a few seconds. He looked at the man before him. He liked this man. Honestly, truly liked him. He had used Kenny a lot over the years and he had never let him down. He had always delivered. He never asked questions and if asked, he had always given Sean good advice.

They had grown close while Sean was making a name for himself. There was a connection between them. It was unspoken but evident to both. Over the last few years, Sean had become a face in his own right, even if he wouldn't admit that himself. His pure love for violence had put him there and kept him there.

There wasn't many a brave man who was prepared to take on Sean Fergus. He looked at Kenny like a kind of mentor, who had taught Sean all about how to find those who are hiding and while Sean was still in the learning process, Kenny helped him out from time to time; when things got too much for him or when Sean's temper got too much for him. Because of this, Sean had entrusted Kenny with certain snippets of his life; Rachel being one of them.

It was Kenny that had taken it upon himself to fish her out. Sometimes Sean's behaviour really worried him and he believed he would become more settled and less fractious if he knew where she was, that she was happy and settled and living a good life. He compiled quite a dossier on her, before he handed it over to Sean.

"Well, speak up boy." Kenny's voice boomed. He was getting slightly impatient, yet intrigued at the same time.

Sean paced a bit more. He took out his cigarettes and lit one. He puffed out the smoke noisily and rubbed his face with his hand.

"James Porter." The atmosphere rapidly altered. "I want you to find me James Porter."

Kenny stared at the man in front of him. He pulled his glasses off and threw them back onto the counter.

"Are you 'aving a fucking laugh? What you wanna go doing that for? That is not a good plan Sean, really it aint."

Sometimes Kenny could sound like he swallowed a dictionary; his articulation and intelligence astounded most people he met. Other times he showed the real east end sewer mouth he had adopted as a child. Now was one of those times.

"You started this Ken. You told me where she worked, where she lived, all about the kid. You went looking. I hadn't. I had left it where it was…"

"You hadn't left it where it was boy and you know it. You aint stopped banging on about her for the last five years, for as long as I known you."

Kenny threw his arms up in exaggeration, deliberately showing the offence he felt. He walked round the counter, past Sean and over to the window, not looking at him as he past. He kept his back to him while he closed the large Indian hessian blinds.

The room went dark, until he switched on the lights by the door. He turned the 'Closed' sign round and dropped the latch.

Sean watched him all the time.

Their eyes finally locked when Kenny stood in front of him and sighed. "I gave you her as a favour, as a present… for peace of mind like… so you can let it go."

"You found her to screw with my head Ken." Sean poked

a finger into Kenny's chest. "It's what me and you do… manipulation. Jeeze we're the fucking bollocks at it…"

"I am not you Sean." Kenny butted in offensively. "I don't take to this as much as you do."

"Bullshit. Fucking bullshit Ken. You love screwing with people, you love the power you feel when you have something they want. It's why me and you work so well together. Who are you trying to fucking kid… eh?"

"You know what you are Sean." Kenny took a slight step closer. "I don't need to tell you. You know it more than anyone. Finding her was so you can put it all to bed son. This is all her fault. You gotta see that? She has made you into this. Has she come looking for you? Has she fuck… this is all in your 'ead. She couldn't give a diddly squat and you… you blunder through your life, punishing anyone that crosses your path, because of what she did to you."

He put his hand up to Sean's face and brushed his lips with his thumb.

Sean looked at him for a second or two and then pushed his hand away roughly.

"Then why is she in my bed, in my house, right now?"

Kenny took a step back. That was a first. Normally he could predict Sean's move but he hadn't seen that one coming. Sean had always said it was a good thing that Rachel had ended it. That his one saving grace was that he had never hurt her like he knew he could. That he would never be able to be around her again.

Kenny never imagined he would actually make contact with her. He looked slightly warily at Sean. He may be the closest thing to what Sean could call a friend but that didn't mean Kenny had forgotten who he was. This was Sean Fergus he had just made an advance on.

"Just find me Porter old man."

He walked past Kenny and unlocked the shop door. Opening it, he turned round and looked at him.

"I'll be in touch… yeah?"

Kenny stared at the young man at the door. Some psychopaths blend in, undetected, in a variety of surroundings; they are intraspecies predators. Kenny found that by conceptualizing Sean as a psychopath, a remorseless predator, helped him to make sense of what often appeared to be senseless behaviour.

He had seen firsthand the dispositions of manipulation and selfishness, the desecration of social norms and ultimately the instrumental violence associated with psychopathic behaviour, he had seen them all exhibit in Sean; but fleetingly he had also seen regret or something like that. It was in passing moments of panic and realisation and his composure was quickly regained but Kenny had witnessed it all the same.

That was enough for Kenny to believe that somewhere deep inside of Sean was salvation; emancipation from whatever it was that obsessed him, was possible. Kenny truly believed that it was Rachel who had made him this way. He didn't know how wrong he was. Sean looked at him for a long second and then walked out.

He got in his car and slammed his fists down on the steering wheel. He cursed Kenny for making things complicated. He cursed him for putting thoughts in his head, which he definitely didn't want to be there. He leant over and opened the glove box. Pulling out a small plastic tub, he looked around the street.

Cutting two long thick lines, he snorted them down within seconds. He felt it slide down his throat and suppressed an urge to gag. Starting the engine, he pulled out into the road and drove away from the shop. He didn't see that Kenny had reopened the blinds and was standing at the window watching the whole scene before him.

* * *

Maureen Fergus was a great hefty woman, with short dumpy legs; her shortness accentuating the ungainly bulkiness of her frame. The traditional floral print dress and starched beige apron that she wore was a long running family joke, her husband telling anyone that would listen that she had seven of them hanging in her wardrobe, one for each day of the week. Her popularity was as apparent as the sky is blue, her house being a free for all. Friends and neighbours knowing the door was always open.

She was involved with the community activities on the modest Brentwood housing estate, as she was the key holder for the hall that sat at the back of St George's church and she loved nothing more than to gather with her cronies and have a good gossip.

To the outside world, she lived for her family, kept a nice home, neat garden and went to church on a Sunday. She had been faithful to her husband throughout her whole marriage and had bore him a son and two daughters. To Maureen, her life was not quite the picture she painted.

The daughters were not the apples of her eye, as she made them out to be and her son, he troubled her, gave her nightmares sometimes. Her mother used to tell her that he was a bad apple.

She often looked back, to when he was a baby, her first born, Sean, such a bonny wee lad with a thick mass of blonde hair and squirming arms and legs. He always seemed to be pushing her away, even from a day old he fought against her embrace.

He refused point blank to be breast fed and whenever

she picked him up, he would scream. It didn't take very long for Maureen to start resenting him. She had wanted him for so long and had suffered a few miscarriages before he had arrived; a strong healthy boy.

As he grew into a child he became more and more distant from her.

She would watch him sometimes, playing with his toys. When he was five years old, he had received a pellet gun as a present from his father; an idea she had not agreed with. He would line all his action hero figures up against the wall and then he would shoot them all down.

Maureen looked over her nice garden with her nice new garden furniture, all paid for courtesy of her son. Her Husband Mick thought he was bloody marvellous. She sniffed loudly. She knew the truth, even if he couldn't see what was in front of his nose. What they had bred between them.

Still, she comforted herself with knowing she had done right with her daughters. Well, better than she had with Sean. At least her daughters loved her. The eldest girl, Alice, was a good girl. She was smart, had done well at school and lived in London working as a legal secretary.

She had a lawyer fiancé, owned her own house and was in the middle of planning the wedding of all weddings. This made Maureen happy, although she would like to see more of her daughter.

Something told her that Alice was ashamed of her family background and she didn't blame her. They lived in a council house on a run down and half derelict council estate. What is there to show off about that? Maureen had made sure her home was always immaculately presented though and, thanks to Sean, she had brand new furniture in every room, all mod cons; surely that should count for something.

Her other daughter, Maisy, was a different entity altogether. She suffered deep bouts of depression, always had done, ever since she was a child. It started when she was about nine years old. She would suddenly just stop talking and stare into space for hours. The only person that could seem to get through to her when she was like that was Sean.

Being five years older than her and the fact he also had tendencies to shut everyone out, it marvelled Maureen that such closeness between them existed. He would sit with her for hours during her bad days. He would hold her and stroke her hair and whisper endearments into her ear. He had a lot more patience than she gave him credit for.

Sometimes she just wanted to shake her daughter and yell at her to snap out of it. She had tried to get her to see a doctor a few times but Sean was always dead set against it. Always telling her to let it be, that any family problem should be sorted out within the family; it didn't do for outsiders to get involved. Sean insisted there was nothing wrong with her but the last few years had been the worst.

Maureen couldn't believe it when her youngest daughter went into labour on the kitchen floor. She was only eighteen. She didn't even know she was seeing anyone, let alone pregnant but sure enough she helped deliver her granddaughter into the world. Tiny little thing she was, still was now, at the grand old age of three.

Maureen and Mick had raised the child since Maisy gave birth; she had never shown any interest in the girl. Maisy never said who the father was and Sean saw to it that the girl wanted for nothing. He spoilt her rotten and that made Maureen feel uncomfortable.

She didn't know why, it was just a feeling that rooted itself in her mind. As she watched the child now playing in the sand pit, in her newly landscaped garden, she counted her blessings the innocent thing had no idea just how fucked up her family was.

She saw Maisy standing at her bedroom window looking down at them. Maureen waved up at her but Maisy didn't wave back. She didn't smile or even acknowledge her mother or her daughter. Another deep sigh engulfed her. Perhaps Sean's visit today would cheer the girl up, she thought, although Maisy seemed distant from him too, since she had the baby.

Back in Maureen's day, they would call it bad nerves. Nowadays it was termed mental health problems. Whatever it was, Maureen knew there was something seriously wrong with that girl. Her head wasn't well. She knew Sean saw her as a stupid old woman but she bore the girl for nine months. She knew when something wasn't right with her own flesh and blood. Just like she knew there wasn't something right with him. Still, she kept her own counsel on that.

Maisy had been such a sweet natured child. She was always smiling and laughing. She had long fair hair, so shiny and glossed it could illuminate the ocean on a dark stormy night; her natural grace and beauty possessing the ability to light up a room whenever she walked in.

Everybody wanted to be in her company, even Sean, especially Sean. Maureen had encouraged it, finally grateful that he was forming an attachment to someone. Then she just switched off the light around her one day and it never came back on.

She looked back up at the window, where her daughter was still standing. An old, matted brown, dressing gown hung off her waiflike figure. Her wrists bore the evidence of past attempts of self harm.

The long shinning hair that was the colour of sunshine, now hung limply around her face. She had such a vacant look in her eye and once again Maureen felt anxious for her daughter.

Sean may not want intervention from outsiders but Maureen knew she wasn't equipped to deal with her daughter's flare-ups. At seventy-three she was a tough woman but looking after her granddaughter full time was taking it out of her and what with Maisy's outbursts, Maureen called them her paranoid, rambling episodes, occurring more frequently, she wasn't sure how much more energy she had with it all.

What had she done in a past life to have borne two such complete loony-toons? She wondered. No surprise they had a bond between them; they were both as barmy as each other.

Sean interrupted her thoughts. She heard him come through the side gate.

"Bit nippy out here aint it mum?"

He strolled across the patio, to where she was sitting, under the huge canvas canopy that he had arranged to be erected.

"The baby needs fresh air Sean." Maureen said bluntly, nodding over at her granddaughter. "She has her coat and boots on. She is wrapped up warm."

Sean turned to look at the small girl, who was playing away with the buckets and spades in the sand. "Where's my favourite angel then?" He boomed, as he walked over to her

Katie squealed with excitement, as her favourite uncle scooped her up into his arms. She was so delicate, such a tiny fragile perfect little being. Sean looked at her with so much love. Maureen saw it and was up like a flash, despite her heavy load.

"Give us the baby, eh?" She reached to take Katie. "Go up and see y' sister. She's 'aving a bad day today."

Sean held onto Katie for a second and looked over at the house. Then he gave her a gentle kiss on her cheek and let his mother take the child from him. He stroked her hair once she was settled with her granny.

"Son, go up and see Maisy... yeah?"

Sean looked at his mother like she was a stranger. It seemed like he was only just registering what she was saying. The boy had such peculiar ways about him. He got stranger every time Maureen saw him. Without saying anything, he walked past her and into the house.

Maureen cursed under her breath and hugged Katie a little tighter towards her. What had she bought into the world and what would become of this little girl. Maureen herself knew she didn't have forever and Maisy was in no fit state to take care of herself, let alone a small dependent child. Especially one she had taken no interest in since the day she was born.

Alice wouldn't want to take her. She was far too selfish for that. She had ambitions and dreams and would by no means be saddled with a child that wasn't hers. Maureen was not expecting any grandchildren from Alice and Benjamin any time soon. Alice was career driven and determined to make sure her dreams happened.

That left Sean and Maureen swore to herself then, it would be over her dead body that he got his hands on this girl.

* * *

Sean opened the door to Maisy's bedroom. He didn't knock, he walked right in. He closed it behind him and turned the key in the lock. She watched him warily, still standing by the window. Despite her appearance, she was a pretty girl, slim and petit.

"Mum says you're having a bad one today?"

He folded his arms, as if he was bored of this already. Maisy looked down at the floor. She linked her fingers together. It was something she used to do as a child, when she had been caught with her hand in the biscuit tin. It was a disguised innocent gesture that annoyed Sean.

"I don't need mum calling me up fretting about you, do I? I am a busy person Maze; I don't have time to run around after you. Do you want to be put in the loony bin? That's where the old girl wants to put ya? She wants to pump you full of chemicals and let the doctors do experiments with your mind."

Maisy shook her head fervently. She didn't want to be sent away.

"Come away from the window." Sean ordered. "Sit on the bed."

Maisy hesitated for a split second before complying and doing as he had asked. He knelt down on the floor in front of her and took her hands. He traced the scars than ran up her wrist. Maisy looked away from him. She tried to go to the place in her head where she felt safe. Where she could block everything out but he wouldn't let her. He dug his nails into the newly formed skin tissue, bringing her back into the room.

"These are healing well." Sean reached to her bedside drawer and opened the top one. He pulled out a pair of kitchen scissors. Maisy started shaking violently.

"No… No… No… No…" It was more a whispered stutter than a repeating of the word. She stumbled to get it out.

"Sshh… good girl. You're my good girl, aren't you Maze?"

He stroked her hair to calm her. To Maisy it was more

of a warning. She nodded intently at him once more. She just wanted to please him.

"Then you know what I want you to do."

Maisy looked at Sean through bleary eyes and then looked down at the scissors he was holding. She slowly moved her hand and took them out of his. She opened them up to the widest they would go and then with one of the points she stuck it into her wrist.

She watched the blood pour out around the blade. It surprised her every time, what a dark colour it was. She always expected it to be bright red, but it's not. It's almost black at first, until the oxygen gets to it, and then it becomes a deep red.

"Not too deep." Sean warned. "We don't want to cause any damage love, do we?"

Maisy closed her eyes but Sean shook her until she opened them. "And again… let the badness out. You know it's the only way."

Maisy sunk the blade into her arms again and again making small criss-cross incisions. She didn't stop until he took the scissors from her. He then pulled out a first aid box from the drawer and opened it up, taking out the bandages he begun to dress her wounds.

"I don't know why you do this to yourself Maisy. I really don't." He said, as he wrapped the clean white fabric around her sliced up wrist.

"It's not normal behaviour you know, maybe mum is right. Maybe you do need to go to a hospital. I mean… cutting yourself for attention…"

Maisy never spoke a word the whole time he attended to her. When he was finished, he pulled back the duvet and helped her into bed. He gave a sleeping pill and a glass of water and helped her to take it. Laying her down, he kissed her gently on the top of her head and tucked her in.

Although, Sean possessed a general lack of empathy and was austerely incapable of understanding the emotional states of other people, he did accept, purely in a detached and intellectual sense, they existed. All the same, people were little more than objects for his personal gratification. There was no discrimination, the callousness extended to everybody, family and strangers alike.

He neglected other people's needs and desires and casually inflicted cruelty as and when he chose. Regular, ordinary people, experience distress when they observe another human in pain, but the callous psychopath, like Sean, feels nothing. It was why he was capable of dramatic performances of cruelty, because he was not restrained and controlled by the horrifying reaction to his prey's suffering.

"No more dramas, Eh Maze. Let's stop being selfish." He unlocked the door and opened it, then he turned towards her and said "And how about you start taking a bit of an interest in your daughter downstairs. She really is a beauty. Would be such an awful waste, if she fell into the wrong hands."

* * *

While Sean was driving back to his house, he reflected on the last couple of days. He thought about Rachel, who was still currently in his house. He had left her sleeping while he had been to see Kenny.

That was a meeting he had not expected to unravel the way it did. He had thought Kenny had found Rachel so they could be together. He had no idea that Kenny felt resentment towards her.

Rachel was his purity. The only one who made him

question his behaviour. The one that made him feel emotions which he thought he was incapable of.

Sean had rested in the belief that his behaviour was innate. He was convinced that his destiny and everything that it contained was pre-ordained. It was why he found it so easy to conform to the stereotype he had become. Only when he was around Rachel did he feel some form of humanity about his past actions.

She made him question whether there was an alternative version of himself. One that she seemed to see, that she believed in, that she loved. If Rachel could see this version of him, then maybe the appalling form could be stopped, eliminated. She had seen it in him nine years ago and still saw it now. Was there hope for him?

Kenny was so wrong, Sean thought. He no longer abused Maisy out of some sexual or power thrill, it was to make sure she did not tell anyone what had happened and what he had done to her.

For the first time in his entire life he felt, to some extent, a little worried. He knew that Rachel would not accept what he had done and this bothered him.

It bothered him more than he cared to admit, which told him that what he was doing to Maisy and what he had done to people all his life was wrong. It was a new feeling to Sean and he didn't like it.

Many psychopaths are superficially charming. They have a great ability to show displays of emotion and manipulate others. Fred West, a prolific psychopath, was described by his neighbours and friends as charming, amiable, charismatic, convincing and persuasive. He murdered ten women and buried them under his patio.

Sean had the ability to display all of those attributes but never genuinely meant any of it. They served a purpose that was all.

Sean however was glib, he possessed an offhand fluency of speech that was often insincere and superficial, he had few social inhibitions, was extroverted, dominant and confident.

He was not afraid of causing offense, being rejected, or being put down. If these things happened, he would tend to dismiss the charming approach and adopt a role of intimidation, coercion and violence to get his way.

Ultimately he was always going to succeed in his objective, so the means of how it was achieved really wasn't of great bother to him. It all depended on what his current mood was.

He was deficient in the ability to be aware of what life actually means, the ordinary and universal emotion or purpose that gives rise to the various personal and social goals and responsibilities that normal people have.

Sean never spent much time weighing up his actions or their consequences, often due to his seeking of immediate satisfaction for his desires. This resulted in short lived relationships, changing plans and committing crimes, all apparently on a whim. He was very reactive to perceived insults and responded aggressively.

There are lots of different personalities. Some are of a sunny disposition, whereas others adopt a more negative vibe and there are various different mediums in between. Ultimately, personality is made up of aspiration, authority, supremacy and control. The level of how much or how little of each of these a personality contains is variable between people.

Sean possessed high quantities of each. He aspired to be important; to be a somebody. He wielded authority, supremacy and control, as his own personal weapons against humanity. The degree to which these owned him, he decided, explained his abnormal and immoral behaviour.

He saw himself in the third person a lot and it helped him to justify the things that happened. Sean believed it all just happened. He wasn't responsible for anything, he just dealt with what life dished out to him.

People are pushed by desire and pulled by conscience. However, Sean was deficient in the latter. He was only pushed by desire and did not have the equilibrium between the two. Desire comes from the part of the personality that contains the basic animal and primitive impulses which demand immediate satisfaction.

They are unconscious aspects; dark, inaccessible parts of the mind. It's the Mr. Hyde revolting from the reserved Dr. Jekyll; that little devil that sits on your shoulder, whispering enticement and prompting you to be driven by a pleasure seeking libido.

Despite it being an unconscious process, this part of his personality Sean knew only too well. He justified it by questioning where we would be without desire. Does it not push you through life; leading you to seek the things you need to survive. Without it people would die.

It is frenzied, occupied with only incensed pleasure and stimulation. It is filled with energy, originating from instincts, but it has no formation, only a motivation to bring about the attainment of the instinctual need. It is present from birth, driven by the pleasure principle, which strives for immediate gratification of all desires, wants, and needs.

If these needs are not satisfied immediately, the result is a state of anxiety and tension. This was the part of him that Kenny referred to back in the shop. The part Rachel had never seen and must never see. He had to make sure of that.

How though, he wasn't sure of. His delusional mind told him, he couldn't fight the instinctive forces that resided in his head; they were too firmly fixed. But maybe he didn't need to. Maybe the goodness she saw in him could fight them for him.

To balance the strong willed desires that exist in everyone, the sense of reality acts as an opposing force. Sean was capable of exhibiting his own awareness of reality but he willingly chose not to, unless he was only around her.

What is supposed to act as an adjudicator, between the demands of a person's desire and reality, in his mind, just didn't. The opposing force negotiates the desire's power, modifying it in order to achieve the gratification despite the limits of reality; like an umpire at a tennis match.

It regulates people's actions and behaviours, in terms of what society believes to be appropriate, ensuring the impulses of the desires can be expressed in a manner acceptable in the real world. It does this through guilt.

If you do something immoral or break the law, guilt sets in. Sean had no interest in conducting his behaviour within society's guidelines. It held no benefit for him; apart from keeping him out of prison and that is where Kenny had always stepped in. He had cleared up any mess that may have exposed Sean and as far as he was concerned; Kenny always would.

This part of a personality is the part regular people usually show to the world but with Sean, inhibiting it, rather than letting it do its job, was more valuable for him; until he met Rachel again that is. She brought out this side of him. The adjudicating principle was allowed to work, to some extent, but ultimately the desire element prevailed no matter what.

Lastly, there is conscience. This regulates the consciousness' ability to control the desire parts of the personality. Usually, a person's conscience arises from their parents and, as they grow up, they internalise the standards that are taught to them; those same standards that make a person feel guilty when they tell a lie or cheat.

Sean's parents were not saints but in their eyes they believed they had taught their children the difference between right and wrong, good and bad.

Ultimately, this had made no impact on Sean's personality or behaviour. Sean knew the difference between right and wrong but had always dismissed it as applying to him. But does everyone have a conscience?

There are certain people, who have gained infamous notoriety because they committed such horrible acts of violence that we sometimes wonder if they were void of conscience. How can serial killers such as Ted Bundy or Fred West commit such horrible crimes?

Do they lack the basic capacity to feel guilt, so nothing really prevents them from acting out their violent fantasies?

He remembered Kenny saying to him once that evil men do what good men only dream of. This had always stuck in Sean's mind; believing that everybody harboured violent, sadistic and brutal desires; it was just that he was brave enough to indulge in them.

As much as he wanted to be the person that Rachel believed she saw, he couldn't entirely turn his back on what really turned him on. He wasn't sure if he would ever be able to do that; fully and whole heartedly. Rachel was trying to make him re-evaluate that.

Kenny had been trying to teach Sean that there were appropriate times when his violent talents were required. Any other time, for mere amusement, it was inappropriate; for lots of reasons but mainly because you do not want to draw unnecessary attention to yourself.

Rachel was teaching Sean an alternative way of living just by being around her. Kenny should have been pleased and it irritated Sean that he wasn't. Granted, Sean had already admitted to himself that he may not be able to give up his way of life completely, but he needed approval from this man and that perplexed him a little.

It also aggravated him because Kenny played on it. It was like Kenny almost thought he could push Sean into what he wanted him to do. Just because he knew some things which Sean definitely would not want to be public knowledge.

He didn't think for one second Kenny would ever grass on him. It wasn't like that, Kenny wasn't like that. It was just a look that Kenny could give Sean which made him feel beholden to the man; that he owed him something.

It was true; Sean did owe Kenny a huge gratitude. He knew he would be rotting away in a prison cell for the rest of his life, if it wasn't for Kenny's shrewd and innovative thinking and that there would be a time when Sean would have to repay his debt. Sean wasn't too sure how that particular day would play out. It was something that made him feel uncomfortable and he pushed the thoughts out of his mind.

He just needed to get back to Rachel. Just knowing she was waiting for him in his house sent shivers down his back. She was his soulmate, she saw what no one else did and he knew, as soon as he saw her again, he was never letting her go. She belonged to him completely. He had let her leave him once before and it had destroyed him.

He now knew that they were intrinsically tied to each other forever and that he must not let anybody or anything ever get in the way of that again. It is why he asked Kenny to find him James, he needed to know where he was, what he was doing. If there was any potential threat of him ever resurfacing to claim his child and in effect Rachel.

Then there was Greg, the other man in her life. Rachel

had already promised Sean she was going to finish it with him. That she just needed some time to work out how. He had to accept that for now but he wouldn't wait for long. The sooner Rachel was finally entirely his, the better everything would be.

The Chronicles
How What Was Came To Be

"Indeed, history is nothing more than a tableau of crimes and misfortunes."

Voltaire 1694 -1778

Chapter 6

May 1995

Maureen bustled through to the living room from the hall way, whilst trying to pull a large wax jacket onto her graceless frame.

"SEAN!" She yelled at the top of her voice. Not waiting for a response she yelled again; this time putting emphasis on to her son's name. "SHORRN!"

She picked up her handbag and car keys that were on the table; patting her daughter's head who was sitting on the floor in front of the TV. She didn't see the distress in her eyes or the tear that rolled down her cheek.

Walking back through to the hall, she stood at the bottom of the stairs. Yelling again, this time with all her muster, she heard the bedroom door open. Sean popped his head round the door and looked down the stairs.

"I am off too work. I am not sure what y' dad's doing, he did mention some overtime. If he decides to come home, tell him his dinner is in the oven. Alice is staying over at

81

Emily's and won't be back till the morning. Don't let Maisy stay up all night long watching tele and Sean watch her will you? Not lock yourself in your room and leaving her too her own devices. I know what you're like. When I ask you to watch your sisters' that is what I expect you to do, exactly that, watch them. I'll be home about eleven… Okay?"

Sean knew she wasn't really asking for a response. He watched her check herself in the mirror that hung by the front door and then she was gone. He waited for a few seconds, until he heard the engine of her car start and her reverse out of the drive. When he could no longer hear her in the distance he walked down the stairs and into the living room.

Sean closed the door that led to the hall way. He then walked across to the other side of the room and closed the door that led to the kitchen. He checked the patio doors were locked and then pulled the thick heavy curtains across them. Looking around the room he was satisfied.

Maisy was still sitting on the floor in front of the TV. She had watched everything he had just done, out of the corner of her eye. She bit her bottom lip, as she thought about what was going to come next.

She had been left alone with Sean lots of times and it was always the same. He would lock all the doors and close all the curtains. Then he would expect her to do certain things for him. It was their special game. Nobody loved her like Sean did and this was how she said thank you for that love. He had told her that she wasn't wanted by mum and dad, for as long as she could remember. She was only ten, yet that idea was firmly fixed in her mind.

He repeatedly reminded her that she was a mistake; that she wasn't wanted because their parents already had a boy and a girl. It was only him that cared about her and thought she was worthwhile. Maisy believed him. Her mother was always so busy, with housework, or cooking, or rushing off to work and her father was out driving his taxi all day and all night, she hardly ever saw him.

Sean told her she was lucky to have him and she accepted that as true. She didn't like having to say thank you though; it made Maisy feel uncomfortable. He didn't hurt her, in fact he was very gentle but his touch made her think he could do so very badly. Something deep inside told her what he did to her wasn't normal. However, the more he convinced Maisy that he was the only one that loved her, the more she felt she had to repay him.

If she hesitated or protested, he said he wouldn't love her anymore and that then their mother would hand her over to social services. He also bound her in silence, by telling her that if their parents found out about their love and their special game, then she would be locked away forever. As a less advanced and tremendously confused ten year old, these threats were exceptionally intimidating.

"Maisy?" He beckoned her.

She turned her head to face him and moved her fringe out of her eyes, in a sweeping gesture with her hand.

Slowly, she stood up and straightened her nightdress. She gradually began to move toward him. Her movement was not exactly hesitant but it was forced all the same.

When she reached him, she took his hand and smiled up at him for reassurance that what she was doing was right. She led him over to the sofa and sat down next to him. He stroked her long blonde hair. It felt so soft and silky, almost like velvet. She didn't look ten. She looked much younger Sean decided.

When Alice was ten she had budding breasts and the mind of an old whore. She had known every swear word going and embarrassed her mother frequently by listing them out loud. She was four years older than Maisy and at fourteen she had the head of a wise old lady. There is no way in the world that Sean could manipulate Alice, in the way he did her.

She just wouldn't have stood for it; she was far too headstrong to be used and abused. It fascinated him just what he could make Maisy do. She was so desperate to be loved that she accepted him treating her however he wanted.

He could push her away and degrade her, yet with sweet whispered words, he could have her begging him to love her again. It amazed him and thrilled him at the same time.

Each time he was left to look after her and they were alone, he would push the boundaries just that little bit more; enthralled to see what else he was able to do. Intrigued by his capabilities, he enticed himself to explore hidden fantasies which he had suppressed.

When they first arose he was only a small boy and he had no idea what the feelings were that spurred him on to torture his sister's kitten. He had a slightly better understanding now, at fifteen, of what they were but he still wasn't fully aware of the power it would yield over him, in the years to come.

For now, Maisy was his learning curve, a subject that was going to teach him about the dominance and supremacy that he possessed.

It didn't matter to him that she was his sister or that she was just a child; that was of irrelevance to Sean. His brain didn't work in the same way as most other people. He didn't appreciate that other people had feelings, or emotions, or hopes or fears. He saw them as tools that were there for his use, they were a means to an end. They held no significance for him.

He didn't understand humanity. He lived by basic needs and wants. He had no empathy, so the pain and sorrow that he caused others, were a phenomenon to him. It excited him and drove him to repeat the experience. Forcing somebody to do something against their will was captivating to him.

Maisy was just the beginning. Sean had no idea of the man he was to become. For now, he was enjoying the emotional exploitation he could inflict; the physical cruelty would come a bit later on in his life. The very essence of Sean's soul was deceitful and manipulative; the social deviant only capable of shallow emotions.

Impulsive; poor behavioural controls; the need for excitement; the lack of responsibility; what was missing, in other words, were the very qualities that allow a human being to live in social harmony.

Chapter 7

January 1997

Sean watched her walk. The grace and poise with which she held herself was unlike anything he had ever seen before. As far as he was concerned, she was exquisite. It was the second time he had seen her around the town; the first took his breath away, quite literately.

She was always on her own, always with a look in her eye that showed she was a million miles away. He watched her stop at shop windows for a few moments and then move on along the busy road.

He had noticed girls before, but not like he had noticed her. Sean was a jack the lad. He had been popular at school because of his exceptionally brooding good looks and over the last year he had taken full advantage of that. The fact he had discovered the monetary gain in drug dealing gave him extra kudos and the seventeen year old girls could not resist the bad boy, to rebel against the system with.

Not one of them had grabbed his attention like the

girl he had spent that afternoon following. Most just threw themselves at him but she had walked right past not even aware he was there.

Brentwood High Street is about a half a mile long with shops, restaurants, boutiques and salons along both sides. It runs from a double mini roundabout and is intersected by about half a dozen crossings. As he leant against the wall of the White Hart, he watched her use one of those crossings to traverse the street.

It was the blonde mass of animated curls which caught his attention the first time he saw her but this time it was the round sapphire-blue eyes. He could swear she was looking right at him, though of course he knew she wasn't; she hadn't noticed him for the last few hours but as she walked towards him, her eyes locked in with his and he was captivated.

He was supposed to be delivering some weed. He was on his way to do it, when he drove down the high street and saw her again. He had quickly parked in the car park that was just behind the shops and almost ran back down the road, in case she had disappeared.

She was bigger than the usual type of girl he went for. Past experiences had been with skinny, still developing teens, clumsy fumbles and awkward sex. She was buxom and curvy and even dressed in the baggy, combat style, pair of jeans she had on, the tight vest top she had put with it exposed her hourglass figure. There was not a scrap of make-up on her face; her natural beauty was overwhelming.

He was so completely entranced by her, it had taken him a few seconds to register that she had stopped walking and was standing right in front of him. It was another few more seconds before he realised she was talking to him, although it was more like shouting.

He was amused and impressed and turned on, all at the same time. She however, was less impressed with him and called him all sorts of names; a creep and a pervert being the top of her list.

Her eyes glistened when she was angry and a small, thin, silvery-blue vein appeared across her forehead, which Sean could only describe as cute. He had never thought of anything as cute before.

When she demanded what he had to say for himself, he could do nothing else but smile, tell her she was beautiful when she was mad and ask to see her again. It had worked, after a little convincing.

He couldn't believe it, when she had said yes. Shag 'em and leave 'em. That was his method. He had never had a girlfriend and had never taken a girl out; never really seeing the purpose. Girls flocked to him, so he had never chased them before.

If they didn't 'put out' he moved on. When they did 'put out' he moved on. This one though, wasn't about that, she hypnotized him; first with her looks and then with her brain.

Even now, three months later, she hadn't lost her appeal. He found her just as fascinating and just as beautiful. He couldn't imagine the idea of not being around her and she seemed to be the answer to his purpose in life. He saw a kind of normality that didn't exist without her. She made him laugh; an entirely new concept to him. She occupied his mind so completely; he hadn't even bothered with Maisy for quite a while.

He had no need to exploit and manipulate his sister. He didn't have the time either; he spent every waking moment with Rachel and every sleeping moment dreaming about her.

Even the fact that they had not even come close to having sex had not deterred him. As long as she was by his side, that was all he was concerned with. Nothing and nobody had ever made him feel like she did.

He wasn't the only one who was pulled in by her physical presence. He had noticed it ever since he first took her out. Men stared at her, as she walked past them. Boys watched in envy, when they saw her sat in his car, while he bombed around the county. What made her even more enticing was, she was completely unaware of the reaction she caused.

It wasn't so bad when she was on one of his errands with him. His customers knew the score. She was Sean's girl; it meant you definitely didn't look. But when they were out raving, or scouring second hand bookshops, or browsing charity shops for quaint little nic-naks, which he frequently found himself doing without the slightest protest, because he knew it was what she loved to do, he noticed it much more.

The first few weeks he found it amusing and revelled in having something nobody else did. But the amusement began to turn to a possessive infatuation. His obsession with her made him anxious. She made him feel things he had never felt before. It was a throbbing ache that griped itself around his chest like a vice, torturing him constantly.

When he took her to the raves, she looked amazing. She would wind the wayward curls into tight, neat little bundles all over her head, each one tied with a different florescent coloured band. It displayed a perfect bone structure that was normally hidden under a mass of tresses. The tightness of the bundles pinned against her scalp and the minimum of make-up that she wore made her eyes dance.

Even with the amount of pills she threw down her throat, she never looked a mess and when she smiled he knew that the receiver of that smile would become hypnotised. Sean was well aware he wouldn't have long with her; that she didn't really belong to him or with him. After always taking what he wanted and never really thinking about whether he had the right, the way he saw him and her was a complete opposite.

But he couldn't bring himself to own her the way he wanted to. There was something in his head that always stopped him. She was his idea of what an angel was; pure and delicate, yet so unbelievably strong. You couldn't keep an angel. They would die in captivity. Angels visit when you need them most and then they leave. They are loaned to you by God. That's the way it works.

Sean wasn't religious, despite his mother's best efforts to drag him to Sunday school and Mass every week, for as long as he could remember, but he liked the stories; parts of them anyway. It was the sermons delivered by the tall, robed Reverend Parson's at St George's, with his thunderous deafening voice, which made him come to the conclusion that if there was one divinity, that had the power the bible said it did, he was doomed right from the start.

But he saw a vision of God when he first saw her and if it was all true, he wasn't about to start fucking around with the main man himself. When he wanted his angel back, Sean would let him take her.

"Always staring!" She said, looking up from the book she was reading.

That was another thing he liked, she read. Like all the time. She read anything, newspapers, magazines, books. There was always a book in her bag and more often than not in her hand. She was clever as well. Not in a 'make you feel stupid' sort of way, but she always explained and introduced him to new information.

If he was honest, he wasn't really that interested in what she was saying but he could listen to her talk for hours and quite often did; her random facts that she would suddenly blurt out could have him in stitches.

91

"I could watch you all day." Sean answered her "Even if you aren't really here, but off somewhere in that thing." He gestured to the book.

Rachel's embarrassed smile sent shivers all the way down his spine.

She closed the hardback. "Sorry. Alice in Wonderland. It's my favourite!"

"It's a kid's story!"

He was mocking her but had a glint in his eyes showing he was secretly endeared by it.

"Don't you ever have a favourite story, from when you were younger? Something your mum used to read to you?"

"No!" Sean laughed, finding the idea ludicrous.

"No, me either. My mum would be too pissed to read me a bedtime story. I was eleven when my social worker gave me this. I had never had a present before so whenever I feel anxious or threatened in some way, I read this. It reminds me that someone cared… *Once*." The last word was almost whispered.

"You worried about next week; the meeting with your mum?"

Rachel looked out of the car window. They were parked in the garage block at the back of Sean's estate. They had been smoking a joint, while he was fitting his stereo; acquired as a payment for a debt he was owed.

"A bit." She shrugged. "It's no big deal."

"It's a pretty big deal. You haven't seen her for years." Sean said.

"I'm used to that. It's always been that way." She replied. It wasn't so much the fact that her mother had requested to see her again, it was more to do with why. "I'm more curious than worried. It's not like they can make me go and live with her again is it. Now I have my own place."

As much as she did love her mother, Rachel preferred

her life when she was out of it. The alcohol just caused too much drama.

Sean had a colossal urge to tell her that he cared, that she wasn't alone anymore, but he couldn't. He had never made such declarations to anyone before. He didn't know how to. They had never kissed and she bantered with him like two mates would. He wasn't even sure if she liked him, like he liked her.

It made him nervous around her. He couldn't be the loud brash vulgar form of his self that he was so used to, because she just laughed at him. It made him feel like he was three foot tall.

She found his drug dealing appealing, but that was as far as the *wannabe moll* went. Rachel was not impressed by the status of being Sean Fergus' girlfriend and often teased him for his female admirers. She saw through the bad boy image and caught sight of something else. Sean didn't know what it was but it had made her stay; made her spend every minute she could with him.

"Rach?"

"What?" She kept staring out the window

He wanted to tell her how he felt. He wanted to shout it out but he just couldn't find the words. It was like something was physically preventing his mouth from forming the sounds. His silence caused her to turn and look at him.

"What?" she repeated more gently. Her eyes searched his, as she tried to read his face.

"Coming for a drive? Gotta drop something off."

She nodded and watched him look away from her to start the engine. He had done that a few times recently. Gone to say something and then changed his mind. It was annoying and frustrating. She just wished he would tell her why he was so insistent on being in her company.

She had worked out quite quickly, that he was well

known. He supplied half of Essex with weed and ecstasy. He could have his pick of girls, but he pursued her; yet he never really tried to take it any further. They talked for hours about anything and everything, apart from them. He never tried to touch her, or kiss her, yet he looked at her like he had never wanted anything more.

She had fallen for him almost instantly. Despite giving him a verbal dressing down in the middle of Brentwood High Street, she had actually been completely flattered that he had been following her, let alone that he had listed several positives to letting him take her out. Nobody had ever taken an interest in her before, especially such as keen one.

They didn't speak any more. Both were wrapped up in their own insecure thoughts. Sean tried to make a conscious effort to concentrate on the road ahead and Rachel pretended to read her book. It only took about five minutes to drive over to Shenfield High Street.

Sean swung into the taxi bay that was at the small entrance of the railway station. They weren't that far from Rachel's flat.

It was a busy Saturday afternoon and the taxis were in and out in a constant stream; dropping off and picking up the hundreds of commuters and shoppers. Sean got out of the car without a word and headed towards the small wooden shack that served as the cab office. Rachel watched him disappear inside. A knock on the windscreen made her jump.

Expecting to see one of the drivers wanting her to move the car, she was surprised to see a friend standing there, grinning into the glass. Smiling, she opened the car door to get out.

"Nathan!" Rachel exclaimed, obviously pleased to see him.

"Watcha kid. Thought that was you. How you doing? It's been a while."

Rachel let the older boy take her into his arms and give her a tight squeeze. She smelt the familiar scent of him. It was a smell that took her back to being young and to a time where her childhood was actually quite settled and happy.

Nathan was the son of one of her mother's many boyfriends. This one however, had stuck around for a few years, both families attempting to take a shot at normality and stability.

For a while it worked, but Nathan's dad was a bigger alcoholic than Rachel's mum was and after two years, her mum said enough was enough and kicked them both out. At the time, Rachel was devastated and she had often thought about Nathan and his dad.

He had been the closest thing she had ever had to an older brother and he had looked out for her like one too; even though he was actually only a few months older than her he had always acted like she was the baby. She couldn't believe that he was standing right in front of her now.

When he finally let her go, he couldn't stop grinning at her.

"How's ya mum, she doing okay?"

"Oh you know mum. Same old. How is your dad?"

The grin disappeared from Nathans face and sadness emerged in his eyes. "Dad died a few years back. His liver finally gave up, I guess."

"Oh Nate, I'm sorry. I didn't know."

He smiled at her again, but she could see it was still a painful memory for him. They had been close, Nathan and his dad and Rachel knew it must have knocked him for six when he died.

Now she looked closer at the boy, she could see his clothes were crumpled from lack of ironing and he sported a few days growth on his face. His skin had a grey tinge to it and he was constantly fidgeting with his fingers.

Before she could ask him anything else, she noticed the look that crept across Nathan's face and then she felt Sean's arm around her back.

"What you doing out the car?" Sean's low voice had an ominous undertone to it.

Rachel observed the cold stare that he was giving Nathan. She didn't like it. An odd, disturbing feeling begun to escalate within her chest.

"I wasn't aware I had to stay in the car." She retorted back curtly.

The hostile response was not lost on Sean and he told himself to keep calm. His eyes did a quick survey of the station and taxi rank. They were not noticed, inconspicuous to the busy activity of a Saturday afternoon.

He pushed Rachel quite firmly behind him and stepped towards Nathan, who in return very quickly backed off a few paces.

Sean willed himself to remain calm but he could feel the rage that was racing through his blood intensify. He made a conscious effort to keep his arms by his side, digging his fingernails into the palm of his hands in an attempt to keep his control.

"Jog the fuck on." He sneered at him. His whole face screwed up in complete repulsion.

Nathan didn't need to be told twice and he scurried away like a gerbil that had been put back in his cage.

Rachel grabbed hold of Sean, her eyes flared in temper and indignation. "We were just talking."

"I didn't like it."

He was husky and importunate; his shoving her backwards, past the car, amplified that bubbling disturbance around her chest.

She let out a small gasp, when the wall she stumbled against broke his force. She looked into Sean's eyes, seeing the urgency and wanting he had for her. Her whole body felt like it was pounding in time with her heartbeat. She felt his grip on her loosen and the concern that he hurt her was written all over his face. She held onto him tighter. She couldn't breathe. Something was overriding her every sense.

He felt it too. She was driving him crazy just looking at him. To be so close to her and not just take her was the hardest thing he had ever done. Sean fought every instinctual drive he had not to kiss her and rove her body with his hands. The more her eyes bored into his, the harder it became to resist.

He knew she was mentally begging him to give in, but he also knew that if he did, he would possess her for the rest of her life; because once he had her completely, he knew he could never let her go.

Rachel's head was swimming. Everything around her was cloudy and insignificant. It was all getting too fervent and obsessive. The voice in the back of her head, which had started off as a slow quiet warning, rising every now and then only to be stifled and pushed away, was now screaming at a crescendo.

"It shouldn't be like this, it shouldn't be so intense." She whispered.

Sean heard the croakiness in her voice and stroked the outline of her face. She had never wanted to be kissed, yet not be kissed in her whole life. The conflicting thoughts and feelings adding to her dizziness.

"I knew him. I've known him since I was little. He is almost family." Rachel protested; her indignation somewhat overzealous.

"I don't like you talking to anyone, especially junked up shit like that. I can't stand anybody else having your attention if only for a second."

She moved her hands up to cover her face. She couldn't think straight. The possessiveness he had over her should have been enough to jolt her into getting as far away from him as she could, but in all honesty, she secretly cherished it.

Nobody had ever made her feel as important as he did. Her every instinct was tingling with desire, longing for him to fight the persistent voice in her head, which still screamed at her to run.

He knew that he had to let her go. He knew that she knew it to. He would ruin her life if she stayed, he was only too aware of that. For the first time in his entire existence, he felt the sting of tears well up in his eyes. He had never had to let anything go before and it was hard. So much harder than he had ever thought.

Sean had always taken what he wanted, but he knew he couldn't have Rachel. She was too pure and unsullied to be anywhere near him. He was actually humbled that she had spent any time with him at all.

"It's over… isn't it?" Sean said, freeing his grip on her completely, to pull away her hands from her face.

Rachel closed her eyes and let two tears roll down her cheeks. "I think it has to be."

She put her hand up to wipe the tears away and when she opened her eyes, she knew he wouldn't be there, that he had already gone.

The regret set in about ten seconds later.

Chapter 8

January 2000

Rachel pulled the bud of marijuana apart with her fingers; the oily residue layering her skin. The smell of fresh nettles wafted up her nose and she stifled a sneeze. Pressing it into one half of the plastic grinder and fitting the other half on top, she begun to twist it back and forth; crushing the contents into a soft fluffy mound that always reminded her of moss covered stones.

Emptying it into a small plastic pot, she began her morning ritual of rolling a joint to go with her cup of tea in bed, before Adam would come bounding in, wanting to play and have his breakfast. At almost three years old, he was the most perfect thing she had ever done.

Taking a Rizla out of its packet, she embarked on ripping open a cigarette and interspersed the tobacco and ground weed on the flimsy paper. With an experienced hand, she rolled it into a perfect cone.

She smoked a lot of weed; she would be the first to

admit that. But since she had made the decision to keep her baby, she hadn't touched any other drug of any kind. She even stopped smoking while she was pregnant. She was determined to be a good mum and believed she was.

Adam had every educational toy there was to buy; she limited his television viewing, made sure he got plenty of fresh air, attended every postnatal appointment and had just enrolled him in a playgroup near where she lived. She smoked weed but she loved her child to the ends of the earth.

Her home in Brentwood was clean, albeit messy; she liked to think of it as 'lived in' and her child was happy, secure and loved. It was in a new housing block that was just a few roads behind the high street. Compared to the damp bedsit in Shenfield, which Social Services had dumped her in a few years ago, she thought she had done okay.

She believed that as long as Adam was well looked after, she was doing a good job. She didn't drink; she hardly ever went out anymore. She lived for her child, so in her eyes she could warrant her cannabis use.

Her bedroom was surprisingly spacious, relative to the rest of the small two-bedroom flat. The walls were a pale yellow, painted on top of woodchip wallpaper. The bed frame, dresser and wardrobe had all been stained in white, giving the room a sense of harmonic stillness. Only the red love hearts, which stamped a border around the top of the walls and the blush red of the duvet set, disrupted the tranquil ambience.

Lighting the joint, Rachel leaned back against the headboard, as she inhaled the smoke deep into her lungs. She looked down at the sleeping body next to her. She would have to wake him soon and get him out. The last thing she wanted was a three year old asking awkward questions, as to why there was a man in mummy's bed.

Children have a funny way of calling things how they are, they learn tact and subtlety much later and Adam was getting more astute by the day. It was fine when he was a baby and unaware of who was around him but trying to hide things from a very inquisitive toddler was a different ball game altogether.

The sleeping man stirred slightly. As she watched him, she thought about the previous night. How he had gone all out to impress her, turning up with flowers, wine, a Chinese take-away and some sweets for Adam, which were put in the cupboard out of the boy's sight and reach. He made her laugh while they ate and paid her compliments throughout the evening.

She knew she should have made him leave when it had got late, but she liked this man. He was kind and he looked at her with complete adoration. Normally this was around the time she would stop things going any further. Since Adam had arrived, she hadn't let herself become attached to any other man.

As soon as anybody begun to get vaguely serious about her she would stop it dead. She wasn't interested in any kind of significant relationship. She convinced herself that, if she just focused on bringing up Adam and providing for his needs, she wouldn't have time to let her mind think about what she had banished four years ago.

It had worked to some extent. If she kept her mind occupied, then she could go a good few hours without thinking about it; about him. So relationships were not part of the plan. She wasn't any good at them. Sean and James had both shown her that. But this one was different. She enjoyed being in his company. She felt at ease with him and they always found they had something to say to each other. It felt natural.

This was a new experience for her and she wasn't too sure

how to handle it. Forming relationships, of any kind, had always been a struggle for Rachel. It's what happens when you grow up in care. Her mother was an alcoholic and had spent Rachel's childhood in and out of various rehab clinics. She never knew her father, so as a result Rachel had spent a lot of her teenage years with different foster families.

Just as she had begun to feel a little settled with one, her mother would decide she was sober again and request her back. Then, after a few months, her mother would resolve to no longer being able to face the world without a drink and hand her daughter back over to the care of social services.

This went on for as long as Rachel could remember. It was a familiar pattern and was probably why Rachel never felt comfortable with anything that was too permanent.

Sex was carefree and abundant. It was something she used to escape the trials of life but men seemed to want more, the ones she had come across did anyhow. So she would conclude the affiliation between them and move on. She didn't see any point in continuing, as they would never be able to take away the longing that sat around her heart.

But the sleeping man, he had turned her head. He hadn't pestered her in a puppy dog way. He had very much left it all up to her. He didn't call; he waited till she got in touch. He didn't sit on her every word or try to impress her with declarations. He looked at her in a way that bore into her soul; it was like he knew she was fighting some inner struggle, which he didn't push her to reveal.

Maybe, she thought, it was because they had some sort of shared history between them. Maybe that explained the connection she felt to him. Something that reminded her of the old her; from before she made the choices that she was still paying for now.

She should have told him to go the previous night but she hadn't. She had let him take her hand and lead her into the bedroom. She had let him undress her and make love to her. He had smelled of fastidious self-maintenance; that detergent fuelled haze that shrouds you sometimes, when you walk past a launderette. It was virtually edible. His hair; limp with freshness. The vanity of youth or perhaps the anxiety of it.

She had let herself fall asleep with him holding her, caressing her as she slept. She wasn't sure if she had made love to him back. But she knew she definitely liked being held afterwards. That was a first for Rachel and she had enjoyed it. She felt safe and relaxed. Now though, she wasn't so sure. He opened his eyes to see her watching him, screwing his face up to the light he groaned.

"Good Morning. How long have you been awake?" He tried to stifle a yawn.

Rachel blew out the last lug of her joint and threw it into the ashtray. She put it on the dresser next to the bed and tried not to catch his gaze.

"You have to go. Adam will be awake soon and he can't see you." She pulled the sheet around herself and moved to get out of bed. "You should get dressed."

He grabbed her wrist and pulled her back into his arms. "Don't do this. Don't give up without even trying."

She didn't want to deal with the confrontation. She just wanted him to go; although she didn't really. The confusion was immense. Being put on the spot made her feel like a giantess who had blundered into the wrong house. The atmosphere became blinded by awkwardness and her discomfiture was so physically evident.

"Greg... I can't..." She tried to push him away but he wasn't having any of it.

"I know I am not him." The words made her stop struggling against him. They pounded into her brain.

Nobody had ever said that to her. Nobody had ever acknowledged him; the elephant in the room.

"I don't try to be, I won't try to be. But I can make you forget him. I can show you there is more, than living half a life; because that's what you are doing. Is that fair to Adam?"

He looked at her so intently and when she leant forward and kissed him in urgency, he finally managed to breathe out.

Greg Carson had known Rachel for quite a while. He knew her from when she was with Sean; that was a particular circumstance which he had never understood. She had always seemed quiet, shy. Not at all like the other girls that threw themselves at him.

Greg had gone away to university and when he came back he had bumped into her again. They had chatted for a while and she had told him about Adam.

He had known Sean from school, although never as friends. Sean never seemed to hang around with the boys, only the girls. They both lived in Brentwood, although Greg's parents lived in a much more affluent part than Mick and Maureen Fergus' modest council estate. The distinctive, post sixties, end terrace house which Sean grew up in, was a far cry from the large detached dwelling of Greg's childhood.

Rachel had not mentioned who the father was and Greg had automatically assumed that he was Sean's. She had not mentioned Sean full stop and that just gave confirmation to what he already thought. It had been the 1990's and the 'raving scene' had exploded across the country. Essex is a small place; inadvertently paths cross.

Greg had met Sean again through some of his friends, when they made purchases from him, so he had also met Rachel. She didn't look twice at him though. She had been too blinkered by Sean and if he was honest with himself, he knew she still was.

Sean had taken Rachel with him everywhere he went. She would always be sitting in the front of his little red Renault 5 GT Turbo whenever he was gallivanting across the county on one of his drug running assignments.

They would be at the same raves that Greg went to, where Sean would have her hanging off his arm. It always gave him the impression that she was worn as a trophy. He had no doubt that Sean had no respect for the new music and culture that was emerging around him; they were just platforms for him to step off from.

To Greg it was the beginning of a whole new world. Raves were free parties; free from the restrictions of the legal club scene. Raves were autonomous, where all the revellers created and enforced the rules.

This meant that drugs were readily available, noise levels were illegally high and there would be no age limit. Clubs had a legally required age limit of either eighteen or twenty-one. The rave scene catered for the population under these brackets.

It was the lack of restrictions and law enforcement that initially attracted, but ultimately it was the music; a new age of music and experimentation. He thought it must have been what the swinging sixties would have been like. The country hadn't had anything quite as dramatic.

It was a new sound and a new scene. Creative art, backdrops, sculptures, mobile visuals, graphics and lasers, such as had never been seen before. It became more than just a few flashing lights and machine generated smoke, as it was in the acid house parties of the 1980's. There was more love, more determination and more loyalty on the side of the ravers.

They would have to travel miles to get to an event. Most

of these parties were illegal. There would be no guarantee that it was even going to happen, as police would often get there before the masses and shut it down.

The location would be kept top secret right up until the last minute in order to try and prevent police intervention. After the chaos that ensued during an Easter bank holiday rave in London, rave organisers were very much alerted to what could happen when the police got involved.

Greg was too young at the time to remember what took place that night, but his older brother Matthew had been there and had filled him in when he was older.

A thousand revellers had been at the rave. Police sealed off the building. There had been no trouble and no complaints, the party was free and open to all, there was no explanation from the police as to what their intentions were, nor indeed any justification for what had happened next.

The police prevented anyone entering or leaving the premises. Anyone who did attempt to was maliciously beaten to the ground. Riot police, wearing padded jackets and helmets, wielding shields and batons stormed the building.

No warning was given. Sledge hammers and a JCB digger were used, to collapse the walls in on people trapped inside. When they finally got into the building, they indiscriminately beat up men, women and children.

People were trying to escape the vicious onslaught from the police. There was panic as people tried to crush through one small exit. Instead of alleviating the crush, the police pushed up hard behind everyone, hitting out and forcing everyone face down onto the ground.

Some people were singled out and given further severe beatings. The police started on the equipment, which had been lent or donated, destroying it needlessly. The local hospital reported hundreds of casualties amongst the party goers; just one policeman injured. Arrests were made, for assaults on police officers and for breach of the peace.

By the time Greg, Rachel and Sean got involved with the scene four years later, raves were arranged on a need to know basis. This would entail a process of first the date and D.J's being advertised on posters. These would be plastered around the county, on walls, bus stops, lamp posts, telegraph poles, on roundabouts, over road signs.

The location would not be advertised, just a mobile number to text. On the night, hundreds of cars would congregate together, up and down the major roads across the county, waiting for the message to be sent through, telling them where to go onto next. This would then be repeated and could go on for hours.

The destination would never be revealed until the early hours of the morning, but when you finally got there, you entered into a parallel universe of unadulterated escapism.

As he kissed her back, that all seemed a life time ago now. He heard Adam call out for his mum and felt Rachel pull away. He saw the reservation return to her eyes. He knew he was on shaky ground with her. She had no real idea of how she felt or what she wanted, but he knew he wanted her. He always had.

This was his chance, the small window of opportunity that wouldn't come around very often. Not with girls like Rachel. He knew she had never looked at him in that way before, her mind and heart too preoccupied by a wasted drifter. But he also realised that she was ready to move on, that she desperately needed to and he was determined to make sure it was him that she moved on with.

"How about I make a cuppa tea and you tell Adam you have a guest for breakfast?"

The subtle insistence that he was not intending to go anywhere had the desired bamboozling effect.

He jumped out of bed and pulled his jeans on. He was out of the door in a flash, leaving her to contemplate what just occurred. As she put on her dressing gown she marvelled at how things can suddenly just change. She wondered at the possibility of this new decade; the new millennium might not be that bad after all.

Chapter 9

April 2001

The constant shrill of the telephone worked its way through to a semi-conscious Kenny. He opened his eyes slowly and tried to focus on the clock that sat on the bedside table.

Slowly, his eyes allowed the red numbers to blur out and the 04:17 finally registered in his mind. The phone was still ringing relentlessly and a sudden fear enveloped him; that it was trouble with one of the children. He reached out and grabbed the phone.

"Kenny… Ken… You there?"

"Who is this?"

"Ken, I need ya help… I… Ken?

"Sean?" Kenny rubbed his temples in a slow circular motion with his free hand. It was still dark outside. He was awake now.

"I fucked up Ken…"

He listened to Sean ramble on about something and

nothing. It didn't make much sense. He hadn't known the kid for that long. But he was up and coming, he knew that. He had met him a little while back through some mutual acquaintances. Kenny had heard of his reputation, so he employed Sean's services, as an inhumane thug.

Kenny hated violence, but that did not mean that he couldn't appreciate its effectiveness and understand the importance of it, especially in the world that they lived in. Sean's other enterprises, such as his sideline in prostitutes, had held Kenny's attention. It wasn't so much the girls that he was interested in, as the boys.

People like Sean and Kenny didn't live by the rules that govern society. They didn't pay taxes, or contribute to the running of the economy; not in the way that regular honest people did.

They lived by a different set of rules, where respect, honour and status were of greater magnitude than honesty, integrity and morality.

Kenny and Sean were entities on their own. Everybody gets a choice in how they will live their lives. Free will determines that for every human. For some people the choice is an easy one.

A nice homely upbringing, which is lavished with love and happiness, normally determines that the choices of that life will be of a similar nature. When that loving and happy childhood is not available though, it can be expected that the choices made in later life will be quite the opposite; a home that is loveless and full of neglect will usually be replicated by a next generation.

They had both made a choice as to how they would live their lives. For Sean, the choice was preordained; the monster that lived inside of him controlled his thoughts, his actions, even his motives. Kenny's choice was different; he had made his out of loyalty and a sense of duty.

Even so, in his eyes, these choices were rarely choices and Kenny was a firm believer that everything was already laid out. There was something about Sean that intrigued him. He was a lost wild beast, but he had a vulnerability buried in the debauched version of himself that Sean had allowed to take form; free will. Kenny had seen it though, in fleeting moments, usually when the drugs had worn off.

He wondered what had happened to Sean for him to be like he was. It was a crazed and demented persona, which would take even the paramount psycho years to perfect. It would need shaping and forming to achieve the fanatical and extreme eminence that Sean portrayed. Yet he was only twenty-one.

Kenny hadn't made any coherent sense from Sean's frantic phone call. He had managed to get an address from him and was on his way to a block of flats, on a housing estate in Harold Wood. Kenny hated this particular suburb of Essex. It was run down, derelict in parts and overrun with Turkish kebab shops.

Even the people that lived there seemed to look run down, life taking its daily toll etched in the lines on their face. Harold Wood screamed out poverty to Kenny and he loathed every second of having to be there. It reminded him of when he had suddenly been thrust into becoming the main provider for his family; a time when there was no money, no food and no warmth.

He had strived to remove his family from that particular depravation and it galled him when he was forced to be reminded of discomforting memories. Kenny saw himself as having made something of his life and couldn't understand people who seemed to want to live this way.

He pulled his car into the entrance of the vast housing complex and parked next to a row of huge metal dustbins.

Communal rubbish, another reason Kenny despised the

destitution of the place. He thought of his own Mock-Tudor semi-detached house in Buckhurst Hill, with its manicured lawn and clean shiny windows and personal wheelie bin, in the sought after tree lined avenue.

Sean was at the car door before he even had a chance to turn off the engine.

"Jeeze lad, let me get out!" Kenny said, as he opened the door. "What's all the pissing drama, to get me out of me nice warm bed, in the middle of the fucking night?"

Sean didn't answer him. He just stared at Kenny. He looked demented; his eyes bulging out of their sockets, red rimmed and bloodshot. He had not shaved for a few days by the looks of it and his clothes were stained with patches of what Kenny decided was dried blood. He looked manic and terrified, all at the same time. He began rambling again, Kenny only being able to make out a few words at a time.

"She looked like her; you see… a bit… I didn't mean to go so far…"

Kenny looked at Sean and then over to the block of flats where he was pointing and back to Sean. Then Sean grabbed his arm and literally dragged him through the communal door and into a ground floor flat. At first Kenny wasn't sure what he was supposed to be seeing.

They were in a one room bedsit. To Kenny's right was a double bed; which sported a discoloured and marked mattress. Large brownish yellow stains were splattered all over it. There was a solitary pillow, which was in the same disgusting state as the mattress; there were no sheets or a duvet.

Against the far wall was a sofa, which had cushions on that did not match nor fit and was quite obviously only suitable for a rubbish tip. In one corner was a sink and a small gas oven, which was practically growing its own version of penicillin. The place was filthy and stunk of stale fried food.

There was a door to the left of the room, which Kenny presumed was a bathroom and he felt no desire to confirm that assumption. He wrinkled his nose under the smell and suppressed the gagging reflex in the back of his throat.

The whole room was minimalistic. It didn't look lived in; it didn't contain enough rubbish to be a squat and it didn't contain enough personal objects to be Sean's base. The windows had been boarded up and there were no carpets on the floor. It was like the bed and sofa had been bought in especially.

Kenny wasn't sure what he had expected to see when Sean had half dragged him into the flat. When it came to Sean, it could be anything, but what he wasn't prepared for, was what he saw emerge out of the door that he correctly thought was the bathroom, a young, naked, battered figure that sheepishly stood in the doorway; a small rancid hand towel keeping what modesty she had.

Her bright red hair glistened in the low light of the room; drops of water fell to the floor. Kenny looked at her and then Sean in almost fascination.

"Fucking Christ! How old is she?" He finally said.

He was in bewilderment. It wasn't often that Kenny was lost for words but this was one of those times. Shaking his head, he sat down on the two seater sofa, then jumped back up again and brushed down his coat. Still Sean said nothing.

Kenny stared at him. He seemed to be in some sort of shock. It was scandalous what he was seeing.

Most people of his ilk could turn a blind eye to things that would usually distress and disturb regular ordinary people, but when it came to molesting children there was an unspoken code, which was universal between his and the conventional worlds; it was bang out of order.

Kenny had a preferred taste for the slightly younger individual but even he had boundaries. They at least needed to make it to adulthood. Granted the girl was not a child, but she was definitely did not look like an adult either and by the look of her, she had not been a willing participant in Sean's depraved and merciless game.

Kenny took off his coat and went over to the girl. He wrapped it around her and led her gently over to the bed. He helped her to sit down. The fact she winced as she sat on her bottom did not go unnoticed. She pulled the coat around her tighter.

She hadn't made eye contact with either of them. Still shaking his head in disbelief, Kenny went out to his car and retrieved a small canvas holdall that he kept in the boot. He walked back into the flat and placed it on the bed next to her. Opening it up, he waved for her to look inside it.

She didn't move, but allowed her eyes to fall down to the bag. It contained a change of clothes and five thousand pounds in ready used notes. It was his emergency bag, in case he ever needed to make a quick exit. He made a mental note to replace it at the next available opportunity.

"Put the clothes on." He gestured. His voice was soft and malleable. The mellifluous velvety tone it assumed brought the girl a little comfort. "Then, if it's alright by you, I am gonna get you as far away from him as I can…that okay?"

She nodded feebly and detachedly watched Kenny grab hold of Sean and march him out of the flat. Twenty minutes later, Kenny was driving the girl up the M11, heading for the Essex border to the North. It was the last time she ever saw the green counties again.

* * *

Ginnie woke up in bed suddenly. She was soaked with sweat. She looked around the darkness and it took her a few seconds to realise where she was. It had been another nightmare; they were becoming more and more regular. She had been having them from a few days after it had all happened. Since she was bought here by a man she didn't know.

She had trusted him though, something inside of her had told her to do so, although Ginnie would have gone with anyone, if it meant they would take her away from the hell that she had found herself in.

He had set her up with a flat and some money and told her she would never see either of them again, on the condition that she never said a word about the night he had found her. She didn't know his name and never spoke to him the entire time he had helped her.

Nightmares at night and flashbacks during the day; she couldn't escape it at all. Ginnie wasn't sure what triggered the first major flashback. She had been in a daze for the first few weeks after arriving in Liverpool. One minute she was sitting, watching the TV, the next she was transported into the middle of that degrading experience which was forced upon her.

She was there, reliving it second by second. It was so very real, she could feel what was happening, hear what was being said. She was unaware of anyone or anything, other than what she was being subjected to yet again; just like the nightmare she just had. She could feel the panic again and couldn't breathe. She struggled against it, wanted to escape but didn't know how.

She was going crazy. She wanted to shout and scream for help; desperate for someone to drag her out of this horrendous nightmare. She didn't want to be there, but the events of those few days enveloped her totally once again. It was really happening again; she was trapped deep in the grip of her tortured mind, unable to move, paralysed with fear.

She could smell him, feel him and hear him as he violated her, abused her and debased her with his actions, his words. How could this be happening again? She was frightened; she didn't know what to do to make it stop. She could hear someone screaming. Was it her? She couldn't go any further, she had gone far enough and she needed to get out.

Ginnie tried to calm herself. She took some deep breaths and reached for the glass of water. It was empty. She climbed out of bed and made her way to the small compact kitchen, at the back of the apartment. She turned the tap and let the water run for a few seconds before filling her glass.

Gulping down the water at speed, she replenished it and held it too her forehead. The cold glass felt cool and refreshing. It helped her to step back into reality and shake off the nightmare she just had.

She instinctively rubbed her swollen belly and felt a trembling followed by some sudden thuds. In some respects, the past eight months had gone quick, but she knew she did not have long left now.

The baby inside her was a heavy, dead weight and it just exhausted her. Ginnie felt a dull ache running along her back and down her legs. It certainly was taking its toll on her. She walked into the living room and sat down on a small arm chair by the window, wrapping a blanket around herself.

She looked down at the silent and vacant street, lit with streetlamps. The flat was part of an old Georgian House. The outside was painted white and had ivy growing all over it. Ginnie loved it. It looked homely. It was on a nice quiet street, away from the city and she hadn't been bothered at all while she had been here.

Most of the neighbours kept themselves to themselves. They would nod as she passed, on her rare trips to the shops. Not liking to go out much, she would buy enough to last a few weeks; the fewer trips out into the world the better. She was beginning to feel safe, until the flashbacks remind her of why she was here.

Ginnie felt the baby move again; a belly full of arms and legs, kicking and punching the limited space. It felt like an alien was growing inside of her; although it was a part of her, she felt strangely detached and estranged from it.

It was just another reminder of what he had done to her, over and over again. She was kept inside that dirty, grimy bedsit for four days before he had come to his senses and realised he had maybe gone a little too far. That was when he had called the man who had come and helped her.

She had honestly believed she was going to die there. Now she was living in constant fear of her life, looking over her shoulder and having to deal with an imminent birth. She was eighteen and terrified. There had been no pre-natal care; no checkups, antenatal classes, no intervention of any kind.

The ache that was pulling at her insides suddenly intensified and she tried to stand, to relieve the pressure that was bowing down in her stomach. As her legs gave way and she fell to the floor, she tried to grab hold of the small table that sat next to the arm chair. It crashed down on top of her.

Ginnie screamed out loud and tensed her whole body as she tried to cope with the pain. What was happening to her? She thought. Surely she couldn't be having the baby now. It wasn't time, she wasn't ready. She hadn't thought about it all yet, not properly. She wanted more time.

Another agonising convulsion hit her, the retrenchment in her belly tore through her but this time she managed to stifle the scream. No one must hear; no one must be alerted. Grasping at the arm chair, she managed to pull herself onto her knees. She clung onto the arms and buried her head in the cushions, allowing herself to moan quietly.

Squatting seemed to help with the pain, which was coming so quickly. It was constant; no waves or lows; intensifying as each second passed. At least Ginnie thought they were seconds, they could have been minutes or hours. She had lost all concept and awareness and could only concentrate on trying to breath. Deep pulling breaths which made her think she may have an asthma attack. When was she supposed to push? Now? Not yet? She didn't know what to do.

She tried to do what she thought might be pushing, although it reminded her of imitating someone doing a poo. If the pain wasn't so prominent, she would have laughed at herself. Then something happened; something shifted inside her. With one all mighty howl, a purple patched, white covered baby, dropped onto the floor with a thud.

Ginnie sat back; legs spread open, smeared with blood and stared at the newborn. It didn't move, just lay there. She felt like she was in a trance. It was shock and a state of bewilderment. It had all been so quick; the immediate onset of labour issued no warning.

It had attacked just as rapidly as he had and it had ripped through her body just as he had. The lack of admonition and the ferocity with which the child was born was so acute, so excruciating, that she had prayed to god to make it stop. In her mind, he answered her.

Then she felt the pain return. Not as bad as it was before but still enough to make her groan in agony and roll over onto her side. As the placenta was delivered, Ginnie threw up all over the rug she was lying on. She had felt the bile rise up to her throat and before she could even think about trying to stop herself, it was out. The trance-like state that had previously taken hold of her had vanished and awareness was very much taking hold.

She glanced back down to the baby. Its colour hadn't changed; it still wasn't moving. She thought there might be some motherly instinct that would kick in and tell her what she was going to do. But she felt nothing; apart from feeling battered and bruised physically. Emotionally she could only describe it as relief and liberation.

Ginnie leant forward and pulled off the throw that covered the armchair. She picked up the baby and wrapped it up in it, then placed it back down on the rug. Slowly, she pulled herself to her feet and it surprised her that she could take her weight quite easily. Picking up the baby, she gradually walked to the kitchen and opened a drawer.

Taking out a pair of scissors and a plastic freezer bag clip she made her way back into the lounge; unwrapping the bundle she attached the clip to the cord and cut it away with the scissors. She remembered seeing it being done on some hospital programme back at the children's home in Essex.

She didn't really understand why it had to be done, she just remembered that the cord was to be clamped and cut. She then wrapped it back up. Her eyes fixed on it, almost as if she was trying to fix the image in her memory. She felt at peace. The most peace she had felt in a long time.

Twenty minutes later a showered and changed Ginnie hauled on her coat. She picked up the bundle and put it inside a small holdall. Zipping it up, she walked out of her flat. It was just beginning to get light. The sky had that dark blue glow to it that told you a new day was about to arrive.

The air was fresh and the sensation gave Ginnie a feeling of extra energy. She got inside the taxi that was waiting for her at the end of the road. Giving the address to the driver, she sat back and watched the world go by.

She wasn't really thinking about what she was doing. It was easier if she didn't. She just kept telling herself, she was so near to the end of the horrifying journey she had been on. It was so nearly over and it hadn't beaten her. She was stronger than she had ever thought possible.

He had tried to break her but he hadn't. She was fighting back now. She was taking back her life. He had occupied enough of it. The taxi stopped outside the entrance to the Accident and Emergency department, at the Royal **Liverpool** University Hospital.

"Can you wait? I won't even be a minute." She asked the driver.

"Make sure you aren't love." The driver replied to her and grabbed his newspaper from the dashboard.

Ginnie picked up the holdall and steadily got out of the car. She walked into the entrance of the hospital and ten seconds later she walked back out again. She got back into the car and the taxi pulled away.

Ginnie had spent a total of one hour with her dead daughter since she was born. The story hit the headlines the next day; it was all over the television. Police requested the mother to come forward, suggesting they were concerned for her welfare and that she may require medical attention.

Ginnie never did.

Chapter 10

November 2002

"Sit yourself down Fergus. No need to stand on ceremony."

A chair was pulled from the side of the room and dumped in the middle. Sean sat down, unsure as to why he was here in the first place. The portacabin on the building site in Loughton, just off the A1168, served as a makeshift office come tea room.

It was a basic set up with a desk, some filing cabinets and a few half filled book shelves. There were page three pins ups from various tabloids stuck on the walls and the aroma of stale cigarettes and mud from the site hung in the air. An old, worn two seater sofa was pushed into the corner, opposite the door, with a small coffee table placed in front.

The two heavies; thick-necked, shaven-headed hardmen, who had abruptly picked him off Epping High Street and bundled him into the dark blue Range Rover, now stood either side of him as he sat. They were dressed in their traditional attire of dark glasses and long, black leather overcoats, ornamenting lots of bling; chunky gold necklaces, fat silver rings and fearsome tattoos were draped all over them.

He tried to look calm and nonplussed, although the knots in his stomach were in serious danger of letting him down, not due to fear but from his body reacting to the lack of cocaine in its system. It was still early and Sean preferred to spend the morning with a clear head.

By lunchtime though, he was normally bored of the mundane reality and would succumb to the inviting package, which constantly lived inside his coat pocket. Now was about the time the itch begun to start.

Trying to take his mind off the substance he craved, he racked his brains as to why he was suddenly summoned by the man in front of him, without realising he could have quite easily pissed him off and he could be about to receive retribution. The older man was a top class villain. Sean had never met him but knew of him. Numerous thoughts were running through his head.

Had he stepped on this man's toes? Quite possibly. Had he threatened or hurt one of his employees? Again, quite possibly. Had he muscled in on a deal, unknowing it was in fact being run by the man himself? Sean did have a habit of suddenly under cutting the highest bidder, right at the last minute, but he was normally quite astute when it came to money.

He would do his homework on his business deals. Know exactly who and what he was dealing with before getting involved with anything. Kenny had taught him that.

He watched the man watch him. Sean knew his quiet calmness was unnerving the two tribal warriors standing by his side; this felt reassuring. If they were unsettled, then they had heard of his reputation. Once they had him inside the car, they had actually been quite polite.

They apologised for their rough handling and explained who had requested to see him. Out of sheer curiosity Sean agreed to go, although you didn't really say no to Ray Jarvis.

Ray Jarvis was an old school gangster. He had started his career as a bare knuckle fighter in 1965 around Spitalfields, when it was still classed as a parish in the Tower Hamlets borough. The east end was notoriously known for being the poorest, most overcrowded and most crime ridden area in London and it gave refuge to an extremely immoral population; women of the lowest character, receivers of stolen goods, thieves and the most atrocious offenders.

The fighting had given Ray the reputation and cash he needed to invest in scrap metal. This career choice served him well for a while, but he was still a young lad with ambition. He had craved the notoriety and prominence that his childhood hero's, the infamous Kray twins, had enjoyed.

Ray had a business brain. He saw the profit in everything. It was what had made him his millions.

They had come to watch him fight once, the Kray brothers; one night down a back alley at Spitalfields Market. Only staying for the fight and not acknowledging him as the winner afterwards. They had bet on the other guy.

That same year, their reign of London's East End came to an end, when they were finally brought to justice for the brutal murder of Jack "The Hat" McVitie.

Ray didn't see it much like justice. He believed that The Hat had it coming and didn't really think it was anything to do with society. Old school gangsters only participated in their own world. The world of ordinary, regular people were quite safe, however the government and police didn't seem to think so and were hell bent on bringing as many of them down as they could.

Ray ran his scrap metal business for about five years before he moved into operating fruit machines. This new business venture was not as much of a step back as it may at first sound. They were fronts for underworld activities, including protection rackets, theft, fraud, stolen goods and usury; where extremely, irrationally, high and illegal interest rates on loans would be charged.

This is what he became incredibly good at, but from time to time he missed the brutality of his fighting days. Occasionally he would suggest to a pub landlord that they should buy one of his fruit machines. Failure in doing so would mean running the risk of having the pub burnt to the ground. Sometimes he needed to exert the harassment and intimidation, for peace of mind. So he knew that people were still scared of him.

At one point he had been arrested for receiving stolen goods but was acquitted through lack of evidence and with the help of a large donation to the Police Fund. After this, he learnt that it was important to have friends in every corner and made a point of seeking out high ranking officers and politicians, just in case an ambitious police scrote thought he could climb the career ladder by bringing him down.

Towards the end of the 1980's, Ray's risk-taking nature progressed further and he began to invest in fraud schemes known as Long Firms. A new corporation would be set up by an associate, who was lucratively rewarded for the prison term he would eventually serve.

The new corporation would direct standard business for some months, constructing lines of credit and winning the trust of suppliers, which would lead to the new business eventually being able to place a very large order on credit. The goods would then be sold for cash, the money pocketed and the company and those involved in running it would suddenly 'disappear'.

Of course all names on official documents pertaining to the new business would have been faked, except for the fall guy, who was always going to end up taking the can for it all anyway.

The reason he was successful and that he had enjoyed a twenty year reign over the East End, was because he had kept his hand in everything he did. If somebody was trying to double cross him, he would know about it. If someone was cheating or stealing from him, he would know.

He had a loyal crew behind him and allies in more than enough faces around the North and South. He paid well and could be trusted. It was that simple.

That didn't mean he wasn't a complete ruthless bastard when the mood suited him, which made him highly feared within his social environment. It was this thought that had Sean's stomach in knots. He wasn't scared as much as uneasy about his situation.

If it came down to it, Sean would fight his way out; already registering the filing cabinets being an ideal object to barge the dense as wood thugs with; they were not a problem for him as far as he was concerned. It was the older man that sat opposite him, behind the desk.

Ray Jarvis, Sean knew would be just as quick and psycho as he himself could be. It was always a sobering realisation, when he came across somebody else who listened to that demon voice that lives inside everybody's head; and it does, no matter how much you deny it or ignore it or fight it, that voice lives inside every single person no matter how good and wholesome you live your life. It resides in your head, rising up every now and then, when you're angry and mad. It whispers at you to punish the cause.

Sean believed it was there in everyone, but it always

surprised him when he met someone else that indulged in it and enjoyed it as much as he did. Ray Jarvis was one of these people. The older man was an out and out thug. If the rumours and stories were true, armed robberies, arson, protection rackets and violent assaults, including torture, were just a few past jobs on Ray's long and comprehensive C.V.

The torture varied in degree of brutality, depending on the crime against him, but his specialty was giving electric shocks until his victims were unconscious, inflicted by a hand-crank-powered generator. The victim had the terminals attached to their nipples and genitalia and were then placed in a bath of cold water to enhance the electrical charge.

Afterwards, if victims were badly injured, they would be sent to a doctor; normally one who was no longer allowed to practice. Ray always saw that as a generous touch. Not harbouring hard feelings, believing he was a fair and just man. Dishing out the punishment and then moving past it.

Also in the Portacabin with Ray and his henchmen was Davie Newman, Ray's right arm. Wherever Ray was, Davie would be too. He was Ray's official negotiator. This is someone who focuses their talents in arbitrating arrangements between two or more parties. Most negotiators act for a particular party involved in the deal.

Davie was the only man Ray had ever trusted and was constantly by his side. He never spoke unless he was spoken to and had the nickname Silhouette as he was constantly Ray's shadow. He was an incredibly articulate man, who could convince you he was the perfect gentleman, yet had the ability to switch to a sewer mouth when the need occurred.

Constantly dressed in black, with a long knitted overcoat and black leather gloves, he had long grey hair that he wore plaited and a Fagin style moustache. Davie's mantra was 'Make them an offer they can't refuse' which he stole from his favourite film, The Godfather. However, unlike Marlon Brando's character, Davie knew the expression did not always need to be immersed in oblique threats and coercion to be of use or valuable.

Sometimes it simply meant coming up with a solution that the other party couldn't turn down. He followed a basic technique that had served him well in his twenty year career. Firstly he would isolate the problem that his solution was supposed to fix. Then he would do his homework, ascertaining what modus operandi's the other party's were currently using to solve the problem and how much that cost. Lastly he offered a cheaper and more effective alternative.

It was all about being able to read a situation and knowing what the other party needed or wanted. In these instances, it sometimes made sense to make an offer that is designed to fail. This is where he played the *Wise Guy*. It is a time-honoured method of good negotiating and effective extortions, to not kill a deal by pushing too hard.

When Davie made an offer that he knew would be refused, what he was really doing was setting the stage for when he made a more compelling offer later on. These future offers then appeared so much more reasonable, in comparison to the offer he initially presented.

Another reason for making an offer that a party may refuse is when the other side starts to believe that perhaps no agreement may be able to be reached, they are often likely to drop their 'negotiating face' and speak candidly. This offers a chance to discover their real motivations.

Once Davie had this information, he would be well positioned to use this knowledge, to make a follow-up offer that will be more acceptable than the first.

But above all else, successful and efficient negotiators

understand that time trumps everything, because time brings power. Davie knew this. He has all the time in the world and will exploit this strength for all it's worth, letting his victims stew. It gives him power and power creates fear. The best way to create fear is to become the bogeyman.

When a sales assistant says, "Those shoes look fantastic on you, but that's the last pair we have, you have just met the bogeyman or when a supplier says, "I'd love to buy your £500 product. But I only have £250 in the budget", that's also the bogeyman.

Any child can tell you, the bogeyman is the thing you fear. And fear, of course, cuts to the core of negotiation. Whether you're an underworld king-pin or a second-hand car salesman, it always pays to have the bogeyman on your side. Because fear, like ambition, comes in all shapes and sizes.

Davie hadn't always been a negotiator. He had made his name by targeting security vans. He had spent a total of twenty-two of his forty-eight years in twenty seven prisons for various different offences. He had been one of the main architects of the Strangeways Riots in 1992, which left two prisoners dead and over two hundred wounded, helping to form the Prisoners Liberation Army. But he also never wanted to go back inside.

He had become a regular visitor to church, finding salvation from his sins. He received huge satisfaction from becoming a reborn again Catholic, believing he could just walk into confession, be forgiven for what he had done and walk back out again. You can't expect to walk into a court, say sorry and expect to walk out again free.

Sometimes he thought about his victims, the people he had hurt. He would look back and wonder whether he should have done that, or question whether he could have handled situations differently, but mostly he came to the conclusion that it was what they deserved and they got back what they had done themselves. Davie had ambition and drive, it was what had made him into the man he was today.

It was exactly this; ambition, that was the reason why Ray had Sean sitting in the small portacabin. He had heard about this boy. The boy without a soul. How he would do anything, if the price was right. He was highly spoken of by some of his more villainess associates and Ray's own curiosity about him had been building for some time.

He knew that Sean was Kenny Maltrowitz' boy, which spoke volumes in itself. Kenny was an old school villain like himself and if Kenny trusted this boy then he knew he could too. Sean's love of violence was well known but just how far would he go? Ray was about to find out.

"I seem to find myself in a bit of a predicament Sean and I wondered if we could have a chat?" Ray said

Sean leant forward in his chair. He slowly rubbed his chin with his hand and took a good long stare of Ray. After what seemed like forever, he finally spoke.

"Firstly, I would really like a line and a Jack Daniels and secondly can we please get rid of the two fucking ugly gorillas standing here." He pointed to the two henchmen with his thumbs. "They really do make the place look worse than it is. If that's possible that is. Then we'll talk."

Ray immediately liked him. His arrogance was stifling yet stimulating. He nodded at the shorter henchman of the two, who on command walked over to his boss' desk and begun to rack up a few lines on a mirror that had once been one half of a ladies compact. He handed it over to Sean, who took it and snorted the potent white powder in a long drawn breath. Ray pulled open the desk drawer and pulled out two whisky glasses and a bottle of Jameson's.

"This do you?" He asked, whilst pouring the brown

liquor into the glasses, not waiting for an answer. The glass was shoved into Sean's hand and the two men walked out of the portacabin.

"I think you may have just hurt their feelings, they didn't seem too pleased with being made to go." Ray said sardonically, quite amused at his henchmen's tantrums.

"I'm sure they will get over it. Brains like goldfish… three second attention span." Sean replied.

Ray laughed heartily. "Goldfish! I like it." The laugh lasted a full minute before he managed to resume his composure and get down to business. He cleared his throat and sat himself up in his chair. "He stays." He said, gesturing to Davie, who stood behind him.

Sean nodded.

"I am sure you are aware, that the Anderson family and myself are not what you would call best pals and that over the years we have had our various turf wars, most of which I have won." Ray continued.

"Are you aware I have worked for George Anderson, on more than a few occasions and at this precise moment Mr Jarvis, I don't know why I am here, so forgive me if my loyalties, at present, lie with him?" Sean interrupted.

Ray took note of the young man's antagonism; secretly impressed. He didn't believe any of what Sean had said about loyalty. He knew as soon as Sean had walked into the portacabin that the boy could be bought; he had hunger written all over him. Hunger for the power and control Ray could give him.

But he liked the front the boy had. It reminded him of a younger version of himself, when he didn't know just how evil the world really was. Sean would learn it, over time, just like he did. The Mr Jarvis reference was also noted. Ray liked that. It showed respect for your elders. He was old school and manners were everything, as strange as that was.

"That I am yes. I am also aware that Anderson pretty much has most of the south-east sewn up. Even you pay a tax for operating on his patch; albeit at a discount I'm sure, but all the same, it must nark you."

"Interesting. I'm listening." Sean leant back in his chair, crossing one of his legs over the other, so his foot was resting on his thigh.

"So it would benefit both of us, if George Anderson was taken out of the picture. His family is nothing without him and quite frankly, these days neither is he. He is an old man like myself, only there is a difference between him and me. I haven't lost it."

Sean gave a half laugh and slightly nodded his head.

"And you want me to take him out." It wasn't a question. Sean knew what Ray was getting at. "Why aren't you doing it?

Ray stared at Sean intently for a few moments. He pulled out a cigar from the top pocket of his suit jacket and picked up a strip of matches from a bowl on the desk. He puffed away on the thick Cuban baton, until it was unreservedly smoking away. Then he gave Sean a huge grin that exhibited a full set of crooked yellowing teeth.

Shrugging he said "I don't need the attention or the glory. I have enough. You, my son, are just beginning. Your name is good but you need to build on that, or do you want to be a pimp all your life?"

Sean took the bait, as Ray knew he would. He saw it in the boys seducing blue eyes. The change in colour to a pale grey was remarkable. It was almost inhuman.

Ray continued to taunt Sean. "It's an achievement, what you've got at your age. You run your girls tight and I like that. Tried a few out myself too, their nice, clean, amenable, but at the end of the day they are whores. Don't you want more than that?"

"Like what? George's role? No thanks Mr Jarvis. I like it just the way I have it. But I must admit I don't like giving him a cut of my hard earned."

"There is a huge difference between being respected and being feared. Respect is easy Sean. You give a little, you get it back, it's simple, it's life. But fear is better. So we have a deal?"

"I didn't say that. What's in this for you? Why you just handing me over a turf you and him have been fighting over, for how long you say? Twenty years was it?"

Ray grinned. The boy sure was shrewd, he thought. Kenny had been doing a good job. He saw what attracted him to Sean, because it was attracting Ray more by the second. It took either a very stupid person to be that arrogant, or a complete nutter. Ray doubted that Sean was stupid, which meant he was more likely the latter.

That could become extremely useful. If Sean felt beholden to Ray, like he was to Kenny, then Ray could pretty much have him at his disposal, anytime he wanted.

Sean however was on the ball. Whether it was the instant rush he felt from the cocaine, or whether he really had been paying attention to Kenny's elongated speeches, no one knew, but he could read what was running through Ray's mind.

"I don't have the patience or the inclination to take over more Sean. I'm past the craving for being king of the manor. I just want my old enemy gone. He is nothing more than an irritating itch now. It would be more beneficial for you to take over. Young blood is what the green yards need."

The stories of Ray Jarvis and George Anderson were almost as old as they were. Sean had heard them many times. Details changed and names were added or omitted but it was generally the same each time he heard it.

In 1982 Eddie Fraiser, one of the Anderson's associates, was shot unintentionally, during a brawl at a nightclub in Norwich. The owners of the club, Bristol based businessmen, had asked Ray to protect the club, in exchange for gaming machines being placed there. At this time, club machine gambling was in its prime.

The Anderson's, not impressed that a club in their jurisdiction was being racketed by an east end face, muscled in on the contract and took over with the protection including the ejection of undesirables; which, presumably, meant Ray and his associates. It is not clear why the club owners changed sides at this time, but it was apparent that their preference was for George to handle all protection matters relating to the club.

It was never proven that Ray pulled the trigger himself and it was never determined which gun and which bullet killed Eddie, but he was more than happy to hold the responsibility for it. He wore it like a badge of pride and escalated the rumour further himself; that he shot Fraiser with a .38 pistol at close range.

The men spent the next two decades fighting and disputing the blame, but they were getting on in years now. For Ray, it was time it ended; he no longer had the drive to carry on the feud.

Sean stood up from the chair and walked towards the desk.

"You're making the mistake that I want to be a don. I don't. I want people to know who I am Mr Jarvis but I don't want the hassle of running half the bloody country. I'm not Tony fucking Blair. I don't aim to be you or Kenny or Anderson for that matter. I'm me. That's it. I am not a gangster, I'm a business man, whose commodity happens to be cocaine and whores. I simply supply a market."

"So you gonna keep paying Anderson his cut. Answering to him. Allowing him to dictate when and where you make your living? It's them and us. Always will be." Ray was goading Sean and he knew it.

But there was truth and reason to what the older man was saying. Sean saw the sense and logic and recognized when an opportunity was being offered, even if he disliked the way it was presented.

"No Ray I'm not." Sean dropped the formalities. He had been backed into a corner but was determined to salvage something from it. "I'll do your dirty work, but not for what you're offering. I'll do it for my freedom. There is one thing I'll take though, as payment like."

"What's that then?" Ray asked even more satisfied than he could have imagined being.

"I'll have Anderson's house. The Sudbury one."

"That it? Just the house?" Surprise showed all over Ray's face.

Sean Fergus was definitely a strange character. George Anderson may be an ineffectual waste of time but he certainly knew how to make money. He thought Sean was stark raving mad for not being tempted by it all. He would have jumped at the chance of being offered that kind of inheritance at twenty-two.

He nodded at Sean and raised his glass up in a toast. "It's yours." He said.

Sean smiled then for the first time throughout the whole meeting. His whole stance changing and those seducing blue eyes returned. He looked almost regular then. Not the demonic fiend his status depicted.

"Just one thing, how you gonna get hold of Anderson's properties and businesses?" Sean asked.

Ray really did smile then; a disturbing smirk that accentuated every sinister crease in his face.

"That, my boy, is what I have been slowly cultivating for the past three years. George Anderson is not going to know what fucking hit him, don't you worry about that. You do your job and do it well and those deeds will be in your hand by the end of that day. You have my word."

The last four words were all Sean needed to hear. Ray Jarvis was a common thug but his word was better than any legally binding document.

* * *

"You wanna do what? You in his fucking pocket or summit?" Kenny asked Sean

Though he was astounded by the boy's eagerness to carry out the job he had just told him about, it was more anger that he felt; at the fact that Sean had a meeting with Ray Jarvis without Ray approaching Kenny first. That was just courtesy.

Kenny wasn't happy at all. He felt stabbed in the back and slighted. Ray was supposed to be an old friend. They went back years. He should have been informed if he had an interest in Sean.

"I am in no-one's fucking pocket Ken, not even yours and don't you ever fucking forget it. I'm doing this for me. Nice little drum that is. Not bad for my first pad. Invest legally. That's what you have been banging into me since I met you. That's what I'm doing. That house will be my first legal asset and the beginning of my retirement." He looked at Kenny then, with a cheeky grin. "Not yet though of course. I aint ready to give all this up just yet."

Kenny rubbed his face with his hands. Knowing, out of sheer stubbornness, Sean would not listen to any reason on his part. Turning away from him and walking over to a small mini bar that stood in the lounge of his four bedroom semi detached house, he pulled out a bottle of Jack and two glasses, pouring a generous measure into each glass.

He picked one up and took a great gulp. Glaring at Sean, he then moved towards the three piece suit that situated in the middle of the room and plonked himself down on a dark green leather armchair, leaving the other glass still on the bar.

Sean mentally smiled to himself and walked over to collect his drink, knowing Kenny was in the midst of throwing a hissy fit. For a hard villain, he really was a big girl sometimes, Sean thought.

He looked around the considerably spacious room. It wasn't to his taste. The room was adorned in dark greens and mushroom creams. He liked the flooring though. It was a solid oak wood floor that screamed out class and sophistication to Sean. He made a mental note to put the same thing in his new house.

A huge, oil painted, portrait of Kenny's late wife Audrey hung above a mantel piece. Sean hated the painting. He found it eerie. Her eyes followed you around the room. She was an ugly woman too, who bore the traditional Jewish nose. Sean couldn't understand the fascination Kenny held for her. She reminded Sean of a dead fish, before it had time to stiffen.

The love he professed for her was just a joke, as far as Sean was concerned, considering he and Kenny's first meeting was about the possibility of Sean supplying him with a constant stream of young men to satisfy his wayward sexual tendencies; the bottom line being that Kenny was a full blown homosexual. Although, this was common knowledge, it was rarely spoken about and would be in hush tones if it was.

"You would benefit just as much by having Anderson off the street. You just don't like it cos it weren't your idea." Sean blasted back at him knowing full well he had hit the nail on the head.

Kenny ignored him and sipped more of his drink. The thick dark liquid burnt the back of his throat. He knew Sean was right, but it didn't make him feel any less covetous. He didn't like Sean pointing out that he didn't work for him either. As much as Kenny liked to think Sean was one of his boy's, right now, it was quite clearly obvious this was not the case.

This aggravated Kenny. He had done a lot for Sean in the year and a half that he had known him and saw this as having it all thrown back in his face.

"Silent treatment?" Sean goaded him. "Because I won't toe your line? Get over it Ken. This jobs happening, whether you like it or not and I will be the one that brings Anderson down. You mark my words."

Kenny gave a deep sigh and then half smiled at Sean. He didn't want to row with the boy. It wasn't something he enjoyed. He could never stay mad at him for long either. But he was determined to try and knock some sense into him.

"Jarvis' word is as good as anything I have ever come across but the clever gits are the ones out here boy, not rotting away on the inside." He eventually said in a resigned tone.

The solemn look then appeared in his eye. A look which showed the vast difference, in knowledge and wisdom, between student and mentor.

"But we are talking murder here Sean. Premeditated murder. That's if you manage to pull it off and what if you don't? What if it all goes tits up and you end up with two of the biggest organised crime families in the fucking country wanting your blood?"

Sean stared into the old man's eyes and in what he thought was a moment of clarity, he saw a lack of faith which, in his demented brain, signalled total lack of respect.

"You don't think I can do it...do you?" Sean's voice was incredulous. He slammed his glass back down on the bar and stormed into the centre of the room. He stood in front of Kenny who was still sitting in the armchair.

"I fucked up once. Once! But you can't let it go; you throw it out there whenever I disagree with you." He was offended and was determined to show it. "How many jobs have I carried out for you with meticulous precision... eh? Fucking hundreds without so much as a fucking glitch."

Kenny felt the intimidation Sean rendered. He wasn't scared by him, he was too confident with his own aggression that he cleverly kept buried to be actually frightened of the boy, but he became aware of how terrified his victims must be when they were on the receiving end of Sean's fury.

"Fucked up? Fucked up? That wasn't just a fuck up son that was an almighty howler. I won't be able to get you out of this one sonny Jim, I can tell you." He took another gulp of his whisky. "There will be no cleaning up your mess this time. It wasn't that long ago I had you on that blower, don't matter how many other jobs you've done since, at the end of the day you fucked up big style. I don't give a cats whiskers if it was only once. Once is one too many boy!"

"I aint your boy Ken. I'm no one's boy. You're fucking deluded. You don't own me and you'll never have me..."

Before Sean could finish his ranted sentence, he felt the full effect of his nose spreading across his face from the force of Kenny's headbut. The pain was so immense he was surprised to still be standing.

The attack had been so sudden and immediate, that Sean hadn't even seen Kenny stand up. He instinctively put his hands to his face and winced as his fingers touched his broken nose.

"Fucking hell!" He exclaimed, punching the air with his fists, in reaction to the pain.

"Don't you ever forget who I am and what I did for you." Kenny voice was quiet but the venom was clearly evident. "Kidnap… rape… I covered it all up, for a kid I barely knew."

He pushed past Sean and walked over to the mini bar, grabbing a clean towel from under the counter and a handful of ice cubes from the ice bucket. He wrapped it up in the towel, silently cursing his protégé under his breath. He had completely lost it, just for a second but he had lost it all the same.

Kenny didn't like losing control of his behaviour. It scared him, what he could do if he wasn't careful, if he didn't manage the side of him that was dangerous. Unlike most gangsters, Kenny hated the violence with a passion, yet the destructive and hostile monster that is the essence of all villains was also in him. No matter how hard he fought not to use it.

He walked back over to Sean, who was by now sitting on the sofa with his head between his legs. Kenny bent down in front of him and offered the ice bundle. He was surprised to see the eyes and face of a young boy, as Sean looked up at him. It was the look of an errant school boy being scolded by a teacher; sorry yet resentful at the same time. Even his bottom lip slightly protruded.

Kenny offered the ice again and, like Ray had witnessed a few days before, he saw the chameleon-like change in the boy's facial expressions. After a few seconds of staring at each other, Sean snatched it out of Kenny's hand and plonked it on the bridge of his nose.

Kenny stood back up and stepped back a little. He

wiped his face with his hand and realised he was sweating. His forehead felt tender from the connection with Sean's nose and he was sure that he felt something in his right hip tear when he had leapt from his chair. He was getting too old for this, he decided, too old to suddenly lose his normally cool exterior to a blind rage.

"I guess I deserved that" The sudden confession from Sean completely threw Kenny. He wasn't expecting that.

Sean jumped to his feet and moved towards Kenny with his hand already out in gesture of an apology. He needed to rectify the hostile atmosphere between them and needed to do it fast. As much as he professed to not needing anyone, he kind of needed Kenny. Why, he wasn't so sure, but he had come to rely on the wisdom the old man had. He had begun to see him as a safety net.

Kenny took the hand that was available and pulled Sean in to a tight embrace, slapping his back to signify all was well between them again. But neither really felt it. Something shifted in their relationship that day. An uneasy truth that now hovered between them.

For Sean, it was knowing that somehow he was beholden to Kenny, maybe for the rest of his life. It was an uncomfortable feeling. For Kenny, it was the reality of knowing the boy was never really his, that he was too much of a wild spirit to ever be tamed; by him anyway.

Chapter 11

Bonita Mashek reached for the telephone. Dialling a number with her long, perfectly manicured and deep red nails, she purposefully licked the front of her teeth and waited to be connected. The voice that answered at the other end was abrupt and coarse.

"Mr Anderson? It's Bonita Mashek." She listened to the unfathomable intonation of the voice change to a more suitable softer one. She smiled to herself. She always had had that infliction on men. It had made her the successful lawyer she had become; that and her thorough knowledge of the entire legal system.

"Miss Mashek, I've been waiting on your call. Everything's according to plan?"

"Yes, everything was finalised a few moments ago. All of your assets are now in the hands of your nephew, a Mr Peter Mambridge. When Inland Revenue come knocking at your door, all they will find is what you want them to."

She heard the deep exhalations which indicated to her that he was relaxed in his mind.

"He aint me nephew, he's my niece's husband. Not like us Andersons at all. That's why I chose him. Wouldn't say boo to a goose. He'll hand everything back when I tell him too."

"Your judgement is impeccable Mr Anderson. I am just glad I could assist you." Bonita responded in her smooth velvety drawl.

"Oh, you assisted me no end Miss Mashek. You appeared like the angel Gabriele, just when I thought my empire was about to come crashing down. Forgive my language but you totally saved my arse. Wish you would allow me to show my appreciation."

She felt her stomach lurch. She knew what he had in mind and it certainly wasn't an experience she would like to partake in. Forcing away the contrite comeback she wished she could unleash onto him, she forged a giggle into the receiver.

"Mr Anderson, you have paid me well over the norm for my services already and, I have already told you, I make it an unbreakable rule not to socialise with my clients. Besides, all I did was expose you to a legal loophole. You did all the hard work."

"All the same, I wish you would reconsider. Goodbye Miss Mashek."

Bonita placed the telephone back into its holder and resisted an urge to gag. She detested George Anderson more than anyone else she had ever met and she had met a lot of villains in her life time.

They fascinated her; their lifestyle, their money, their violence. It all gripped her attention solidly. She picked up the telephone again and made one more phone call.

Opening her desk drawer, she pulled out a small mirror

and checked her make-up. It was flawless as always. She opened a few more buttons of her dazzling white blouse, to expose a small glimpse of her huge breasts. She slightly hitched her skirt a little and crossed her long slender legs. Then she waited; her eyes fixed firmly on her office door.

Bonita was in her late forties but didn't look a day over thirty. Her father, a former foreign diplomat, had been of Lebanese decent and her mother was Spanish, giving her a striking European appearance. She had jet black hair, which she wore wrapped up in a bun and her dark brown eyes were encased with thick, curly lashes that gave her the sultry elegance men craved for.

She was raised in a wealthy, devoutly Roman Catholic family and had travelled the world due to the nature of her father's occupation. She studied International Relations at university in Mexico and worked for three highly established law firms, before she ventured out on her own fifteen years ago.

Her complete working knowledge of the legal system, her intelligence and her extreme beauty however, were not what had attracted her to Britain's Gangland. Her ability to find a get-out clause in almost everything had given her credibility with the hard men. Her reputation for discretion and acumen was renowned and trusted.

She managed to knock back villainous suitors, of which there were many, with such graceful and endearing style that, most of the time, the hardened men were not aware they had been slighted.

All but one particular one; she didn't want to knock him back. He fuelled the fire that burned between her legs. He always had, ever since she first met him almost twenty years ago. But this man was a loose cannon and none of her feminine wiles had managed to tie him down. She had tried them all and, where most men would normally succumb on the first, this particular man had resisted every step of the way.

He flitted in and out of her life, normally in it only when he wanted something or she was useful to him. He spoke to her with no regard for her feelings and showed her absolutely no respect and she let him; she had no other choice.

Why? Because she was hopelessly in love with him and nobody else had ever come close. He invigorated her every time he touched her, even when he was rough and demanding. When it came to him, Bonita's cool and professional persona turned to a complete jellified mush.

If the other villains who vied for her attention knew what this man did to her, she was sure she would not be held up quite so high, on the pedestal they put her on.

He had kept her a secret for two decades. Nobody knew of their alliance. She was more valuable to him that way. She knew the financial ins and outs of the majority of the south-east most prolific gangsters and that information was gold dust; especially to her man.

Bonita repositioned herself on her swivel chair and glanced down at her watch. It was almost eight o'clock and the street lamps outside had just come on. Her office was a quaint one storey building in Braintree, close to the Freeport shopping outlet. There was no signage advertising the business she ran; that, combined with owning the property, ensured privacy for her clients.

She got up to close the venetian blinds and as she lowered the last one, her office dissolved into darkness. As she turned, to walk towards the light switch, she felt his hands grab hold of her waist.

"Ray!" She breathed huskily.

"Thought I told you to be sitting on your chair, with those tits and legs on show." Ray sneered at her.

He slowly licked the length of her face and she pulled away in disgust, wiping her cheek with her hand.

"Ray... don't... please..."

"Ray, don't please... what?" He imitated her voice in a high pitched tone, mocking her.

"Don't talk to me like that. You know I hate it when you are like this. Foul mouthed and dirty minded."

Truth was, she actually craved the way he spoke to her. His rough handling of her only turned her on more. Shoving her against the wall, she heard the ripping of material as he tore open her blouse; buttons blasted off in all directions.

He pushed her white lace bra up around her neck and ignoring her cries as the wire grated over her supple downy skin, he watched as her huge tremendously shaped breasts sprung free.

There was no drooping from them at all. They looked tight and firm, not the breasts you would expect on a middle aged woman. But then, Bonita was not the average woman in so many ways. Even Ray appreciated that.

He grabbed her breast brutally and squeezed her nipple tight. The dark areolas surrounding his fingers bulged under his pressure. She let out another cry and he put his free hand over her mouth, stifling her moans of pain.

His touch changed, from the fierce abrasive handling, to a more controlled teasing stroke. Keeping his hand over her mouth, his other hand slowly massaged her breast and nipple simultaneously. He watched her close her eyes in pleasure and felt her body relax against him. She wanted him, she always did.

No matter how hard she tried to fight it, he could always make her succumb to his touch.

Maybe it was because he made damn sure she didn't allow anyone else to touch her, so she was so desperate for the contact on his visits that she allowed him his way. He didn't really care why. He just enjoyed the control he had over her.

He grinned sleazily when she bit down on his hand; the pleasure he created in her caused his groin to protrude from his trousers. He dropped her breast and unzipped his fly. Grabbing his penis he began to pleasure himself. His hand that was covering her mouth moved down to her shoulder, in an attempt to force her to her knees.

"Show me how much you've missed me then." The deride sounded just as disrespectful as it was intended.

Bonita fought back slightly. She grabbed at his hand that was gratifying himself and pulled it between her legs. His rough fingers automatically finding their way under her lace panties. She moaned out loud, as he thrust them inside her.

"Please…" She begged, her voice gruff from the way he made her feel. " Please make me come… I'm so close… please…"

She gyrated against his hand; his fingers became wetter and wetter as they slipped in and out of her with case. He put his other hand back over her mouth and slammed her back against wall.

"I want your fucking lips around my cock." He barked at her.

His demands made her wetter, he could feel it. "You like the dirty talk really." The sneer and the final thrust inside her made her explode all over his arm. He liked making her come. He felt the absolute power he had over her and it made him feel like a god. It was probably the closest he had ever come to actually loving someone, not that he was aware of it.

Just as demanding and as rough as he made her orgasm, he grabbed hold of the back of her neck and this time physically coerced her to her knees. Her rounded globes for breasts bounced from his force. He imposed her mouth with his penis, compelling her to take the full length of him, which she did with no trouble.

There was no gagging and spluttering like with the whores. Bonita's throat didn't reject him and when he shot his warm salty load into her there was no spitting it out like they did.

Their sex wasn't unusual for them. It was frenzied and rough, always rough. There was never kissing or caresses. There was no loving spooning afterwards. It was primal, animalistic sex and nothing more. But for those few minutes that it lasted, Bonita knew that he was solely hers.

Ray pulled his trousers back up and tucked in his shirt. Within seconds he was smartly presented again. He grabbed his packet of cigars out of his back pocket and lit one. Bonita watched him, knowing her time was over. It was back to business now and back to the real reason he was in her office.

"So all the papers are signed and the nephew scrote is now the new owner of Anderson Industries?" He asked her formally; the villain now firmly back in the room and her man gone.

She looked down at her dishevelled state. Her blouse was ripped and ruined and her skirt sat around her hips. She pulled her bra back down over her breasts and stood up to straighten herself out.

Her hair had fallen from the perfect bun she had arranged that morning and now hung down around her shoulders, giving her normal sultry look more definition. She really was beautiful and it took Ray's breath away that she loved him. For a short while he almost felt guilty of his treatment of her, but it didn't last very long.

"Yes Ray. Everything is in place. All you need to do is get hold of Peter Mambridge and get him to sign it all over to you. There is nothing George Anderson can legally do about it. Officially, he no longer owns the properties or the businesses; Peter does. I have all the paperwork ready so, as soon as you have Peter, we are good to go."

Ray grinned, showing those crooked yellow teeth. They would put any woman off him, but not Bonita.

"Just what I wanted to hear." Rubbing his hands together, rather like a small squirrel who had just found a hoard of nuts. "I think this deserves a celebratory drink."

Bonita reached for her suit jacket. She had taken off her torn blouse and replaced it with just the blazer. She looked the epitome of class. With her six inch high heels and tight knee length skirt, she didn't look like the average gangsters moll.

Ray took two glasses from the small drinks cabinet and poured out a generous measure of straight gin into each. He handed one to her and she took it smiling. She perched her bottom on the edge of the desk and watched Ray down his in one gulp and then pour himself another. The thick smoke from his cigar curled away in the ashtray, filling the office with a Cuban aroma.

"It feels good doesn't it?" Ray sighed, after downing the second shot. "After three years of planning and you infiltrating Anderson's crew, we are finally at the end. In a matter of hours, all he owns will be mine and he will be nothing more than another rotting corpse in Epping Forest."

"We certainly pulled it off. I admit I didn't hold out much faith, when you first came up with this crazy plan, but George Anderson fell for it all."

"Don't underestimate me Bonnie. I'm a shrewd prude when it comes to business and even more so when it comes to Anderson." Ray pointed his finger at her and she knew it was a hidden warning. "A pair of tits, long legs and an intelligent brain is a lethal combination for any man; even me. Anderson never stood a chance. What with you, slowly convincing him that Customs and Excise and the bloody Inland Revenue were hot on his tail. You single-handedly turned him into a paranoid loon."

He reached her within a few steps and shoved his hand inside her jacket, gripping hold of one of her breasts and giving it a hard squeeze. "He trusted every fucking word that comes out of your pretty mouth, the mouth that sucks *my* dick. You, Bonnie girl, pulled a blinder."

It was Ray's, not so subtle, way of ensuring she knew; she had signed George Anderson's death warrant, just as much as he had.

"Make sure you're available later tonight. I'll call when I need you." He slapped her cheek and then, grabbing her chin, bit her lip in a kiss like action. Then he was gone, leaving her alone once more.

* * *

Peter Mambridge was in a right mess. His hands were literately tied. His face was a bloody mess and some of his teeth were on the floor in front of him. He had been beaten to within an inch of his life and was now sitting on a chair, in a kitchen of a house he didn't know.

He didn't know where he was either. He had been set upon in the car park of his office in Kempston, where he was blindfolded and gagged and then bundled into a dark green Range Rover. He tried to figure out the direction he was being driven but they had gone round roundabouts three or four times before turning off and he got confused. They drove for what seemed like hours, but for all Peter knew, he could still be in Bedford.

He had never been so scared in his entire life; he didn't know why he was there or what he had done. He got no answers to his questions but when Ray Jarvis walked into the kitchen with the attractive lawyer he had met with earlier that day and another meathead dressed from head to toe in black with a pick axe in his hand, he actually thought he was going to die of fright. It slowly dawned on him, that he had somehow got himself mixed up in one of his wife's uncle's exploits.

"Hello Peter old boy, fancy seeing you here." Ray said to him in a very jovial manner, like he had just walked into his local pub and bumped into a friend he hadn't seen for a long while.

The two brutes who had shoved him into the car and then proceeded to bounce him around the house burst out laughing, amused at their boss' humour and the horror that was written all over his face.

His trepidation was unmistakably palpable; you could almost smell the fear. Ray felt sorry for him; Peter was a good man. He was honest, he paid taxes and had never broken the law in his life. His only crime, was guilt by association.

Ray never really understood why people were good. He understood why people were bad, but the good fascinated him and he did have passing moments of empathy for them, when they wound up involved in the murky world he existed in.

"I don't believe we've met in person. I'm an old acquaintance of George's." Ray said. "Corrr… they messed you up a bit, didn't they. My boys get a bit rough sometimes. Still, your hands are okay aren't they? I mean you can still write can't ya, just your signature like? That's all I need, then you can be on your way."

Peter finally had the light bulb epiphany; that clarifying moment when the fog cleared. For a millisecond he felt euphoria as the confusion vacated, until the fear and horror set in, at the realisation of what he was involved in.

"No… Please… Fucking hell… I can't. He'll kill me."

The two thugs that had pounded into him laughed out loud behind him. It wasn't so much as Peter's fear that they found amusing, it was more the spluttered attempt at pleading with a mouthful of blood and missing teeth.

"He won't kill you Peter; because he won't be alive to." Ray shook his head, his voice cajoling. Then with a malicious snort he added "The others will probably get you though, the moron brothers who will peck and fight over the scraps that I leave behind, like vultures."

Peter begun sobbing, long snotty tendrils hung from his nose. He knew he sounded pathetic but he really didn't care. If crying saved him his life, he would cry for England.

"Please…" He wailed.

"Of course." Davie, *the meathead with the long grey plait*, started to speak. "We're not going to let that happen. We look after our friends and as you are going to assist Mr Jarvis, we look at you as our friend. You are our friend Peter, aren't you?"

Davie's voice was calm and gentle. It had a soothing quality to it. Peter nodded frantically, like Davie knew he would. Fear, terror, dread and panic all make a man incredibly willing and agreeable. It was a magnificent weapon to yield.

"Good lad. All you have to do is sign your name where the lovely Miss Mashek tells you too and you'll be on your way, with half a million squid. That should be enough to get you and your pretty, expectant wife far away from here. Don't you think?"

Peter looked up at the man standing in front of him. He grasped the hidden indications in what had been said to him. He took in the fact that he was no longer safe with his wife's family. He also took in that he was being told he was not safe with the men that were in the kitchen with him, but the hint towards his pregnant wife and her safety was enough to make his decision.

He cursed the day he ever met his wife's family. He had no idea who George Anderson was until his wedding. Now, he was unwittingly involved in a gangland turf war. He didn't want to have George's assets signed over to him. It was a dodgy tax evasion and he wanted no part in it, but he had no choice. You didn't say no to George, the same as you didn't say no to Ray Jarvis or Davie Newman.

Peter knew he was screwed either way, but he also knew that, if he didn't take the money, he was dead and he couldn't do that to his wife, not his Patsy. The woman he adored over anything else. He couldn't leave her alone to raise the baby.

He looked over to Bonnie, who was standing in the doorway of the kitchen. She smiled at him politely, like this was just a normal business deal. She had been the same that afternoon, in her office. She was as villainess as the men in the room. A few hours ago he thought she was just a professional and that somewhere along the line, what George was doing was legal.

It had to be. He had a top notch lawyer and everything seemed above board when she had explained how it all worked to him earlier.

It dawned on him just how naive he had been, but then again, so had George. He obviously had no idea that the beautiful lawyer was working for Ray Jarvis, anymore than Peter himself did. She had done the pair of them over.

It briefly crossed his mind, when would she screw the main man himself over, because, in his eyes, she would eventually. This was a comforting thought. He tried to return the smile but due to the broken jaw, it wasn't the easiest thing to do.

Looking back at Davie and Ray, he gave a loud resigned sigh.

"Show me where to sign." He said, slowly shaking his head; the product of a beaten and defeated man.

Ray smiled and clapped his hands together. "Miss Mashek, do the honours."

Bonnie walked into the kitchen and pulled out a chair from the table. She sat herself down next to Peter and pulled out a brown cardboard folder from her briefcase.

She didn't look at him, she just begun to proficiently reel off technical legal jargon, while handing him one piece of paper after another, to sign away his life. He wasn't listening to her. All he was thinking about was how the hell he was going to convince Patsy to run away six months pregnant, but then again, once she saw the state of him, she might not take much convincing at all.

Bonnie noticed his blood stained hands. It was funny but violence never bothered her. It's not that she enjoyed it like Ray did; she just had a strange detachment to it. It all seemed so staged. She felt the same way about it as a hen pecked husband does about his wife's nagging. It was that quick raise of the eyebrows, here-we-going-again, boys-will-be-boys tolerance.

Ray watched, while all of George's legal assets were handed over to him. The illegal ones Ray just intended to waltz in and obtain. You don't need a lawyer for that kind of takeover. He waited until the last of the papers were signed and then he called Sean.

Everything he had planned over the last three years had finally come together in the space of a day and a night. He couldn't have wished for a more successful outcome. He now had what George had spent a lifetime creating and, once the night was over, he would be rid of the thorn in his side as well.

The only downside was that Sean didn't want to take over. It meant he would have to split the businesses up and get his own crew to work them. It meant spending further time in Essex and that was not Ray's intention. He wanted to get back to his own terrain, as soon as he could. He wasn't that keen on this particular area and missed the smog and the noise of London.

Still smiling, he walked over to Peter and gave him a friendly slap on the shoulder.

"Well done lad. Mr Newman here is going to sort out your payment and then he will take you home. If I was you, I'd leave tonight."

"Ttt…tt…tonight?" Peter stammered.

"Yeah, tonight. By morning Anderson is gonna be on the missing list. This time tomorrow I will be informing the rest of his family that I am the one that took it all away, right from underneath their noses."

Peter had never felt fear like he was feeling it right now. It crept up from his toes and spread all through his body. His heart pounded against his chest and his lungs seemed to deflate, refusing to let oxygen back in. His head was thick and heavy and the room felt like it was closing in on him, getting smaller and smaller by the second.

Ray turned to Bonnie. "Fergus' papers ready?"

She nodded and gathered up the folder and documents. Ray waited for her to secure them in her case and then gently grabbed hold of her arm and led her out of the room, leaving Peter contemplating his future and his past.

* * *

Sean poured out a full tumbler of vodka and knocked it back like it was a glass of water. Kenny watched him. Sean had been sniffing coke and swigging vodka for the best part of three hours. He had paced the length of Kenny's living room in an almost military trance waiting for his phone to ring.

Kenny knew he was psyching himself up, he knew the thoughts that would be running through his head; the questioning, the reasoning, the justifying. Beating a man, maiming him, it pales into significance compared to taking a life. No matter how much of a sociopath you are, the enormity of what you are about to do will always enter your mind, even if it is only briefly.

What Kenny didn't know was that although he was right in his suspicions about what was going through Sean's head, Sean had only considered them for about the first hour. After that, all he was thinking about was how the older men, Ray, George and Kenny all thought they could run him.

The more he mulled it over, the more he began to fixate on it. As far as Sean was concerned, he was going to end all of the control. He was going to show the old school the new school. Taking the contract on George was about demonstrating his worth, not as an employee or a protégé, but as an equal; just as shrewd, just as brutal.

Ray needed to be shown not to back him into a corner and Kenny needed to be shown that Sean will do whatever it takes to get what he wants. George was going to be the one that delivered the message.

He checked his watch every few minutes, his whole posture fidgety, giving a glimpse into his restless mind. It worried Kenny slightly how quiet he was. It was unlike Sean to be a silent thinker. He normally showed his thoughts quite clearly but as Kenny watched him do another lap of his living room, he begun to have serious doubts as to the nights events being a success. He wondered, not for the first time, what had got him involved with Sean Fergus and why.

When Sean finally spoke, the calmness of his voice certainly didn't match the edgy and impatient bearing he had been presenting. It threw Kenny even more than Sean already had.

"It's time to go."

Kenny looked at him straight in the eye. Sean saw the meaning behind it. It pleased him, that Kenny was second guessing him. After tonight, he and Ray would know, just how far he was prepared to go.

He was going to show his worth. It wasn't about the monetary gain anymore, although George Anderson's house was a major factor in it, it was about moving up the ladder. Sean no longer wanted to work for the main men; he wanted to be one of them.

He implored the power and fear that he could yield. He had a taste of it from running whores and now he wanted it from the older guys too. He wasn't concerned with what they had; he didn't want what was theirs. Sean had no interest for owning nightclubs, or managing protection rackets, or even being the social worker for the community, like Kenny was.

All of that involved having a firm, working in a team. That wasn't Sean. He was a loner, always had been. He was indifferent to teaching people, or helping them along the way. He loved running the girls, but even that wasn't for the money. That was for the power. It was all about the power and control.

Finding a new girl and breaking her in, stripping away their innocence and making them completely dependent on him, he loved it. It was the constant thrill of how easy it was.

The pathetic and weak ones he put on the street, where they risked their lives getting into strange cars all day and night, to pay for the drug habit that he had forced upon them. He got half their money for their bodies and the other half for their drugs. He owned them in every way.

The more savvy and slutty ones he put in the houses, where they had regular vetted clients, health checks and security, these girls earned him a fortune. He appreciated that and rewarded them, by paying them a decent wedge and looking after them. Sean especially looked after his top girls; the ones in charge of each house.

They run all the other whores. It was always one of the girls, never one of the boys. Rent boys fight and scrap more than whores. They don't have the temperament to be in charge. It's just their nature.

He was more than happy with his way of life. Tonight was about gaining the fear and respect of those around him. Above all he wanted and needed equality. He needed to feel adequate. He hadn't felt that in a few years, not since he was seventeen and it had left a hole inside him.

He masked it with aggression and violence but it didn't fill it. He fucked his way through women in an attempt to cancel out the emptiness that threatened to explode. They became a toy for him, something to relieve the boredom, frustration and longing.

It was vital for Sean that he made himself a name; he had to be a 'somebody'. The opportunity to take out George Anderson couldn't have been dismissed, not just because it was Ray Jarvis doing the asking, but because in Sean's eyes it was his way of showing the world who *he* is. That he had been successful.

Ultimately, he was showing her; the girl that created the void in the first place.

Kenny watched Sean walk out of his house; the boy adamant he was going alone. It was coming up to one in the morning and he was dog tired but he knew he wouldn't be sleeping; his mind pre-occupied with how the night will unfold. He needed something to relax, to take his mind off the anxiety. He reached for his phone and sent a text.

If he was going to be up all night, he would much rather be in the company of an affable and willing young man than wearing out more of his solid oak flooring by continuing the pacing Sean had been doing.

His young friend would help take his mind off it all for a while; until Sean called to say it was done, or that it wasn't. Whichever way it went, Kenny was sure that nothing would ever be quite the same again, for any of them.

While he waited for his male prostitute, he thought about the last few years and his life since Sean had come into it. A mutual associate had introduced them one night in a pub in Basildon. Kenny had taken an instant shine to him, which was strange because he normally made a point of staying well clear of the straight ones. But there was something about Sean that Kenny couldn't resist.

It wasn't the arrogance or the confidence that attracted him so much; it was more of a look that Sean would throw at him every now and then, that said Sean felt a connection too. It was always momentary and it had never been discussed, but it was something that had kept them together.

Kenny knew Sean didn't let people get close to him and he was probably the closest anybody had got; in his growing years, this made him feel unique and elite. But then, Sean was good at making you feel like that, when he wanted to.

Sean hadn't so much as blinked when Kenny had enquired into whether he had boys for sale as well as girls. He had just smiled his charming smile and told him he could get Kenny whatever he wanted. There was no disgust or repugnance in his eyes. He had never mocked Kenny for his tastes and in Kenny's mind that meant Sean was not homophobic.

He was secretly flattered, that Sean had called him when he had raped that girl; that he had needed Kenny's help and expertise. But Sean had also come a long way since that night and tonight Kenny knew he was about to find out just how far. It was nights like this, that either makes you or breaks you. You learn to live with the consequences of your actions or you crack up.

Sean had never really mentioned the rape, since it happened. He just carried on as usual. It had got to Kenny though. He thought about the girl a lot. Her haunted face came to him in his dreams. It had affected him more than he liked to admit. The revulsion he had felt when he saw what Sean had been doing was so intense, it took all his will power not to batter the life out of him.

But it was this strange connection between them that had stopped him. If anybody else had called him in the middle of the night and landed him in the shit Sean had, they wouldn't be standing now. Because it was Sean though and because of the feelings Kenny harboured for him, he covered it up and played it Sean's way.

The doorbell interrupted Kenny's thoughts and he sighed heavily. He needed the diversion that was on the other side of the front door and decided there was nothing he could do now, apart from wait and see what happens. In the meantime, he was going to let the prostitute weave his magic and make him forget about Sean Fergus for a while.

* * *

George Anderson looked straight down the barrel of the shot gun. Then he smiled at Sean.

"Not my chosen weapon." George said jovially.

It wasn't what the boy was expecting and it unnerved him slightly. Considering he was straddled over the man, who was lying in bed and had just been woken up, with a gun poked in his ribs.

Sean wasn't about to show his disconcertment though and smiled a cheeky grin down at George.

"Completely misunderstood the shotgun is; a bit like me really. This beauty has more than a few advantages. For a start she is reliable, with still and moving targets, just in case you make a run for it."

He stroked the barrel tenderly and then continued chatting away, knowing that if he kept his cool, he would unnerve George a lot more. He was, after all, at the advantage. He had the gun and he knew that George was alone in the house; the house that would very soon be his.

He had been watching the place for the last two hours. He had scouted every inch of the vast grounds that came with it, investigated the two large outer buildings that sat at the back of the house and had a good look round the various rooms inside, before he had ventured up to George's bedroom.

The first thing he was going to change was the security system. He had just waltzed straight in. No security lights, no burglar alarm, nothing; not even a dog. Just a normal lock, that set Sean back about thirty seconds. He wasn't sure if George was really that stupid, or whether he was just so cock sure nobody would ever come after him.

"It has gigantic stopping power at short range, you see; more than the hand guns and rifles. Gotta know how to handle one though." Sean jumped down from the bed and pulled the sheet off, exposing a naked and vulnerable George.

"People think the shotgun is great for untrained shooters, amateurs, but truth is, at close range like now, the distance from me to you, the spread of the shot is not very large and the skill in aiming is essential." He went on, enjoying the confusion in the older villain's face, watching his facial expressions change, from disbelief, to a final realisation of what was really happening. That this was a hit.

"Whatever you're getting, I'll double it." He pleaded.

Sean just laughed. "There isn't a price tag on this job George. This is about my freedom from you all. Now... let's take a little walk shall we."

George slowly rose from his bed and looked around for his robe, more an automatic move, rather than a need to cover his dignity.

Sean guessed what he was doing. "You don't need to get dressed mate, come as you are."

He shoved the end of the gun against George's chest to show his impatience. George took the hint and instinctively put his hands up. He stood, a little unsteadily and nodded at Sean.

"Outside then, son." He beckoned in the direction of the bedroom door. The sarcastic 'son' reference was not lost on George. It was what the older villains called the up and coming talent. He himself had referred to Sean as son, or boy, many times and Sean's ironic affront had not gone unnoticed.

The cold eastern wind whipped itself around George as they walked from the house, across the garden and over to one of the outer buildings. Once inside, George immediately realised that Sean had been here, before coming to get him. He also realised that Sean had no intention of letting him die a graceful and quick death.

An overwhelming smell of sulphur clung to the air. In the centre of the floor stood a tripod with a small handheld video camera and a tin bath tub filled, George correctly guessed, with sulphuric acid.

Wide eyed and panic stricken, George turned round to face Sean.

"There is no need for all of this. Just shoot me and let that be it."

"Oh I'm gonna shoot you George, don't you worry about that old boy." Sean shoved George towards the bath, his eyes begun to sting from the overpowering aroma.

It didn't seem to affect Sean though as he walked over to the camera and turned it on. Then he pointed the shotgun back at the naked man. He didn't say anything. He knew his silence would make George babble like a baby and he was right.

"This really doesn't need to happen Sean." George began, almost straight away. He kept looking at the gun and then back at the bath behind him. "I can give you your freedom. We can take out Jarvis and the Jewish cunt together. I can give you whatever you want."

"Why would I take out Kenny?" Sean's voice boomed around the building. It echoed out into the night, where the dark blue sky was slowly beginning to lighten.

The dawn chorus had begun, indicating the day would soon be upon them. Sean raised the gun to his eye line.

George began to sob. He pleaded and begged with Sean, to spare his life. He even went as far as to say he would work for him, that he would give up his position and hand it to Sean, in exchange for his life.

It fascinated Sean, how panic and fear could reduce the hardest of men to a quivering mess. He had an uncanny knack of tuning into people's weaknesses and insecurities. Dying happened to be George's and he suspected it was Ray's too. The film was to be sent to Ray afterwards, to show him just how far Sean would go.

The tin bath full of acid served two purposes. It showed Ray that Sean was outrageously crazy and it also disposed of the body quite nicely; apart from the teeth and some tougher bones. Sean could transfer them unnoticeably later.

"Not Kenny, then... but Jarvis. We could get rid of Jarvis?" George was so desperate. He had one hand offered out to Sean in a protective; yet trying to persuade him, way and the other hand was covering his short fat penis.

"You see George, now I have a problem. Now I think you want to take a hit out on my old friend Ken. All this talk about taking people out; it's just not sociable."

He watched George fluff and gaff his way through a series of stuttered apologies and assurances that it was not what he had meant. It was all rather amusing but Sean, as always, quickly became bored.

He fired two shots into George and watched him fall back into the acid filled tub. The sheer size of the man caused a huge splash and the acid spilled over the sides, fizzing around George's blubber. Sean put the gun down on the floor and picked up the camera and tripod.

He repositioned them, to the side of the bath, filming George's body being slowly eaten away by the chemical. He watched in enthralment, as the absorption process began to take hold. Science really was a wonderful thing.

When the body was fully submerged in the acid, the fumes finally besieged Sean and he had to go outside. He covered the bath with a plastic tarpaulin and walked out of the building, leaving his former employer to dissolve into a liquid sludge.

As he walked across the long stone drive that led round the side of the garden, he saw Kenny walk across the lawn. He knew he would turn up. The old man had gone the whole night without a word and as much as he protested that Sean was out of his depth, he knew Kenny wouldn't leave him.

"No phone call?"

Sean saw the look of apprehension in the man's face.

"Took a bit longer than I thought." Sean replied indifferently. "It's done now."

He went to walk past but Kenny grabbed his arm. "You reported in to Jarvis yet?"

Sean pulled his arm free and thrust his face into Kenny's. "When I'm ready."

Kenny couldn't help looking into Sean's eyes. Somewhere under that madness was a normal person. Kenny was sure of it and for a few undisturbed seconds, he held the boys stare but Sean's expression didn't alter. His features didn't soften. The look of admiration and the need for approval had gone from his eyes and Kenny felt for the second time that week, the shift in their relationship.

"This stops now. The hold you have over me, it stops here and now. I'm no longer under you. I want you in my life Kenny, but I don't need you there"

He went to walk away and then turned back and pointed his finger into Kenny's chest.

"I done this for my freedom. From Anderson, from Jarvis and from you. From here on in I don't work for nobody but me. The girls are mine, the drugs are mine and Essex is mine. I'm not interested in anything else."

"You need a woman; not a fuck, a woman." Kenny said.

Sean burst out laughing then. It was the most ridiculous, random thing to come out of Kenny's mouth.

Kenny started to laugh as well. It was a strange sight to see, two men holding onto one another, standing on a plush manicured lawn at five o'clock in the morning, giggling like school girls.

Kenny slapped Sean on the back. "Well then, we better go and tell Jarvis there's a new kid in town."

"Nahh, I got a video that will tell him all that." Sean patted his jacket pocket. "Let's go get some breakie and get this couriered over to Ray. It will be a nice little delivery for him to wake up to."

Trial and Retribution
When You Dance With The Devil

*"What we call the beginning is often the end,
and to make an end is to make a beginning.
The end is where we start from."*

T.S Elliot 1888-1965

Chapter 12

October 2005

By the time Sean had driven back, from Brentwood to Sudbury, it was quite late in the afternoon. The sun was low in the sky; giving a red glow to the Essex-Suffolk countryside. Sean loved this part of the country; with its clean air, green trees and fields that stretched out for miles.

Whenever he had a tiresome or monotonous day, like today, it always managed to clear the dark melancholy void that devoured him. He hadn't intended to be away from home for as long as he had. He only anticipated visiting Kenny to give him a little job; the desperate phone call he had received from his mother afterwards, forced him to take a detour back to his old house.

Why his sister had to cause him so much aggravation he didn't know. He had planned to slip back into bed next to Rachel, without her ever knowing he was gone. Now, he wasn't so sure she would still be there. He had just left without a word, or a note. What did she think when she had woken up and realised he wasn't there.

Would she have felt rejected? The thought tightened itself around Sean's chest. He would never reject her. Didn't she know that? This thought unnerved him. What if she had left? What if she had thought she had been discarded and abandoned? Had he blown the one chance he had been so franticly desperate to get?

He had never fought for her; all those years ago when she had left. He had never told her that he couldn't breathe without her. Why had he not gone looking for her himself? Essex was a small place. It wouldn't have been hard. Why had he not? Why had he just let her walk away, into the arms of somebody else? She hadn't left. She had moved around, to different areas, but ultimately stayed within the county borders.

But, if he was honest, he knew the answers to all his questions. He let her walk away and had not sought her out because he knew, if she ever become conscious of who he really was, she would hate him and he could never bear to see that in her eyes, on her face. She was the only one that ever saw a glimpse of decency, kindness, wholesomeness; she was the only one that ever loved him.

The reprieve and liberation he felt, when he walked back into the house and saw her sitting on the stairs in the hallway, was tremendously overpowering.

"You're still here. You stayed!" He couldn't contain the delight and relief he knew was projecting all over his face. Then she smiled at him. It was all he needed. The affirmation was so extreme.

"I wasn't sure if I should go or stay? Mind you, I don't really know where I am, so calling a cab wasn't an option. I tried to find a letter or something with the address on but you don't seem to have anything lying around."

168

"I guess I don't really receive much post." He walked over and sat down next to her on the stairs.

As she turned and looked at him, he traced the outline of her face with his finger. It was such a delicate and intimate move and for a few seconds, he totally bore into her soul.

"I waited so long to feel like this again Sean. It never went away, no matter what I did."

He kissed her then. When he reached for her, she was astonished again at how she responded to him. It was as if the being disconnected for years had created a dire urgency for each other; after missing one another, yearning for and craving one another. They made love until the sun had disappeared and their bodies were downy with sweat.

Later, they slept in each other's arms, something neither had done with anybody for years, if ever. Rachel was at peace and did not know why. She did not care. Sean was back in her life and she was determined that was the way it was going to stay.

She awoke to find him watching her. Half sitting half lying, with his head resting on one arm, smoking a joint with the other, he looked startling. It was dark and the only light that came through the window was from the security lights outside of the house; causing a beam of white yellow to glow the room. The sleep in her eyes felt thick.

"You're still here." It was almost a whisper. Her stretch was such a small and feminine movement; the shine to the room gave her naked body a fresh, sun tanned look.

"I didn't think I would get away with disappearing again." There was a hint of playfulness to his voice.

Smiling, she closed her eyes again; sleep beckoning. She wanted to fight it; to spending every minute she could with him.

Sean put the half smoked joint in an ashtray and placed

it on the floor. Nestling down beside her, he kissed the top of her head.

"Why do I not scare you?" It was almost a murmur, the words were spoken so quietly.

Rachel was awake now. Her eyes were open and she saw the confusion that was running through his mind; his eyes were dilating with the torment. For a second, she thought maybe he had taken something and this was the beginnings of a paranoid rambling, but the sincerity in his face, the lines that showed the consternation of his question, wrenched at her heart.

She fell absolutely in love with him in that instant. It had always been there, the wanting, but at that moment in time, it all became so definite. She knew what she meant to him. She always had, in the depth of her heart and mind. It was not that she sought the power she knew she had over him, it was the way he became somebody else, only for her. She knew she was the only one that received that treatment; it was reserved only for her. Nobody had ever made her feel so special, so exceptional.

"Why would you scare me?"

The expression changed in his face, to a solemn but earnest one.

"I have done some really bad things Rach. It's like something inside of me head takes over and I do nothing to stop it. I just sit back and watch it unleash. I feed off the retribution I think I need to dish out."

"Would you ever hurt me – or Adam?"

The urgency in his look manifested itself in his eyes once more. The silence in the room was tangible. Every breath, every blink, could be heard.

It seemed like forever before he spoke. "No, I would never hurt you Rach but I make choices other people don't. I have to. It's the life I lead."

"When you love someone, you'll stand by them through thick and thin, forgive them for their mistakes and you'll never give up on them… no matter what. Everybody gets to have a new life Sean; to start again. Maybe this is your chance. Maybe this is our chance."

"You can't change the life you've lived, but you can change the life you're living." The profundity of Sean's response surprised her. It wasn't like him to come out with such a philosophical statement. He half laughed at her and half at himself.

"Someone said it to me once. I never really got what it meant but it's always stuck in my head. I kind of get it now though."

"I like it. Who was it?"

Sean shifted uncomfortably. He wasn't too sure on how to answer her. He decided on limited information probably being best.

"Just a wise old man… who tries to keep me on the straight and narrow."

"Hmmm… I would like to meet him."

"Maybe… One day"

She leant in and kissed him then, but not the fervent, animalistic kiss that came from passion. It was slow and gentle; it blew him away quite literally. He knew it would always be her for him. No one else could do this to him; no one else could make him see a different life; life without inflicting degradation and mortification.

Feebly, he pulled away from her; as much as he wanted to stay entranced in the kiss, there was so much he still needed her to affirm.

"Our chance? You said maybe it is our chance."

She had said the words without even thinking about them, a Freudian slip. But she had meant them all the same.

Maybe it was their turn, their chance, their one shot at happiness.

Neither of them had found it being without each other. Was the answer so obvious? Was it blatantly staring right at them? Neither had been able to forget one another. Both had searched for anything to fill the emptiness that excavated away at them.

She had pushed other suitors away, building barriers between herself and anybody who tried to come near. She knew he had done bad things, Essex was small and Sean's name was well known.

She had worked in enough pubs, bars and restaurants to have heard the stories. But she was back in his life now and he no longer needed to do the awful things he did.

"If you want it? It's there..." Her voice sounded more confident than she felt.

This surprised her. She knew, above anything, she needed to be with Sean. Laying her hopes on him was such an enormous gamble.

"More than anything Rach."

Kissing her, he repeated it over and over.

"More than anything, more than anything, more than anything..."

She had him then; completely, utterly and entirely. Sean Fergus was wholeheartedly and unreservedly enwrapped in her presence and it absolutely terrified him.

* * *

James Porter looked at the time; it was gone seven. He rubbed his eyes and sat back, in the chair he had been sitting in for the past twelve hours, staring at the computer screen that displayed a spreadsheet of data. It had made sense to him this morning, when he started to analyse it. At lunchtime, it no longer made sense and he had to start from the beginning again.

He had just been promoted to Risk Assessment Manager, at an insurance firm in Kirkdale, a few miles from Liverpool city centre. This was his first major client and he didn't have a clue what he was doing.

Tiredness and hunger had set in and he wanted to go and get pissed. He was supposed to have a preliminary report compiled by the end of tomorrow for his boss and he wasn't even through with the data yet, let alone near to producing a comprehensive analysis with recommendations.

Deciding he wasn't going to get anymore done tonight, he switched off the monitor. He would come in early again tomorrow. The pub was beckoning him and sleep wouldn't be long after that. Besides, the cleaners had been hovering outside his office for the past half hour, so he took that as his cue to go.

He grabbed his jacket and walked out of the building. It was dark. It had been dark when he arrived at work, just before 7 am. It occurred to him, he hadn't actually seen daylight all day. He had sent out for a sandwich at lunchtime and, since he quit smoking, he no longer had the advantage of cigarette breaks.

Crossing the road and heading towards the bus stop, he saw the number 39 bus proceed down the road towards him. The beauty of living in a city was that you never waited longer than a minute for a bus. They were never late. Back in his home town in Essex you could be waiting an hour between buses; sometimes more.

It was strange to suddenly think of home. It wasn't home anymore. He hadn't been back there in over eight years. Kirkdale was home now. He had friends here and his parents and brothers visited quite often. He had bad memories of the last time he was there, sitting in his bedroom with Rachel.

He didn't ever want to go back. He didn't want to think about her either. She broke his heart. He really had been in love, although he had never told her. He knew he was the rebound shag to her, but he would have gladly taken any attention she threw his way.

He was scared when they found out she was pregnant; he was the first to admit that. But he would have come round to the idea. He would have been there for her and the baby. She had frozen him out though, went and had an abortion, without discussing it with him. It was his baby too.

Didn't he get a say in it? She blanked him out after that. She wouldn't return his calls or his texts. So he came back to Liverpool, finished his apprenticeship and had been working for O'Donnell Insurers ever since. He had done well there too. It was just in this new role, he was struggling a bit.

He watched the lights from the shops whiz past from the bus window; their colours hurtling into one another, shattering and exploding into fragments of bright white. There were still lots of people milling around the streets; dashing along in a hasten mode or dawdling in a sluggish, deliberate manner. A man carrying a billboard, advertising a second hand book sale, smiled at him as the bus sailed past. James didn't smile back. He ignored him and carried on staring; nothing making an impact, or dragging his attention to anywhere else but here.

All he was thinking about was getting to the bar and sinking a few pints, so when the bus came to a screeching halt, James nearly fell off the seat. He silently cursed as he settled himself again. More passengers got on. An elderly lady sat herself down next to him. The smell of urine was overpowering. It made his eyes water and he instinctively put his hand to his face to try and mask it.

The ammonia nestled into every pore of his nose; how did people get themselves into this state he wondered. He got off the bus two stops early and walked the rest of the way to the pub, no longer able to stand the odour that had permeated the enclosed space. It was a busy night and he had to fight his way through the crowd to reach the bar.

It was one of those places that had recently under gone a refurbishment, so from the outside it looked like a traditional English public house, but when you stepped inside you were bombarded with modernity; laminate flooring, glass display cabinet's and black and chrome finishing's.

Mirrored pillars replaced the original dark oak style and big lounger sofa's were strewn in unorganised fashions; not a bar stool or wobbly table, steadied with beer mats, in sight. As he waited to be served, he finally caught a glimpse of why he was in such a rush to get there.

She was a mirage as far as he was concerned, a complete fantasy. With long curly hair, the brightest red you had ever seen and florescent green eyes that seemed to sparkle in the glowing light. She was the first woman to have caught his attention since he had moved here. In fact, she was the first woman since Rachel.

Meeting her a few months ago, when she had started working at the pub, was an answer to his prayers; not that he was religious. But if he was, he was certain this girl was it. James was the sort of person that accepts what life dishes out to him. He didn't try to change things he wasn't happy with, or prevent things he didn't want from happening; preferring to just observe from a distance and accept.

If he was completely honest with himself, he wasn't happy. He was forlorn in Kirkdale. He was miserable and lost and isolated from his family and friends. It had been his choice, but that didn't make it any easier. He was too proud or too scared to go back. He wasn't sure which one and his accepting disposition just made it all the more worse.

They had spoken a bit over those months, the pretty girl

with the cardinal, ruby, red hair that emitted passion. It was the colour James thought of when he thought of love. It's vibrancy, brutal with aspiration and expectation. It had just been general chitchat but lately James began wondering if it could lead to something else. Her name was Jane Fitzgerald and she was originally from Romford in Essex.

James supposed this was why he was initially attracted to her. She was a little bit of home for him, although James no longer thought of Essex as home. But as soon as he had heard her accent, he had to talk to her. He did not know why, just knew that he had to and since that day he had been popping into the pub every night, for a few drinks and to see her.

She smiled as she saw him. Finishing up clearing the table and picking up the empty glasses, she walked towards him, still smiling and still holding his gaze.

"James, you made it!" The exclamation was as if she had been waiting for him to come in. She seemed pleased to see him, he thought, almost excited in fact. This thought made his stomach do somersaults.

"Yeah, eventually. It felt like the bus was never gonna get here though!"

"Well, you are here now and I am glad, because that means I can have a drink with you. I am just about to finish and I have a large glass of wine with my name on it!"

"That's great... I mean..." James was very aware he suddenly sounded eager. He knew he was grinning like a Cheshire cat but couldn't stop himself. "I mean..." He faltered.

Jane laughed. "How about you grab that table I just cleared and I'll bring the drinks over?"

James just nodded and cursed himself silently. Now she

was going to think he was some sort of love struck puppy, he thought.

This was, in fact, the exact impression Jane had of him, but in Jane's eyes it was not a detrimental insult. A love sick puppy was just what she was looking for; someone kind and caring.

She saw that in James. She didn't know why. She hardly knew him but she would like to get to know him better. He seemed lost somehow, trying to survive in the big bad city. It is how she felt. It is how she had felt since she had arrived here five years ago; lost, alone and scared.

Blocking out the thoughts in her head was an instant reaction she had learnt, to not let herself think about her life before. That girl no longer existed, Jane told herself. She was dead and buried, keep her that way. It was how she managed to keep living and surviving. It had given her protection over the last few years.

She wasn't that girl anymore, that girl who did an awful, awful thing. She was somebody else now. She reinvented herself and had almost come to like the new girl. It was the new girl that the nice guy sitting opposite her was interested in and Jane was determined to only ever let him see that one.

She knew he would not want to be anywhere near the other girl. She was tainted and damaged and carried an appalling secret around with her. Jane was certain that James would not be smiling at her, like he was right now, laughing and enjoying her company, if he knew who she really was.

"Is everything okay?" He sensed that the atmosphere had changed and the distant look in her eyes had not gone unnoticed either.

Jane smiled at him and looked into his face for a few seconds. "It will be."

"Is there anything I can do?" The offer was sincere, she

knew that and she appreciated it. He really was a lovely man, she thought. She picked up her glass of wine and took a small sip of the cold liquid.

"You're doing it." She smiled shyly and her eyes dropped from his gaze.

He thought she was exquisite. Her long red hair fell across her shoulders and partially obscured small but spherical breasts that were squeezed into a low cut, figure hugging blouse, which sported the pub logo; the loose curls that hung over her eyes framed her face perfectly.

"Can I take you out for dinner or something?" James was more shocked and scandalized than anyone when he heard the words come out of his mouth. Where the hell did he find the confidence to ask her out? He was so taken aback that Jane burst out laughing.

"Yes. That would be really nice." She managed to compose herself. She finished the glass of wine in front of her in one swift gulp and stood up. Holding her hand out to James. she beckoned him with her green speckled eyes. "Shall we?"

He took her hand and let her lead him out of the pub. Once they were standing on the pavement outside, she turned to face him. Before he knew what was happening, she leant in and kissed him delicately. It was so slow and attentive; it made his head swim with a sensation of giddiness.

"Promise you won't hurt me." She whispered onto his lips. It was so simple yet beseeching and insistent and James plummeted under her feminine wiles there and then. She had captivated and enthralled him with the mystery that surrounded her. Jane Fitzgerald was just what he needed.

Chapter 13

March 2006

A s the next few months passed and the cold late winter turned into a warm spring, giving the impression that summer was almost near, Sean and Rachel were in the midst of a romantic haze. She had ended her relationship with Greg almost straight away. She had not wanted to drag it out, or cheat on him for that matter.

She loved him, in her own way and was so thankful to him for loving her over the past five years. It had literately broken her heart, sitting him down and telling him she was leaving him for someone else. He had been so gracious; trying to make it easier for her. She didn't deserve to know such a considerate person.

He told her that he knew this day would come. That she would leave, to be with him. He couldn't believe he had got to have as much time with her and Adam as he had. That was when he notified her, that he knew Sean was Adam's real dad. Rachel was flabbergasted. They had never spoken about who the father was.

Rachel never imagined that Greg had thought it was Sean. It was understandable, she supposed. He had never known James. She was with Sean when he had gone away to university and had a kid by the time he had come back. It was perfect logic to assume Adam was Sean's.

The relief that was evident in Greg's eyes when she explained the truth unnerved her. He didn't seem to be too bothered who the father was, once he learnt it wasn't Sean. Although he was willing to let her walk into the arms of a crazed psychopath, he was less willing to let her take the child too. He had bought Adam up as if he was his own.

He had spent five years being the boy's dad and was not about to let Sean Fergus take over that role, whether it was his biological right or not. Greg loved the boy with all of his being. He had taught him how to read, to swim, to ride a bike. He had taken him to his first football match and stood on the sidelines cheering him on. He had patched up his knee, when Adam fell out of the tree house and he made a secret pact with him not to let Rachel know, as she would have no longer let him play up there.

Adam was Greg's son. That was the way he saw it and there was nothing and nobody that was going to change that. He made sure he had kept an active role in Adams life, since the split with Rachel. He had him for most of the weekend and saw him a couple of times during the week too. This drove Sean crazy. As much as he enjoyed the time he had alone with Rachel, he was not best pleased about the fact that Greg was still around.

He had expected him off the scene as soon as Rachel had given him the boot, but he was still there, in the background, hovering. Sean knew he was being watched; that Greg was waiting in the wings, positive that he would fuck up, to be on standby to swoop back in. Sean was certain that was why he had been so amicable about the split.

The thought that Greg didn't take their love seriously infuriated Sean. It enraged him to think that Greg didn't see it for what it was; or that he didn't see him for what he was and what he could do. He was exasperated at him arriving that half hour earlier to pick Adam up, which always resulted in Rachel offering him a cup of tea.

It wound him up immensely that Greg would stay just that little bit longer when he dropped off Adam; chatting to her about their day, making her laugh with stories of what *their* seven year old got up to. It was this that inflamed Sean's paranoia of losing her to him again.

The boy was Rachel's first and main priority and he was Greg's too. This put Greg ahead with an advantage. Sean had to show Rachel that he could be a good role model for Adam. He hardly had anything to do with the kid since he and Rachel got together and he knew this was more Greg's influence than it was her saying she wanted to take things slowly; that she didn't want to confuse the boy too much.

Greg was standing in his way and Sean didn't particularly take to people obstructing him very well. Sean saw Adam as the key to keeping Rachel forever, the closer he could get to him, then the more successful he would be in possessing her.

The very fact that Greg saw this too however, unsettled Sean. It wasn't often he came across people that made him feel anxious and a little frightened. These were emotions that he inflicted onto others; they were not to be directed towards him. Greg always looked at him straight in the eye; his gaze always held an air of assurance and poise.

It was as if he didn't fear him. This was a completely new concept to Sean; that he might not be feared. He didn't like it. It was unfamiliar and filled him with self-doubt, which was another ugly quality that had manifested itself due to Greg's whole demeanour with him; gorging away at him.

Greg was threatening his future and Sean knew it. He knew he would not be able to get near the kid, while the ex boyfriend stuck around. He had thought about paying him off, but he wasn't sure Greg would take it; no matter how much he offered him. Greg was a man of principle.

The thought made Sean feel sick. He hated moralistic do gooders. It was quite ironic really; Sean had never seen him as a threat before now. When they were kids, Greg had never once given him the impression that it would be him who tried to take him down.

That was how he saw it. For the last few weeks it had been building up inside him. That is what paranoia does to you; it creeps up slowly and before you realise it, it has completely consumed you.

Paranoia doesn't run alone either. It is accompanied by jealousy and suspicion. All these traits already encompassed Sean, but you add love and obsession into the mix and you have all the right ingredients for a very deadly cocktail of psychotic tendencies. This is rarely a good thing, at any time, but was especially bad when it came to Sean Fergus.

There was no way was he going to let Greg win, or even stand a chance of gaining Rachel back. As soon as he found out what the score was with James Porter, he was turning his full attention towards what he saw as the demon that threatened his future.

* * *

Kenny was taking his time. Sean had been waiting in his car outside a lorry park on the A1060 between Chalk End and Margaret Roding. It was a very rural part of Essex; it sometimes amazed him how the vehicles managed to get down the country lanes. It was mainly small holders and transits, which would be hired out to the public.

The place was deserted now; in the middle of the night. The security guard was in the small hut at the rear of the park. Sean had watched him walk in after his routine patrol. He wouldn't emerge again for another forty-five minutes. Sean had done his homework and watched him before. If he got the news he was hoping on from Kenny tonight, then it would serve him well.

Checking his watch again he sighed deeply. He was agitated; he didn't like to be kept waiting and Kenny knew this. What was taking him so long? He pulled out a CD case from his car door and removed the small paper parcel from his coat pocket. With a small sharp pocket knife, he began the process of slowly grating shreds off the pale pink rock; cutting himself two chunky lines.

He sniffed them up his nose within milliseconds and waited for the sensation of exultation to take hold. Cocaine did not give him an awareness of euphoria, like a drug such as Ecstasy or Heroin did. It gave him a sense of control; of power and invincibility. He lit a joint and saw the headlights of Kenny's car pull up behind him. It was about time, Sean thought.

For a man fast approaching seventy, he found Kenny's natural agility astounding. It was a shame his time management was not quite so agile. He had no sooner turned off the engine than had jumped into the car next to Sean; dressed in an Italian fine cut tailored suit.

Kenny liked to wear expensive clothes. It made him feel important. He had never quite shaken off the feeling of poverty, from when he was a small child. He knew he looked good and definitely didn't give the impression he was collecting his pension. He gave Sean a huge grin, displaying a set of perfect white teeth; another expensive purchase that Kenny had indulged on.

"You take the piss." Sean was riled and didn't attempt to hide it.

Kenny merely shrugged and took the joint out of Sean's hand. "Yeah yeah…"

He puffed on it and inhaled a deep lug into his lungs, then released small perfectly formed circles out of his mouth; a big one and then a smaller one that skilfully drifted through the larger one. He looked at Sean and gave him a wink.

"Me Pa taught me that, when I was eight. I never forgot how to do it."

Passing the spliff back, he pulled out a large white envelop from his jacket pocket and handed it over.

Sean smiled. "What did you find then?"

"Not much, to be honest with you Sean. The guy is squeaky clean, not even a speeding fine. He is up in Liverpool, been there for the past eight years. Works as a Risk Assessment Manager for an Insurance firm, whatever the fuck that is. Earns a decent wedge, has a pension plan, home and contents, life insurance all that. No financial problems, unmarried. No girlfriend from what I could tell."

"Yeah yeah… all fucking interesting Ken, but I don't want to fucking choose him as a life partner do I? Fuck me. What about the kid?"

Kenny wasn't too impressed by the cut off Sean had just directed his way. He huffed noisily to show his discontentment.

"What about the kid?" He shrugged again, implying he found all this rather boring. "He knows nothing about the kid. As far as I could find out, he had left to go do some apprenticeship. Either she never told him she was pregnant,

184

or he done a runner. Whatever way, it looks like he is out the picture."

Sean digested what Kenny told him. It was nothing really but it was good news. If James was not aware of Adam then he was not a threat. He began to nod his head slowly, almost rhythmically, the coke beginning to take its full affect.

Leaning forward, he picked up a pair of black leather gloves that were on the dashboard. He began to put them on, making sure each finger was secured inside tightly. He lifted the hood of his jacket, up over his head and turned to look at Kenny. His eyes were flickering all over the place, their gaze fixed but not on him.

He was looking straight past, into something else. Kenny didn't know what. A feeling of fear encircled around him; for a second or two he wondered if it was him that was about to be on the receiving end of Sean's mania.

Picking up the knife that lay between his legs on the car seat, he jumped out the car and started to run towards the lorry park entrance. Kenny sat in the car, not sure what had just happened. He hadn't told Sean anything to send him off on a crazed bender, not even with all the crap he shoved up his nose. He knew he had to follow him.

He got out of the car and walked in the direction to where Sean had run off. He saw the small lit hut at the back of the park, the door was wide open. Kenny walked in, just in time to see Sean slit open Greg's throat with his knife.

As the injured man instinctively put his hands up to hold his neck together, Sean plunged the knife deep inside his stomach.

He turned around, to face a completely horrified Kenny. He gave him a hearty chuckle and patted his back as he walked past him. Kenny stood, staring at the man on the floor, who was desperately trying to hold his sliced up body together.

He watched him struggle for a full five minutes, before he finally gave up and lay still.

Kenny watched him die and then walked back out of the hut. He gulped at the night air but it didn't stop him spewing his guts up all over the floor.

"Jeeze Ken… Evidence!"Sean's voice rumbled behind him. "Last thing I need is your pissing DNA everywhere"

Kenny looked up from where he had just emptied the entire contents of his stomach to see Sean walking over to him with three other men. He recognised them immediately as being three cousins that Sean used now and again, when he needed help with a slightly bigger job than normal. The larger one out of the three laughed as they reached him.

"What's up old man, something you ate?"

He thought he was hilarious and threw his head back with laughter, until he became aware nobody else was laughing. Rick, not famous for his brains, more his physical strength, looked at his other two cousins for support. They weren't meeting his eye and were staring at the ground, like it was the most fascinating thing in the entire universe.

Kenny, if he wasn't feeling so rough would have had the boy on his knees normally, for the disrespect, but right now, after what he had just witnessed, he wasn't sure if he had it in him. Instead, he made do with giving the younger man a long glare that told Rick that it would not be forgotten and would be addressed at a later date.

With the same glare, Kenny turned his attention towards Sean.

"What the fuck are you doing?" It was said in a very deliberate slow manner

The boys could feel the tension between the two men and were buzzing with adrenaline, from the anticipation of what might happen between them. Sean and Kenny were both big names; the boys just starting out in their criminal pursuit of life.

They had heard the rumours of both of them and to have front row seats at one of their performances was an opportunity that rarely came along. Sean held his stare. It threw Kenny off guard that he had such an air of controlled confidence. He had come a long way, from the shell shocked boy that Kenny had found in the flat in Harold Wood.

"Burn it down. All of it!"

He was talking to the three men, but his glare didn't leave Kenny. The other men stood still, not wanting to miss a minute. The fuel filled seconds felt like an eternity, until Sean begun to move; he walked back past Kenny and towards his car. He got in, started the engine and drove off. He didn't look back at Kenny at all. This was noted by all four remaining men.

* * *

Sean was sitting in Kenny's living room, bold as brass; drink in one hand and a joint in the other. He gave Kenny a grin when he walked in and an even bigger one when he saw it wasn't returned.

"Don't agree then, I take it?" He asked simply, like he was asking the most normal question in the world.

Kenny stared at him for a long while. Sean always managed to flabbergast him with his audacity.

"Agree with what exactly? The murder, the arson or the complete lack of respect you just showed me. I'm not your employee Sean. I was doing you a favour. You should have told me." Kenny was angry.

The quiet volume of his voice and the fact he had not

sworn told Sean just how angry he was. It was when Kenny became really quiet he was at his most dangerous.

Sean leant forward from the arm chair. He stared at the floor for a few seconds and then looked straight at Kenny. "You would have tried to stop me. Not part of the code. Killing civi's, is it Ken?"

"Not part of the code? What the fuck? Sean what you just did was a senseless murder. The press will have a field day when they get hold of this. You left the fucking body for fucks sake."

"Course I left the fucking body. He couldn't just disappear. Too many questions. A security guards body adds to the attempted robbery and arson don't it? It was a botched job gone wrong. The guard died in the process."

He puffed on his joint and leant back again into the chair.

"I don't tell you everything Ken, the same as you don't tell me."

Kenny shrugged in a defeated manner. He knew it was pointless pursuing it further with Sean. He walked over to the sofa and dumped himself down into it.

"I don't get it. She had left him. She chose you. Why kill him now?"

Sean looked down into his drink. He swirled it around in the crystal glass and gave a half laugh, half snigger.

"I didn't scare him."

Kenny watched as Sean searched inside himself, for his reason for killing Greg. He had a faraway look in his eye and his stare moved from the glass to in front of him; although the glazed look told Kenny he wasn't focusing on anything in particular.

"He looked at me like I was nothing, like he was so above me. There was no fear in his eyes. He would have got her back, eventually. I know he would. He'd chip away at her, ever so subtly, making her doubt her choice."

Sean's stare finally moved to Kenny. He suddenly looked vulnerable. Kenny hadn't seen that look in him for a long time. It reminded him of the boy he used to know.

"I mean come on... how long is it before she discovers who I really am? How long do I really have? I just bought myself a little more time, that's all."

Kenny didn't answer him. Once again, Rachel had made him lose control. This, Kenny began to think, was becoming a habit. It was bad enough when she wasn't around, but being on the scene hadn't improved anything.

Sean was getting worse and Kenny was convinced she was the contributor behind every evil deed Sean had ever carried out. She was going to be the man's downfall; Kenny would lay money on it.

Chapter 14

September 2006

Sitting in her pyjama's, at a small oak table in their kitchen, Jane wrote her signature on the pad in front of her. Mrs Jane Porter. Then she wrote it again. It looked strange but felt remarkable. Mrs Jane Porter. Mrs. That was something she thought would never happen to her. But here she was, six months after meeting him; married.

She didn't think she would ever be this happy. She had a brand new name. There was nothing left to tie her to her old life. This was now her future; a new name and a new life, in a city a million miles from where she used to be. It was perfect. Everything was perfect.

It had been a whirlwind romance. She had fallen for him, James, her husband, almost straight away. He had been so shy and awkward around her, she had found it almost impossible not to warm to him. He was gawky and lumbering, which just endeared him to her even more.

She had begun to look forward to him popping into

the pub where she worked more and more. The more she saw of him, the more she thought about him. It seems he felt the same way, considering he went down on one knee and proposed, during a very romantic moonlit walk along the Mersey.

Jane smiled at the memory. James clocked it as he walked into the room. The kitchen was a considerable size. A burgundy island that housed a sink and draining board stood in the middle of the vast open plan room. There was almost a farmhouse feel to it that was disrupted with flashes of modernity.

Fitted chrome units slotted against the far side wall, giving way to a gap in the middle where a cream cast iron Aga cooker resided. The small oak table sat in front of two magnificent French patio doors that opened up on to a modest mass of green and shrubbery.

He flicked on the kettle and took two mugs from the draining board.

"What you smiling at?" He spooned heaped coffee into the mugs and grabbed the milk from the table.

"My name…" Jane answered, with a big grin. She lifted the pad to show him. He laughed and returned to making the hot drinks.

"It looks so weird. Mrs Jane Porter."

"It doesn't sound weird." James responded. "It sounds perfect."

"Yes it does. It sounds perfect and feels perfect and I am your wife! I am *a* wife!"

He laughed at her then, not in a cruel way but in a wholeheartedly kind way. It caused her to jump up from the kitchen table and throw her arms around him, nearly knocking him flying.

"You have made me the happiest woman alive, do you know that Mr Porter?

"Mrs Porter, the feeling is quite mutual." He replied, leaning into her clinch.

Their embrace lasted for as long as Jane allowed it to. When she pulled away, James knew that the moment had passed. She was very much in control of what affection and contact could be made between them.

She could be so loving towards him and then something seemed to switch in her head and it would be over; just like that. They could never just lay and cuddle for hours, she always stopped it.

She held back from him when it came to intimacy. Sex was scheduled and routine, but still good. He was a man though and guessed he would think that; it was the impression she had always given him anyway. It was the closeness and proximity she pulled away from. James often wondered, what had happened to her to make her like that.

He worried sometimes, when she would wake in the night screaming. She always told him she never remembered the nightmares. He knew it was a lie, just like when she drifted off to the place in her head daily and he asked her what she was thinking about; the answer would always be the same. That it was nothing, or she didn't remember.

She would never talk about her childhood or her life before she met him. Wasn't that strange, he thought. His parents had found the whole shot gun style wedding very peculiar. How Jane was insistent on getting married here in Liverpool and dead against going back to Essex. Then how she reacted, when he found her birth certificate while they were sorting through personal papers, to collect their marriage certificate; she had almost snatched it out of his hand

There was her reaction, to when he told her his parents thought she was pregnant and that's why they were getting married so quickly. He had thought it hilarious but she hadn't. She was insistent that he put them straight right away. The whole idea of having a baby seemed to horrify her. Again, for the zillionth time, he wondered what the hell had happened to her.

He had noticed that her name was Geraldine Fitzgerald. It was quite a strange name he supposed. He assumed she was embarrassed and didn't want him to know. She called herself Jane and it suited her. Sometimes she acted so aloof and he really didn't have a clue as to why. His new wife intrigued him though.

He knew there was so much more to learn about her and, if he was really honest, he couldn't wait. It had been a very long time coming for him to feel contentment and joy, like he did with Jane. He had been stuck in a mundane and ground hog day life, since he had come to Liverpool and Jane had put the rose tint glaze to it that he had needed; the excitement and anticipation of a new chapter in his life.

For Jane the memoires were all too fresh in her mind; the day she arrived in Liverpool, what had happened before she got there, what had happened after. She had been through such a harrowing experience, that she didn't think there would ever be a time she could talk about it. She saw the way James looked at her sometimes; the confusion and perplexity that ran through his mind. She was sorry for this. Sorry that she couldn't open up and tell him who she really was.

She was certain he wouldn't understand; that he would stop loving her, if he knew what she had done. It was an appalling act that happened at her hands. Jane couldn't comprehend that she herself was the victim in it all; that it wasn't her fault, that she had had no control over it and that she was just a child herself. She wouldn't allow herself the freedom from her own persecution. She only hoped James wouldn't push to find out more.

Watching him make the coffee she forced the bad thoughts out of her head. She returned to the chair, sitting down with one leg bent underneath her. She wouldn't let him win; the monster that had caused the devastation and desolation. He had taken enough and was still taking from her, all this time later.

It had been over five years ago. Why did it feel like yesterday? Would she ever have a day where it didn't take over her mind at some point? Where she wasn't transported back to the sickening episode?

James interrupted the daily introspection her brain was undertaking. He put the mug of hot coffee in front of her and kissed the top of her head gently.

"How about we go out for dinner tonight?"

The simplest act of trying to make her feel better was not lost on Jane and she loved him entirely for that. It was like he knew what to say to her to make her see what she had. That everything was different now. It was worth a thousand I love you's. He was not aware of just how much her saviour he was. But then, she was not aware of just what a saviour she was for him. Jane had no idea, that it was her that had enabled James to trust again; to let his heart love.

She made him see a future to look forward to, instead of just another day to get through. Destiny and fate are philosophical in nature. Something had caused these two to cross paths. James and Jane were each other's allies. It was a supernatural power that had entwined their lives; only neither of them knew it just yet.

Fate will predetermine and order the course of events; defining events as inevitable and unavoidable. It implies no choice, no free will. It will happen, no matter how hard one tries to prevent it. For Jane and James they had no idea how much their fate was connected, or just what their destiny was waiting to bring.

She grabbed hold of his leg, as he turned to walk away from her; a yearning swirled around in those bright green eyes. The immense disappointment he felt, was because he knew it wasn't the same yearning he had for her. Hers was a longing for understanding, without any explanation given. Desperate for him to grasp the underlining reasons for her defences. His was a web of built up frustrations, from the constant barriers he had to encounter.

"Dinner would be good." Her smile, although genuine, never quite met the edges of her face.

James felt the stirring sensation low down in his groin, the feeling intensifying the longer she kept her hand on his thigh; the thin cotton of his trousers offering no protection from the warmth of her skin. His body unblushingly throbbed in communication to her touch.

She noticed the shift in his eyes before his physical reaction to her. She felt the familiar dread wash over her, as she recognised the intimate gaze. As she tried to move her hand away, he clenched his fist around it, his grip pulling her closer. His other hand lifted her chin up, forcing her to look at him.

The way she looked right now, with her mass of red hair twirled and pinned on top of her head, loose wayward curls escaping from the clasps, her face fresh from paint and the pure innocent grace with which she sat, was putting James' untamed desires onto overdrive.

He lent in to kiss her, resisting the urge to give in to the animalistic passion he was consumed with and adopting a gentler, loving touch. He felt her kiss him back, her lips responding in time with his. Pulling her up off the chair to her feet, he forced her mouth open wider with his and allowed his tongue to slowly explore the wetness she possessed.

This was when he felt the familiar resistance. He had been waiting for it for the last few minutes. He felt her push against him and try and free herself from his embrace. James held on to her tighter, his breathing jaggered.

"Shall I stop?" Whispering against her lips, he worked his tongue inside them once more. His hand had a firm lock on her jaw this time, not so much as a forceful grip but more of a guiding lead.

Jane shook her head and forced herself to relax. The guilt and self-reproach she experienced daily was once again manifesting itself inside her head. She felt shameful that she couldn't give herself totally to her husband.

That he had to resort to asking her, for a piece of herself. But every time he touched her she was transformed, back into that girl. The girl she had spent a long time leaving behind.

She felt his hand move down, from her face, to the buttons of her pyjama shirt. His fingers gauchely fumbled the plastic discs free. Fighting back her initial tangible reaction, she allowed his hands to roam over her shoulders and down to her small symmetrical breasts.

The involuntary convulsion, fuelled with repulsion, was as pungently evident when his clumsy hands cupped around the soft formed mounds of flesh.

He pressed himself against her as he held onto her breasts; they felt like they were a separate entity. A nauseating sensation swarmed her entire body, as he gently flicked her nipples with his thumb. His mouth, finally giving hers a reprieve, worked its way down her neck nibbling a little firmer the more aroused he became.

She could feel how much he wanted her, that it was her that caused him to put himself inside her and shoot that burning liquid high up between her legs.

She made him want it, need it. She knew it was all her fault. She feebly tried to push him away but his grip on her just tightened, forcing her back a few steps until she hit the island that stood in the middle of the kitchen.

Putting her hands down instinctively on the surface edge to regain her balance, allowed James to rip off her shirt in an easy one handed movement.

"James…" She murmured, squirming against his hold. "James… please…"

He pulled away from her slightly, only enough so he could look at her face. She looked confused and unsure. Her youthful and inexperienced appearance drove him crazy.

Nuzzling back into her neck, his teeth sunk into the smooth suppleness, his hand finding her breast again. The other hand delved down into her pyjama bottoms and slipped a finger inside her.

As much as she physically convulsed and shuddered against him, she was always surprisingly moist whenever he managed to get this far. Surely her half hearted attempts to stop him were false indicators that she didn't want him? Slowly sliding his finger in and out resulted in her becoming wetter, but she still showed no reaction that resembled pleasure.

He purred in her ear. Jane, not really registering what he said, had gone to the place far back in the depths of her head; a place where she was somebody else, somebody normal. Where the things he was doing to her felt normal, because no matter how hard she tried to force it to happen, she couldn't and would never enjoy the feel of him touching her.

She let him because she knew he wasn't to blame. Why should he be punished, for something he had no idea about? Her body was just reacting to the stimulus James provided. Her mind had gone somewhere else the second he had kissed her. It always did, no matter how hard she tried to stay in the realms of reality, the castle in the sky always beckoned.

She felt her pyjama bottoms being peeled away from the lower half of her body and James pulling her down to the floor. The square marble tiles felt ice cold under her slender build, their rough surface scraped along her back as he thrust himself into her. She remained silent and stiff. Her rigidness fought against his hardness, her walls bared down around him, impulsively trying to push him out.

He clung on to her shoulders to keep himself inside her. She knew it wouldn't be long now. He never went long. A few quick impulsions and he collapsed on top of her, the erratic breathing gradually slowing down to a more restful balance. He felt her body judder, as he slipped from inside her, the vacant stare still transfixed across her youthful face.

As much as he craved to be close to her, he longed to be wanted by her. Seeing the look in her eyes killed him. Feeling her shake and jerk against him literately tore him up. He didn't get it one bit.

At times it was like he had married two different people. One was loving and tactile. The girl he first fell for in the pub; the sassy and witty redhead that had spun his world around. The girl that, for around eighty-five percent of the time, was still there, until intimacy was involved and the other girl took over. This one was quieter, subdued; almost a reverted childlike version.

All he wanted was to be able to make love to his wife, instead of feeling like every time he touched her he was raping her. Even now he could feel her discomfort, at having her naked body pressed against his half dressed self. She turned her head away from him, fixing her gaze on the far side of the room. Waiting for him to move, to let her know it was over. That he had finished playing with her. James mentally shook his head in disturbance.

"This isn't right." He said as he pulled himself up from the floor. Grabbing his trousers from round his ankles, he yanked them back on. Looking down on Jane he watched her curl herself up into a foetal shape ball "It's not normal… This *is not* normal!"

The tears fell out of her eyes at an alarming rate. There were no sobs or staggered breathing; just titanic saline droplets. She knew more than anyone that she wasn't normal. She felt it every day.

* * *

Maisy finished the last sentence of the letter she was writing. Signing her name, she folded it carefully and slipped it inside of the envelope. She addressed it and put it inside the back pocket of her jeans as she walked out of her bedroom and down the stairs. Her mother was hovering in the hallway. Maisy ignored her when she called out to her and walked out of the house.

It wasn't an act of rudeness, it was just that her mind was so focused on what she was doing that nobody else was filtering through to her. Ever since she had first thought about it she hadn't been able to let the idea go. It took hold of her entirely and the day had finally arrived for her plan to take shape. Once she had posted the letter, a feeling of reprieve took over her.

The post box was at the end of the road, Maureen watched her daughter walk all the way there and all the way back. She nearly had to sit down, at the shock of Maisy smiling at her as she returned. There was something different about her daughter lately. She seemed a little more together; almost sane sometimes. She had begun to talk more; conversation that made sense instead of paranoid ramblings. She even took an interest in Katie.

Maureen had begun to leave her to look after her every now and then; pleased that mother and daughter were finally bonding. Katie had taken to her immediately, grateful and thrilled at her mother's attention. Revelling in the time spent together. It was almost as if the small girl knew who she was and that she didn't want her.

It had broken Maureen's heart to watch Maisy reject her granddaughter. Katie was such a beautiful little thing, that Maureen could not help but despair, at the time Maisy was losing out on with her. As much as she adored her granddaughter, it didn't alter the fact that she should be bought up by her mother.

It was the natural order of things. Her husband kept his own counsel; never one to cause friction in his home. He ignored most of the daily dramas that occurred; preferring to leave it up to his wife to sort out, wanting to enjoy his retirement in peace.

Watching her daughter now, almost skip around the kitchen making a sandwich, marvelled her. It was like somebody else had possessed her.

Maisy saw her watching. "You ok mum?"

Maureen smiled at her daughter; not wanting to upset her in any way. She always felt cautious when talking to her.

"Yes love. You still feel alright to look after the baby tonight?"

Maisy nodded and continued with making her sandwich; concentrating on spreading the butter to the very edges of the bread.

Maureen continued chatting.

"I won't be long, I shouldn't think. I wouldn't go but ya dads quite insistent on it tonight. Says we aint been down the club together in a long time now; and what with you feeling so much better…"

"Mum, it is fine. It's no problem." Maisy interrupted her.

It was short and impatient. Maureen knew that was enough and that it wasn't to be pressed any longer. Not wanting her to change her mind, she dropped the subject willingly. She really was looking forward to going out. It was not something that happened often anymore, now she had Katie to look after.

There was a time she would have been at every social function going, but not anymore. So tonight she intended to really enjoy herself. It had been a long time coming and, without wanting to be selfish, she believed she was owed this one night of liberation; it was just she couldn't quite get rid of a feeling that something bad was about to happen; that an event beyond her control was about to take place.

She tried to ignore it and pushed it to the back of her mind. She busied herself with preparing dinner and getting Katie fed, bathed and settled in bed. She wanted everything organised, so Maisy didn't really have to do anything, apart from listen out for her.

She had showered herself and was now just applying a slight touch of blusher, to make her cheeks glow. Mick Fergus stood in the doorway, watching as she brushed her hair.

It was a dark grey mass of curly locks, although there was a day when that dark grey was as jet black as the sky. She still did it for him, his old woman. He had strayed over the years, sought out alternative companionships, but not one of them was a patch on his Maureen.

It was only sex, he justified himself, not love. Normally when she had been pregnant and not wanting to fulfil his needs; which was all they were, basic instinctual drives. There was nothing for her to worry about; he would never have left her. He loved her far too much. He had just liked a bit of different over the years.

That was all a long time ago. Mick didn't have it in him

anymore to chase skirt. He was more than content with a few cans and an early night with his girl.

"Are you not ready yet woman?" His voice made Maureen jump.

She smiled at him with her reflection in the mirror.

"Yes, stop nagging."

It was said light-heartedly and taken that way too. It showed a lifetime of understandings and perception. She followed him out of the bedroom and down the stairs. Maisy came out to the hallway from the living room.

"Have a good time."

Maureen smiled at her daughter. Although she was pleased to be going out, she still couldn't shake off that bad feeling. She didn't know what it was. It felt like she should be panicking, but she didn't know what she should be panicking about. Mick was hustling her out of the front door.

She let him do so; sighing inwardly, she decided to not fret about what she didn't know, not tonight anyway. Tonight she was going to forget all their troubles and let her hair down. She giggled as she snuggled into her husband's arm. She felt like she was courting again.

Maisy closed the door and stood in the hallway for a few moments. She just wanted to take it all in for a while. The silence and emptiness of the house enthralled her. Her heart was beating so soundly. She felt so calm, so tranquil.

She went into the kitchen and put a small saucepan of milk on the top stove. Waiting for it to simmer, she pulled out a small medicine pot from her cardigan pocket filled with a mixture of sleeping pills, pain killers and anti-depressants; all prescribed by Sean. She had been storing them up for months.

Dispensing them out onto the work surface, she set about crushing them into a powder with the back of a large metal mixing spoon. She then transferred the powder into the steaming milk and poured it out, into a mug and Katie's beaker. Turning off the oven, she went upstairs.

Her daughter was sitting in her bed, holding her favourite bear in her lap. She was looking at a book that showed a picture of a fairytale castle. It reminded her of the stories her mother used to tell her when she was little; before everything had changed.

Maisy separated her life into two parts. There was the first part; where she was a normal little girl that had the devotion and attention of everybody around her, just like Katie did and then there was the part after that where her brother took away that simplistic life and replaced it with a distorted corrupt version.

He was going to do the same again, to a different little girl, she was absolutely certain of it. He had come to her one night, a few months ago and told her that they had the chance of a new life. That both of them could start again.

It was the closest he had ever come, to saying out loud that what he did to her was wrong, that how he had manipulated her all for all those years was wicked. Not that he had actually said that. What he had in fact said, was that *he* had the chance to start again and have the life *he* deserved. That he didn't need her screwing it up by her obsessive and tedious tangents.

He told her he would leave her alone, if she stopped making her mother so concerned about her. Be normal he had instructed; like she knew how to be. How come he got to start again? How come he got to walk away? She couldn't. She was trapped with a constant reminder of what he did to her.

The mind games he played; the physical harm he induced. Then there was the other stuff. The stuff her mind had blocked; the stuff no brother should make a sister do.

He mustn't get to walk away from that. She wouldn't allow it. The more he had stayed away, the stronger she had felt herself become.

She had planned this night, in detail, repeatedly in her head. The taking an interest in Katie, presenting herself in a positive light, talking to her incessant mother, leaving the house, albeit for a short time only; putting every element in place.

Her family thought she was crazy. They didn't know the half of it, she thought. At this very moment in time she had never felt saner.

"What are you looking at?" She asked Katie. She walked over to her bed and sat down on the edge. The little girl turned the book around to show her mother.

"What's it about?"

Katie shook her head. "I like the pictures."

Maisy looked at her daughter. She was the spitting image of herself at that age. It is a strange feeling looking into the eyes of a child and seeing you. The innocence and purity that Katie held was overpowering. She didn't love the child. She was incapable of loving anything. Sean had seen to that.

She felt responsible towards her however. Maisy understood that Katie hadn't asked to be born out of a sadistic act between siblings. It wasn't something she was a willing participant in either. It was something that had happened beyond mother or daughters control. But there was something that Maisy could do about it now.

She could protect herself and her daughter from the hands of him. She could make sure that he could never hurt either of them again and in doing so she could bring him down; expose him for what he was; a vile revolting predator.

"I made you some milk. Why don't you drink it up and I'll read some of your book to you while you fall asleep?"

She handed the beaker of warm milk to the little girl, who snatched it up eagerly and jumped into bed; settling herself under her duvet and sucking at her cup, she waited for her mother to begin reading. Maisy gulped at hers.

It tasted normal. It was the sugar that masked the vast amount of sleeping pills that were dissolving away. She put her legs up and rested against the headboard of Katie's bed. She started to read the story, stopping intermittently to drink.

As the time wore on, the words begun to jump around the page; dissolving into one another. Rubbing her eyes didn't help. They felt so heavy and her vision was getting increasingly blurry. She tried to turn her head to look at Katie but she couldn't make it move. It wasn't just her eyes and head that felt heavy, it was her whole body.

It felt like a tonne weight was on top of her. She wasn't sure if she was still breathing. She couldn't hear it or feel her chest move. Her eyes were forcing themselves shut. She didn't fight it; she didn't want to. When the delirium came, she welcomed it, greeting the hallucinations with a relish, knowing the reality she had been forced to bear was slipping away.

She saw herself as a child, playing on the swings in the garden with her sister; the image so real she tried to reach out and touch her younger self. As her fingers touched her own small hand, the image blurred into a vacuum of swirled colours eventually settling on two figures huddled in the corner of the room. The elation turned to a vehement fright, when it registered in her mind that the two figures were her and Sean.

Again she was a child, older than the girl on the swing, but still a child. She remembered the scene the delirium was creating; being huddled in the corner, her knees pressed so tight against her chest, her head buried on top. He was bent over her, his hands poring at her legs and over her back; his words telling her it wouldn't hurt as much next time.

Maisy felt her body vault, mentally withdrawing from the recollection of what she was desperately trying to escape.

The walls of the bedroom rushed past her, turning into a ferocious sea of surplus illustrations; painting the pictures of her hopeless existence. Redundant memories, of laughter and smiles, mixed with uninvited depictions of degradation. Katie's angelic face a prominent and recurring image.

The small child standing in a blackness, screaming out in terror at her own hallucinations, until she felt the strong arms of her daddy picking her up. Even in her death, Maisy was subjected to his persistent presence.

Sounds of ice-cream vans and excited thrills, merged with his sinister tone of her name. He called it out every so often, reminding her he was there; that he would be to the end. The fused clatter rose with each wave of new and old images; swirling and flashing, grabbing out at her as they passed each one franticly trying to pull her into their world.

The delight she felt, as she let the darkness surround her, finally finding the peace and stillness that she wanted so badly. They were safe now; his toxicity no longer binding their existence.

Maureen found her daughter and granddaughter the next morning, lying side by side, static and motionless; their bodies cold and rigid. To look at, they were sleeping silently. She heard the screaming but didn't know it was coming from her. When her husband had come running into the room, she collapsed in his arms.

Mick Fergus lost his wife, his family and his world

that day. The massive coronary she suffered, at the scene before her, took her away from the long exertion of her life. Her heart could take no more. For Mick, the rest of his days would be spent in a psychiatric clinic, staring out of a window, rocking too and forth, mumbling incoherent nothings.

Chapter 15

October 2006

R achel had buried four people in a matter of weeks and one of them was a baby; she still couldn't get over that. Katie was such a delight. How did they not see how deranged Maisy had become? The girl should have been seen by some kind of medical professional by now, she didn't understand why not.

Maybe Maureen hadn't seen it; being left to practically raise the child herself and getting on in years. It must have been hard for her. Rachel knew Sean had popped over when he could; he would come home telling her what his raving loony sister would be doing. She had laughed with him, at his stories of her sitting in the garden in the pouring rain in just her underwear, or when she had locked herself in the cupboard under the stairs and refused to come out; how Sean had to sit there for hours negotiating with her.

She knew he had done his best for her but he was a man and didn't realise the severity of her situation anymore than anybody else did. They had to accept that nobody was aware of how ill Maisy was and that they all played a role in Katie's death. As grim and ghastly as it was, the sooner they all admitted that to themselves the better.

Rachel felt apprehensive and troubled. Life wasn't working out the way she thought it would. She thought her world would be complete when she met Sean again, but their idyllic life wasn't turning out quite so idyllic. Were they being punished for trying to be happy? So many people had died, in such a short space of time. Were they cursed?

Maureen's heart attack and Mick's breakdown were just the latest. What was next? Rachel wondered. Having to bury Greg was bad enough. She didn't realise she had so many tears. That day had gone by in a daze. She didn't really remember much of the funeral. When the police had come to the bistro to tell her he was dead, she thought they were talking about someone else.

She didn't know he had taken on an extra job. It made sense; he now had to pay for rent on his own and had still given her money each week for Adam. The police told her it was a burglary that had gone wrong. They assumed Greg had tried to stop a robbery and ended up being targeted by the gang.

The fire had destroyed all the CCTV equipment; there was no chance of ever having his killers brought to justice. It was all just so senseless. She couldn't identify his body; there was nothing left to recognize, apart from a few personal possessions that hadn't perished in the fire.

Just two solitary items to tell the world who he was; a signet ring that had hers and Adam's date of births inscribed on the back and a watch that she had bought him as a Christmas present one year.

She had gone alone to Greg's funeral, not thinking it was right to arrive with Sean. He had stayed away at her request and took Adam out for the day. Greg's parents were pleased to see her and his father, Jimmy, held her hand all the way through the service. His family had all kindly paid her their respects, treating her like the grieving widow.

Rachel felt guilty at this. It was not a role she felt comfortable taking. As much as she grieved and hurt, she felt she didn't deserve to be made as much a part of the family as she was.

She made her escape into the garden once they had all gone back to Greg's parent's house after the funeral. It had been raining and Pauline's tiny, perfectly attended patio glistened in the sun that was determined to out shine the misery of the day. The small patch of green lawn shimmered, as each blade seemed to stand to attention underneath the warmth of the late summer sun.

Rachel thought about the many summer barbeques herself, Greg and Adam had spent in that garden and how Greg would chase Adam around the washing line, while Pauline fretted about there being no room for games like that and that Adam would get hurt. She smiled at the memories of laughter and burnt sausages. The hickory-smoke filled evenings of traditional family time.

It was her first experience, never having anything like that herself. Jimmy and Pauline had welcomed her and Adam into their fold and showed her what it should have been like. She would always be grateful for that, for the love they had shown her and Adam. For a brief moment she wished it was different; that she could love their son, the way he had loved her.

Footsteps interrupted her thoughts and she turned to see Greg's brother standing behind her. Matthew was four years older than Greg but they looked like twins. It was uncanny. When she had first seen him at the funeral, it had taken her a few moments to register it wasn't Greg. Their eyes and jaw

211

line were almost identical; a few creases around Matthew's mouth were the only signs that gave away the difference.

He smiled at her but his eyes didn't quite meet hers. He looked awkward. His hand reached out to her, offering her own jacket.

"I thought you might be cold. You have been out here a while now."

Rachel shook her head. "I'm not cold. I was just remembering the summers out here…" Her voice trailed off, as the gripping pain tightened itself around her chest once more.

"You mean before you broke my brother's heart and he was murdered."

The words fell out of his mouth with a malice that shook Rachel to the core. She stared at him in disbelief. She wasn't sure how to respond.

Matthew smiled at her again and Rachel realised this time that the first smile had been just as dry. He hadn't come out to check on her, he had come out to have a go at her.

"Bit of a coincidence, don't you think? Six months ago you and Greg were happy as Larry and then in walks your old gangster boyfriend. Within days, you're shacked up with him and my brother's dead." Matthew stepped a little closer to Rachel, blocking her path back to the house. His six foot two frame obstructed her view of the patio doors, hindering anybody inside the conservatory to see the altercation taking place in the garden.

"I… I'm not sure what you're trying to get at Matt. Sean and I have nothing to do with what happened to Greg. It was a robbery that went wrong."

Matthew nodded. "That's what the police said too."

"Matt, what is this? I know you're upset and angry but this isn't my fault." Rachel reasoned. She didn't like the way he was looking at her. His face was screwed up into a disparaged sneer and his eyes told her he knew more than what he was saying.

"I told him not to go near you years ago, but he wouldn't listen. I told him you were damaged goods, but he reckoned he could fix you. I don't like things that are broken. They just aren't the same afterwards."

Rachel was astounded by Matthew's sudden attack on her. There had never been any animosity between them before.

"Matt, I know you're upset, we all are..." She tried to reason with him, but he just cut her off again.

"You have no idea just how upset I am." He moved even closer to her. Rachel could smell the whisky that permeated from his breath. "It's funny; you should have said you were up for taking on other men. I would have had a go. Greg said you could be a right go-er."

"Get the fuck off me." She spat out at him, pushing Matthew away from her as hard as she could. Her strength surprised him.

"There she is; the tramp with the sewer mouth. I knew she was in there somewhere."

Rachel stared at him for a long moment. "What is wrong with you? This is Greg's funeral."

She went to walk round him but he caught her wrist as she passed, pulling her into his strong arms. To anybody that was watching from the inside, it looked like a comforting embrace between two grieving family members.

"Fergus had something to do with Greg's murder. I know he did."

Rachel struggled herself free of him. It took all her strength to do so and she had to step back a few paces to steady herself. She wouldn't look at Matthew. She couldn't meet his eye.

"There was a reason you ran from him in the first place.

You saw what I see now. I know you did." Suddenly, the nastiness was gone from his face and it was replaced by an urgent and imperative need for her to agree.

Rachel slapped Matthew as hard as she could round his cheek. Snatching her jacket out of his hand, she walked back into the house, leaving him outside in the garden. She didn't know or care if anybody had seen; she just needed to get out as soon as she could. She felt suffocated by the guilt and thoughts that were running through her mind.

She tried to push everything out of her head. As soon as she was back with Sean and Adam, her perspective would become clear again. Matthew had startled her and thrown her mind into chaos. Rachel left Jimmy and Pauline's, almost immediately after. She wouldn't allow her mind to fester any further, on the poison that Matthew had tried to inject.

* * *

Rachel reminded herself she loved Sean more than anything. She always had. He had been her rock. Even when he had received the phone call about Maisy, he hadn't crumbled. He was strong, in mind and in soul. Rachel felt so comforted by it; that he could cope with anything that was thrown their way. It made her believe they would survive. He made them strong and he would protect her from anything.

Somewhere, out of all the recent tragedy, something good was going to come of it all. She was sure of it.

Sean wasn't feeling strong though, he was beginning to lose the plot, if he was honest. He was desperately trying to hold everything together but it was all unravelling about him. He was incensed at what Maisy had done; enraged at her nerve. Taking Katie with her was a slight for him. It was personal, he knew that.

Maisy was telling him she had won in the end. She had got one over on him and taken away all he ever truly cared about; power and control. The saving grace for Sean was that she was dead, which meant nobody would ever know the truth. Even so, she had taken with her that beautiful little girl, who had put sunlight into his world. He would have throttled his sister's bare neck if she wasn't already departed.

It had almost finished him off, having to play the bereaved brother and son. It was an emotion that was alien to him and he surprised himself, at how well he managed to keep up the pretence. Now it was taking its toll though. Sean wasn't sure at all how much longer he could keep it all together.

His sister's death had affected him more than he realised it could. Killing Greg was a means to an end and it had worked. Rachel had let him swoop in and play the hero to her and Adam. He had become intricately engaged into Adam's life almost immediately and Rachel was too absorbed in grief to think, or see things for what they were.

Sean's plan was coming together and then Maisy went and pulled a stunt like that, which in turn took his parents out too. Sean only had Alice left and they hardly spoke to one another. Alice hadn't even turned up for their mother's funeral. She had sent a note with some flowers, explaining she didn't see the point in making two trips down to Essex and that she would see everybody at Maisy and Katie's. Like it was some kind of family gathering she was excusing herself from.

They couldn't all be buried at once due to the nature of the deaths. Maureen's body had been released first, so they had to have two separate funerals. They had hardly exchanged two words to each other when they met; although Alice was secretly impressed with her brother's house.

Whatever way he had made his money, he had certainly invested it wisely. She was also impressed with the relationship he seemed to have with his girlfriends' son. She watched them in the church, during the service. Sean had scarcely taken any notice of the proceedings and seemed more occupied in entertaining the boy.

It was the same during the wake, back at his. Everybody was milling around quietly, sombrely; while Sean was running round the garden with Adam on his shoulders, pretending to be an aeroplane. The scene took her back, to a time where it was Maisy being entertained. Alice shivered as she felt a dark potent awareness came over her. It never felt right, the attention he frittered away on her sister. There was something unnatural and twisted about it. It wasn't that Alice was jealous; she definitely didn't want or require the same interest. She knew it was wrong.

It dawned on Alice she didn't know half the people at her sister and niece's funeral, there were a few odd family members, not many, but the rest were there for Sean she guessed. She didn't know it for sure, but suspected she was sharing the room with some of South East England's finest criminal masterminds; all there to show respect and loyalty to Sean.

As much as she was disgusted with the whole idea of her brother, she had to begrudgingly admire him for his success.

The missing presence of her father vibrated the room and Alice felt sadness at the tattered disaster her family was. She and Sean were the only ones left; they only had each other now. It was a sobering thought.

Alice always believed she didn't belong to her family. Even as a child, she pretended she was adopted. Her sister was a complete nut job and the devil possessed sociopath her brother developed into, only gave her more reasons to believe she really didn't belong; their lives incompatible with each others.

Alice thought very highly of herself and despised her humble beginnings. The humiliated shame she felt, of her council estate childhood, was obvious to anyone that took the time to scratch her surface.

She believed she was worth more than her brother and her sister. Why should she just accept what life handed out to her. In her mind, she was entitled to the life she had now created for herself, judging herself better than them. She had gone to college and gained qualifications.

She now worked for a top solicitors firm in London, their offices a short walk from The Gherkin and she was about to marry into one of the wealthiest families in the country. Her engagement had been covered by Hello magazine; a two-page spread detailing her upcoming nuptials to one of England's most eligible bachelors.

The very fact she had to leave her idealic life and be reminded of where she came from, who she was related to, infuriated her; bound by a sense of duty to pay her respects. Truth was, she had no respect for her family. Respect is earned, not automatic.

She had not been looking forward to telling her parents she did not want them at her wedding, so recent events were a saving grace. She still had to tell her brother though. That was something she really wasn't looking forward to; his reaction when he found out that her fiancé's brother would be giving her away.

Alice sensed someone behind her, assuming it was her fiancé Ben, she paused a while longer, watching Sean and Adam frolicking. It wasn't until she heard the female voice that she spun round to face Rachel, standing in the doorway of the imposing and luxurious open-plan kitchen.

"I'm sorry; I didn't mean to make you jump." She spoke again.

"It's okay. I was just lost in my thoughts there for a while." A half smile, half awkward grimace worked its way over her mouth.

Rachel stepped into the room a little further and looked beyond Alice, who stood at the window that gave view to an impressive manicured lawn. She saw Adam, standing on the stone wall that lined the decked path, leading down to the garden. He was fearlessly throwing himself off; the confidence evident that he knew Sean would catch him. Rachel smiled at the scene.

Alice clocked the puppy-dog look on her face. "He is good with him?" The question was hidden.

"Yes he is." Rachel nodded in agreement. "To be honest, I don't think Adam and I would have got through the last month without him."

Alice resisted the urge to scoff at the praise of her brother. She watched Rachel for a few seconds, absorbing the sentiment the woman obviously represented. She felt a fearful anxiety low down in the pit of her stomach; not quite sure why, but it was enough to make her act on it.

She reached Rachel within a few strides; the urgency with which she seized hold of her and spun her round, put her off guard.

"You do know he's not who he makes out to be... Don't you?"

Rachel wasn't sure of the question, or whether Alice really wanted an answer. She narrowed her eyes and slightly tilted her head.

"You see it, don't ya...? That hollowness in his eyes?" Alice's controlled voice wavered slightly, the Essex twang rearing through on certain words.

All those elocution lessons Ben's family insisted she

took, rapidly letting her down. She silently cursed herself that she allowed all the hard and sometimes painful work to be undone; immediately blaming Sean for the speech downfall. She felt Rachel try to tug herself free of her tight grasp but saw the quick flicker of acknowledgement, before she showed a feigned confusion. Loosening her grip, she let Rachel back away.

Before any more could be said between the two women, Sean and Adam crashed through the heavy oak door that led out into the garden; the little boy whishing past his mother and through the kitchen at top speed, excitedly yelling at Sean to follow.

"I promised him a re-match at that football game he loves."

For the first time, Rachel saw him look ill at ease He stood in the middle of the room, with a look of almost surprise that people were in his house and now, whilst explaining their sudden eruption into the room, he looked awkward. There wasn't any other word.

Alice had unnerved her. It wasn't just what she had said, but the ease in which she managed to put into words what lay in the dark depths of her own subconscious; things that had never been allowed to become fully formed thoughts.

Alice seemed to be unnerving Sean too. He wouldn't quite meet her eye, yet she stared right at him. It was the quietness of her which he found unsettling and she knew it. She had learnt that, if she waited long enough, he would always speak first. It gave her an upper hand over him. She needed that with Sean, always had.

He would lie his way out of any trouble he got himself in. The less someone accused him of something, the more he began to give himself away. This useful quality she became skilled at, proved to be quite a hit with her employers, which in turn had led her to meet Ben.

She knew her brother had something to do with her sister and nieces deaths. She also knew, she had absolutely no proof of any of her inner thoughts. As much as she was embarrassed by the rest of her family, she despised her brother with a strength that was much more dominant; she struggled to control her reactions in his presence.

It stemmed from a permanent memory; they were just sounds but she couldn't get them out of her head. She was about eleven or twelve and it was the middle of the night, she had been woken up by a low *ssschhing* and whimpers from Maisy. Their small shared bedroom meant their beds were head to foot. The memory told her nothing, it gave her no hint of what it meant and for years she told herself she hadn't even heard it; that she had dreamt it.

But she knew she hadn't. She knew in her heart that it was real; that night was real. She wished that she had turned round to the noises. That she hadn't shut her eyes again and drifted back off to sleep. Lately she wished that more than anything. But then, she was also glad she hadn't. If those sounds were what she suspected they were, if what happened in her worst nightmares did actually happen, then as a small child still herself, she thanked god for making her stay facing the other way.

The graceless silence that had begun to build in the room became almost tangible; an invisible black smoke swam in and out, consuming each of them with a thick toxic hold. Sean spoke first, eventually, just like Alice predicted he would.

"You look good? Y'know… not bad. How's things?" It was lame and they all knew it.

Rachel was even more thrown by Sean's sudden flustered ramble. What did sister have over brother?

Alice smiled then and Sean seemed to relax a little. She didn't answer him though, just smiled at him with a smile, which looked like her sister's, but didn't quite have the same shine as Maisy's did. Alice, although an attractive woman, didn't have her stunning looks, or her slim, petit build, taking after her mother for her dumpy form, but she did have Maisy's look about her. The resemblance was there.

Before Alice could reply to her brother, Ben walked into the kitchen, holding an empty whisky glass; completely oblivious to the tension that was so clearly visible.

"Ahh, there you are my love. You will never guess who I just had a rather interesting conversation with. Only Kenny Maltrowitz."

All three of them turned to the door, where Ben had appeared. This was the first time Sean had ever actually seen his sister's fiancé. His parents and Maisy had met him, when Alice bought him home once, but he had yet to have the pleasure. The man standing in the doorway was not what he had expected.

For a start Ben was black. No-one had mentioned this fact. Not that it bothered Sean. Some of the best cocaine importers he had dealt with over the years had been black. He quite liked them, but it was still a shock all the same. He wasn't prepared for the sheer size of the man either.

At over six feet tall, he towered over all of them and it struck Sean that, when together with his sister, they must look a rather strange sight. Alice was short and plump, compared to this incredibly well manicured, gigantic man.

"I do apologise. Where are my manners?" Ben's thick, dense voice purred off his wide lips.

Placing his glass on a side-board by the door, he walked over to Sean, who noticed the Savile Row label, as he reached into the inside pocket of his blazer jacket. Ben brought out a business card and shoved it into Sean's hand with a strong, firm handshake.

"I do not believe we have met. I am Benjamin Marshall-

Howard. Please let me offer my sincere condolences for your recent loss."

While turning away from Sean and introducing himself to Rachel, Sean looked down at the card.

Allen & Marshall-Howard
Criminal Defence Lawyers
9 Carmelite Street - London - EC4Y 0DR
Benjamin Marshall-Howard. *Senior Partner*
Tel: (020) 7222 1234   Fax: 020 794 5333

The articulate and eloquent voice denoted the poles-apart difference between Sean and Ben. It demonstrated not only the class distinction but the variations in social status and social confidence. Ben took centre stage in a room. He commanded attention, but not in the aggressive, volatile way that Sean would, more in an authoritive, holding court way. It wasn't something that could be forged. It showed years of grooming, prepping and moulding; a life that was consumed with brushing shoulders with society's elite. Ben's natural grace threw Sean off guard completely. Already wary of his sister, he now had to contend with her upper-class significant other. He didn't like it when he felt threatened and although Ben's demeanour was friendly enough, he felt out of his depth with this man. His eloquent speech conveyed the intelligence he possessed and it was that which scared Sean more than anything.

Alice noticed Sean's discomfort and it pleased her that Ben had that effect. She had hoped he would and, as usual, her fiancé did not disappoint her. She thought about letting him squirm under the awkwardness for a little while longer, enjoying the scene before her, but decided it could wait for another time.

She had been around her brother for far longer than

she had originally planned and now all she wanted was to go home, back to her world and wash off the stench of her past.

"We really should be going dear," She said to Ben, lightly touching him on the arm. "If we want to get back to Chelsea before it is dark."

"Right-o." Ben replied

"It was nice to see you again Rachel. We must meet for lunch or something soon. Maybe you could come up to London for a day." Alice directed to Rachel.

The invitation wasn't as fake as it sounded. She said it partly to wind her brother up and the quick twitch of his eyes showed her that she had succeeded, but she really did want a chance to spend some time with the woman on her own. Why, she wasn't too sure of, but she felt a connection with her and that was something which didn't happen very often in Alice's life.

Rachel just smiled and returned the hug that was offered before Alice and Ben left the kitchen, leaving her with Sean. His familiar stance was restored, as soon as they had left. Giving her a quick kiss on top of her head, he walked out of the kitchen, yelling at Adam that he was ready for their re-match.

Rachel stood alone and mulled over the last half an hour. There was something definitely going on between brother and sister that much was evident, but it was the way Alice had been with her that had been unsettling. Rachel knew her from when she was first with Sean but they had never been friends. The urgency with which Alice had grabbed hold of her had left a panicky feeling inside her chest. But she did not understand what it was.

* * *

223

Mick was suffering more than anybody. He had just lost his entire universe. Maureen had been his constant, throughout his whole life. She was such a pretty young thing when he had met her; vibrant, effervescent and pulsating. She loved life, always laughed and dressed in outrageous bright clothes; that was the swinging sixties.

She was a big girl even back then, but Mick had loved it; something to get his hands around and grab on to. When the paramedics had told him his wife was already gone and that there was nothing they could do, he thought his heart would stop beating. The tightness that had clenched it felt so hard; like it would squeeze the life out of it.

He looked at his wife's bulky frame, on the floor of the bedroom where she had collapsed and over to his daughter and granddaughter, who looked like they were sleeping. Then his brain switched off. The psychiatrist had said it was a coping mechanism. PTSD it was called; Post Traumatic Stress Disorder. They were told is it caused by the experience of a traumatic event but one of the nurses at the institute, where Mick was now staying, had explained it better to Sean and Rachel.

"A traumatic event, such as experiencing the death of someone, can in turn overwhelm the individual's ability to cope; producing severe negative feelings of helplessness or horror. Your father is displaying all the classic signs."

Sean laughed at this. When it came to the Fergus family, crazy loony toons behaviour was unquestionably 'classic'.

Chapter 16

November 2006

Dear Rachel,

I am not entirely sure as to why I have chosen you to be the one I bear my soul to. I do not feel as if we have ever had a bond of any kind, so you may be a little perplexed as so am I. However, it seems to be that you are indeed the one I need to tell my story to because, you see I am now safe, whereas you are definitely not. In fact, you are probably in the biggest danger of your entire life.

I know this doesn't make much sense but please let me start at the beginning and I hope then you will start to understand.

My brother abused me from as far back as I can remember. He isn't the sweet gentle giant you think he is. You couldn't be further from the truth. He is a monster. He was born this way and he will never ever change.

He completely manipulated me, made me believe that he was the only one that would ever love me. He made me do sick things to him, that a brother should never make a sister do.

225

He kissed me in a way that was wrong, eventually all the touching and kissing led to him raping me for the first time when I was eleven. After that, it was something that would happen quite frequently, until he met you.

But when you left him, it started all over again, until you finally came back. Then he became scared that you would find out, that's why I guess he stopped. But he still continued tormenting me and making me hurt myself.

Have you not guessed yet? My awful secret. His awful secret.

Katie is Sean's daughter. She is his blood. Another innocent life created and destroyed by the same person. An evil, wicked, malicious and sinful being.

It is not just this I need to tell you though. He may have stopped having sex with me, but he hadn't stopped creeping into my room in the middle of the night, climbing into my bed and whispering nasty disgusting words into my ears.

Most of it would be utter filth, the kind of stuff he wished he could do with me but was no longer able to because of you. He saw that as betraying you. But he said some other things too.

Like how he sliced your boyfriends' throat and then burnt him alive; Greg was his name was wasn't it? He was in the way you see, of you and Sean. Sean will exterminate any obstacle that he believes is in his way. Greg was in his way.

Sean has a friend; his only friend come to think of it. His name is Kenny Maltrowitz. He was there the night Greg was murdered.

Kenny was also the one that found you. He had been watching you for quite a while by all accounts. He told Sean where you were. I don't think he would have come looking if it wasn't for this man. In a way I am grateful to Kenny for that, because once Sean had you again, he stopped wanting me. Just like when we were kids. When you were around he never wanted to do the bad things to me.

I am warning you my brother will end up killing you; either directly or indirectly. All the same it will happen.

He executes everything he sees as an obstacle. Annihilating and eradicating. Mark my words my girl, you will die at his hands unless you GET OUT NOW!!

It is not just you that you have to think about. You have a son as well. Sean will see him as a threat soon enough. How long before he turns?

It is up to you now. You are the only one that knows the truth. The whole beastly account.

Take care and good luck,

Maisy

It must have been the hundredth time Rachel had read the letter. The first time none of what Maisy had written went in. The second time she threw up and the third time she slowly begun to absorb and comprehend the dead girl's words.

The more times she read the letter, the more it had all begun to make sense; the things that she was saying happened to her. Sean? It couldn't be; running it through in her head. Sean wasn't that monster; was he?

The more she read the more she tried to find logic in Maisy's letter. He had raped his own sister, had been doing so for years. He shattered and crushed everything around him. He had murdered Greg. Why? She didn't understand; she had left him, she had chosen Sean. Why kill Greg?

All her instincts were screaming that she knew what Maisy was saying was true, but she still continued to search for hidden indications that the girl was well and truly off her rocker. But the letter was so concise and had been written involving details that just couldn't be made up or imagined. It didn't sound like the ramblings of a mad woman. It sounded too sincere and raw.

She ran into Adam's room and started to throw clothes into a small rucksack. Grabbing Greg's T- Shirt that he had taken to sleeping with at night from the bed, she snatched her keys up and ran out of her tiny flat. She jumped into the car and headed straight over to Adam's school. She wasn't really sure what she was doing, but she needed time to think; to process. Above all, she needed to get herself and Adam as far away from Essex as she could.

Sean found Maisy's letter on the table where Rachel had left it. He didn't need to read it; already knowing what it would contain. His brainless and weak sister was having the last laugh, from beyond the grave. Only she wasn't so brainless; that's what really galled him. She had planned all of this for god knows how long; to kill herself, to take Katie with her, to make sure Rachel found out everything.

He cursed her and himself. Why had he acted the big 'I am' and boasted to Maisy about what he saw as achievements? He wanted to scare her, to show her what he could do. That people could just disappear if he wanted them to.

Once he became conscious that some of Rachel's and Adam's belongings were missing, he knew he was running out of time. He grabbed his phone. The call to Kenny was quick and concise; he was coming to pick him up.

He knew where she was heading; the only place she had left to run to. Only, she didn't know that Sean knew all about it.

Chapter 17

In Plato's 'The Symposium' Aristophanes narrates a story about soul mates. Aristophanes describes how humans initially had four arms, four legs and a single head made of two faces, but Zeus was anxious their power could destroy him so he divided them all in half, denouncing them to spend their lives searching for the other half to complete them.

Rachel had learnt about it at school. She remembered thinking how stupid it all sounded. That there was one person destined to be with another, seemed to her a little farfetched. Then she had fallen in love with Sean Fergus; the minute she first met him. It had only taken a few moments and she was smitten.

It was a love that had lasted a whole decade of being apart. He completed her. They were still kids when they had first met; their whole lives ahead of them. She had caught him staring at her a few times, before she decided to confront the boy that made her feel awkward and self-conscious.

Was that her mistake right there? If she had never spoken to him that day, would that have prevented everything which had happened since? It may not have helped Maisy, but Greg would still be alive, they may have been able to be happy together.

He had hypnotised her; captivating any common sense she may have held. She had the same affect on him too. They were so young; so adolescent and naive to the power that existed between them.

Rachel tried to shake the thoughts of old memories out of her head. They weren't helping her to think clearly. She had to see him for what he was. She had to. She tried to concentrate on the road ahead. It felt like she had been driving for days; her whole body felt drained and unattached somehow.

She didn't want to deal with any of it. She knew she had to though, but her first priority was getting Adam somewhere safe. She needed to make sure she took him as far away from the situation as possible. She wasn't ready to deal with the repercussions of Maisy's letter; she wasn't ready for what she was about to do either.

She had always decided that she would let Adam choose when he wanted to meet his real father; never expecting to just turn up on his doorstep unannounced. No warning. So she didn't think about it. She pushed further thoughts out of her mind. Sean wandered back in though, no matter how hard she tried not to think about him.

An image or his voice. His smile or those irresistible eyes. The thing about suppressed thoughts is that the more you try not to think about something, the more the thought will enter your head. It is a rebound effect. While part of the brain will try to think of anything but the thought it's supposed to be suppressing, another part is searching for information that will enable the suppressed thought to re-emerge. This constant loop-like action was what was happening in Rachel's brain right now.

The journey was taking its toll on her and she rubbed her eyes. She had been driving for four hours solid and had made not one stop since she had frantically collected Adam from school; telling them there was a family emergency and that he needed to leave right now. They were almost there.

They had left the elongated and far-reaching M6 a while ago. Rachel had only been here once, when James had first moved there. She didn't even know if he was still at the same address. It had been eight years. But it was the only option she could think of.

She looked in the mirror at her sleeping son on the back seat. He didn't deserve any of this. She had let Sean into his world, when she should have been protecting him. But how could she have known. The Sean Fergus she knew, the one she had been exposed to, wasn't the person that had done such dreadful things, ruined so many lives.

The Sean that had held her in his arms, that made her feel safe and complete. The Sean that made her laugh and showed her the sensitive side of him he kept reserved only for her. That Sean was her world; had always been her world. That Sean, Rachel wasn't so sure she could turn her back on.

Stopping the car outside James' rented house she shuddered silently. She never thought she would be back here again. She had to admit to herself, she wasn't looking forward to this; to all the questions and accusations. She didn't really have time, to give the answers she knew he would want.

Gently shaking Adam awake, it slowly begun to dawn on her that she had made some pretty wrong decisions in the past ten years. Hindsight is a funny thing. But then so is fate, if you believe in that, Rachel reasoned with herself. If fate and destiny exists then her decisions made no impact.

This day was always predetermined. It was always going to happen because someone, or something, somewhere had already decided. From Rachel's knowledge of fate and destiny, which was derived from films and soppy romance novels, believers subscribe to the idea of an event in one's life that is preordained; inevitable and unavoidable.

Fate lays emphasis on the illogicality and inhospitable nature of events, whereas destiny focuses on the concept of an irreversible direction of those events. Fate and Destiny conclude ultimately in Doom. This is especially relevant to the final ending, always unhappy or terrible, all directed by fate and destiny.

She blocked that thought instantly. Had Maisy possessed free will? Rachel's mind was working overtime. Her letter sounded like she had liberally made the decision in what she did. It was almost as if she was at peace with herself; or was it all inescapable and necessary?

Necessary for what though? Why had she met Sean, fallen for him? Why had Maisy told her what she did? Rachel just couldn't think straight anymore. It was all just too confusing. She had to get Adam settled and safe and then try to unpick the huge, wrangled knot her life had found itself.

Standing at the door, she hesitated to knock. Adam looked up at his mother, still a little dazed from being woken. She smiled but he sensed her uncertainness. Grinning back at her, he knocked on the door himself. Was that fate; her seven year old son knocking on his father's door? Was that his destiny or did he freely choose to do so.

Adam was a child. He did not understand any of what was running through her head. He was quite used to his mother behaving irrationally, if not quite so erratically, before now. He had always had Greg though, to explain it all too him. He didn't know what to make of being taken out of his classroom and going on a very long car ride with his mum.

She had told him they were going on a little trip, that he was going to stay with her old friend for a few days and then she would be back to get him. Adam, being quite a laid back child, thought it was all quite exciting; especially when he discovered that Rachel had packed his favourite backpack. He thought he was going on an adventure.

James had doubt his legs weren't about to give way underneath him when he opened the front door. They felt as if they had turned into two pieces of string, dangling under his upper body.

"Hello James. Can I come in?"

He stepped aside the door to let her pass; all done automatically and unconsciously. Rachel walked into the house. The front door led into a small living room. There was a young woman curled up on the sofa reading a magazine. She smiled at Rachel and Rachel returned the smile.

"I am sorry just to turn up, it's just…" Pausing, she took a good look at James. She forgot how good looking his chiselled features were. He looked well. It surprised her to think that. She hadn't ever really thought about him like that but right now, standing in his house, she was quite amazed at how he affected her.

"I need your help. We need your help." Rachel indicated to James that she had someone with her.

James wasn't sure whether he had noticed the boy at first or not. Now he couldn't help but notice him. Adam smiled at the two adults, whose house they were in. James instantly found himself smiling back. Jane however did not. She was a little miffed at their visitors. She didn't like the way her husband was looking at this woman. There was something between them that was for sure.

"Why don't I take the boy and get him settled in the back room. There is a TV in there, I am sure we can find something for him to watch. Then maybe you can tell my husband and me what this is all about."

Rachel took a mental note of the word 'husband' but allowed Jane to take the boys hand and he obediently followed her into the other room. Jane returned to where James and the woman were, just in time to hear him ask the question that shattered her world.

"Is he mine?"

Rachel just nodded. She didn't know what else to say.

* * *

"Well well well…"

The man walked through the front door and stood behind Rachel. She turned towards the cockney voice. She didn't recognise him. She didn't see that Jane did either.

"Miss Marsden, Mr Porter and Miss Fitzgerald. All in the same room. That's a sight I never thought I'd see. All just in time for the main man himself. You just couldn't keep away from each other could you? All four of you, reunited at the end."

"Do I know you?" Rachel searched the man's face for some recollection of meeting him before. Finally, after a few seconds, the penny dropped. He had been at Maisy's funeral. The man seemed to know all of them.

The soft moaning noise that was coming from Jane interrupted Rachel's confusion, before it then added to it. The woman looked terrified, not scared or frightened but petrified. James looked just as baffled. He tried to put his arm around his wife to comfort her and was shocked by the ferocity with which she shook him off.

She had a wild, defensive look on her face and he instinctively backed away. The moaning continued. It wasn't loud or penetrating, it was an almost hum. As if she found doing this therapeutic.

The man stepped forward a few paces. Tilting his head, he looked at Jane.

"You stayed here… this whole time?

The humming stopped. Jane nodded slowly. Her fixed stare took a more defiant tone.

"I thought you would have gone, as soon as you got your 'ead together love."

He spun round to James.

"You and her? Well… that's new."

James looked at Jane, but she wasn't seeing him. She was staring back at the front door. He and Rachel both followed her gaze.

Rachel knew, before her brain had registered it, that it was Sean. James however, was surprisingly quick on this particular turn of events. He ran his fingers through his hair and let out a deep blowing sigh.

"What the fuck is going on?" He said. "First you turn up with a kid I never knew about…" He pointed at Rachel. Then he turned to Jane.

"Then you and them?" Gesturing towards Sean.

Jane couldn't stop the vomit that projected out of her mouth. She was sick all over the living room floor. They all stood and watched her, as she composed herself; each waiting and anticipating the next moment. She looked around the room at them.

Kenny started to slowly clap his hands. "Can always count on you to make an entrance, eh boy! What happened to you staying in the car?"

Sean didn't say anything. He was staring, an intent look boring into Jane. Not even Rachel could interrupt. James watched his wife and the men who had abruptly and unexpectedly walked into his home; perplexed by the commotion unfolding. They all knew each other.

Somehow Jane knew Sean and the older guy; James had managed to work that much out, but how, why and where from he had no idea. Rachel had come to him for help; help for what? He needed some answers. Why they were all here and why his wife was acting so strangely.

She was staring just as intently at Sean, as he was at her. James' mind began to go into overdrive. Had Sean Fergus got their first again? Was he Jane's first love too? What the hell was Rachel doing here?

Just when he thought his head was going to explode, from all the mental questions he was forming, Jane dropped Sean's stare and turned to him.

"What do you want to know?" It was a helpless defeated response; the sadness in her eyes that had always been there seemed to burn through even more reverently than before.

None of them predicted what happened next. Sean, pulling a gun out from the back of his jeans, instantaneously leapt across the room, shoving it in Jane's face.

"One more word." His piercing blue eyes dilated in the low lighting of the flat. The threat hung in the air. Nobody said anything. Jane pushed the gun away from her. Her strength shocked Sean.

For a few seconds the gun had startled her, but after the initial shock, an immense anger took over. She no longer felt scared. The exhilaration of finally being released from the fear she had carried with her, impelled her to fight back. This time she wasn't going to let him control her.

"Shouldn't we explain how we know each other?" She

was taunting him. He knew that. "Everybody here wants to know who's who, so let's start it all off shall we?"

He hadn't prepared for this. The very fact she was standing in front of him was enough to send his mind spiralling. He was struggling to keep it together. She wasn't shutting up. It was like she was goading him to let out the real him. To exhibit the monster to everyone in the room; the monster that Jane knew first hand lived inside him.

"It was tough you know… at first… to believe it was me that you raped." She paused for effect; the slight shift in her eyes told him that. Let the information sink in.

"I tried to put it to the back of my mind. If I didn't think about it, it couldn't have happened. I was in denial."

Sean aimed the gun at her once more, warning her not to go on. She had said enough. Rachel took a step forward. He had a gun. Where did he get a gun? This all felt too unreal. Adam was only feet away.

"Rach, No!" James leapt in, interrupting her thinking and making her stop still.

Jane put her hands up as if to block them both. "Rachel? You're Rachel?" She stared at the woman in front of her and then turned her attention back at Sean. "And it all starts to make sense."

He knew he had to make her stop; the crack of her jaw when the back of his hand struck it resounded around the substantial living room. The clump knocked her off her feet and she dropped to the floor.

Sean had the gun in James' face before he could even respond. "Do not fucking move."

Jane spat out a mouthful of blood and felt the side of her face. It felt swollen already and her cheek was throbbing like mad. She pushed herself up from the floor and forced herself to stand up. She wasn't finished and she was determined to make him and everyone else listen.

"I would wake up, not knowing what to expect. I couldn't talk to anyone. I was scared to go out, in case I saw you in the street. I couldn't trust anyone after what you did. I mean I had trusted you Sean, hadn't I?"

She felt her mouth fill with more blood and she spat it out again.

"But you betrayed that trust so badly. I didn't have any faith in my judgement any more. I still feel dirty and ashamed. I still blame myself for what had happened. But it wasn't my fault. I was eighteen."

Sean turned towards the man that had come in just before he had. "What the fuck is she doing here Ken?" He was wavering; the gun trembling from the shakes in his hand.

Kenny had seen this Sean before; the Sean that gets scared and panic stricken. It wasn't often he ever let this side of him emerge. The last time was, ironically, when he had to call Kenny because of Ginnie. Here he was again, in nearly the same state as before, because of the same person as before.

She hardly looked any different. Her eyes were still the dark emerald green they had always been. They still had the orange speckles that made them sparkle. Her hair was still long and the deepest red. She was getting to him. He hadn't expected to see her again; ever. He never asked Kenny where he had taken her, that night he had called him in a blind fear.

He didn't know what he thought had happened; he just assumed Kenny had disposed of her. When he walked into James house not ten minutes ago, he was prepared to convince Rachel to come back with him. He had spent the last four hours rehearsing his side of the whole story.

Of course he was going to lie his way out of it and blame it all on Maisy. He had convinced himself it was the truth, so he thought it was going to be easy to persuade Rachel. Now, Ginnie had opened her mouth and there was no going back from there.

She hadn't finished her tirade yet though. Jane had plenty more to say.

"Four days you kept me locked in that flat." She then beckoned to Kenny. "Even after he bought me here, the flashbacks were still there."

James and Rachel hadn't moved the whole time Jane was talking. No one dared to stop her. Not even Sean now. She had a lot more to unleash on the psychopath that stood before her.

"The flashbacks were so intense. Sometimes I would scream or shake so violently. Had I reacted that way then? Had I Sean? I would beg you to stop, plead for you not to hurt me, crying out in agony as you hurt me more. I sobbed while you took no notice of my cries of "no, please no more" whilst you violated me."

Jane was releasing memories which she had pushed deep into her subconscious because of the pain and fear she knew she would experience, when she eventually let them bubble back to the surface again.

"You're a twisted fuck. That is the only way I can describe the fantasy that you relived over and over, whilst you raped me again and again. You actually believed I was her."

Rachel's heart felt like it had stopped. Jane was pointing at her.

"You were who your sick mind led you to believe you were. Your eyes were crazed, as you took great delight in describing what you were doing and why. You did it. You. I was so scared. Scared because you were no longer the person I thought I knew. It would have been bad enough, just to have had regular sex without consent, but that was something else. It was like you had gone crazy. You couldn't tell reality from your fantasy."

Rachel watched the dead look in Jane's eyes; it was eerie. Her own face was expressionless. Everything she was hearing was so unreal. Part of her wished so very badly that she had never opened that letter, earlier in the day. Or that Maisy had never written it. Parts of her wished she had never witnessed Sean assault Jane, or hear the sickening words that she was disclosing.

She needed it to all stop; there was just too much happening today and she felt like she was drowning. Nobody looked as if they were willing to be the ones to stop any of it. Sean, the man she had lived half a life for; for so long he had been the cause of so much pain and destruction. She hadn't seen it. She should have seen it.

James looked as if he was frozen where he was standing. It occurred to Rachel that he had only moved when she had stepped towards Sean. He was looking at his wife now, like she was a complete stranger. He never was very good with confrontation, she knew that, but he looked just as scared and hesitant as he had the last time she saw him.

Jane appeared half demented. By the way she spat the words at Sean, Rachel guessed she had never spoke about it before. It was funny but, like herself, Jane didn't seem scared. James was actually the only person in the room that wore a face of sheer terror. Kenny looked more amused by the proceedings than anything but it was Jane that Rachel was growing concerned for.

She just kept on with her tirade, of what Sean had done to her. It was like she was reminding him of what he was. She needed confirmation that it had happened, Rachel supposed, but that didn't make it any easier to listen to. And still she went on.

"I was the one listening to what you were saying, I was

the one who was there; who was having those things done to her. I was the one in the real world. You were lost in your own imaginary world." She began to pace a little, no longer able to stand still. Her body was pounding from the fall and the smack she had received from Sean, but it spurred her to go on.

"A world where you could take what you wanted knowing that there was no comeback, after all I was nothing, someone to use and abuse, like it was your right. Your status empowered you to do anything you wanted, to force me to do everything you wanted, to threaten people I cared about if I didn't do what you wanted...Oh the power you had."

Throwing back her head, she spat out at him. It landed right between his eyes; a thick, stringy, blood congealed phlegm.

"You revelled in it. Now you know why I didn't struggle, why I didn't scream out for help. You were crazed, incapable of hearing me, even if I had been able to say anything. I was the one who was there, watching your face, seeing the arrogance, the satisfaction, the hatred that you were showing towards me. The only thing was Sean, it wasn't Rachel you were making love to; you were raping me."

Sean aimed the gun at her once more. She smiled at him then. It was a disturbingly sinister smile that was filled with intimidation. He wasn't used to this being projected onto him, especially by a woman. To be made to feel inferior and substandard.

"It was only once you had run out of coke and were on one of the biggest comedowns of your life, that you began to stop. When you sat on the end of the bed, with your head in your hands, was the point where you came back to reality. Does that sound like a man who had consensual sex with someone? No, not in my book. Sean, face it, YOU RAPED ME!"

She was screaming at him now, tears pouring down her face.

"The demons pushed it deep into your subconscious, with a lot of the other baggage that you dare not face because of the consequences. But one day you are going to have to face everything. So you want to shut me up. Pull the trigger Sean. Let's see what a man you really are."

Rachel felt herself move. She walked in between Jane and Sean. She saw the chaos and turmoil in his eyes. She put her hand up in front of the gun and closed it around the barrel.

Chapter 18

"Get out of the way." Sean pleaded with Rachel. What was she doing? Was she stupid? Why was she putting herself in front of the gun? He didn't know if he had what it took to fight the beast inside him, the beast that was telling him to pull the trigger and shut the fiery redhead up for good.

"No." She tried to pull the gun down, towards the floor, but Sean's hold was too strong.

"Please baby, I don't want to hurt you." The words were whispered so sincerely, it took everybody in the room aback. But Rachel stood fast.

"No." She said again; shaking her head. "This time no one is getting hurt Sean. You came here for me... right?"

Sean faltered. Was she still looking at him like she loved him? It had all seemed so simple in the car. He had a plan. He had repeated it over and over to Kenny on the way up.

Kenny was to go into the house and remove James. He would then persuade Rachel to come home with Adam.

Ginnie was not part of the plan. Why had they not known about her? It was just as much Sean's fault as it was Kenny's. Neither thought James needed to be watched any further, as neither saw him as a threat. Unbeknown to them, in the six months that Kenny had stopped investigating James, Ginnie and James had got married, only Ginnie was now Jane. It was all too surreal.

"James, take your wife and Adam and get out of here."

Her voice sounded a lot more confident than she was actually feeling. Her stomach felt like it was going to empty any minute and she desperately needed to sit down.

Sean wrenched the gun out of her hands and pointed it at James.

Rachel grabbed Sean's face in her hands and forced him to look at her.

"I was always coming back. I just needed to get Adam safe first… Sean, look at me; I was coming back. Let them go."

He lowered the gun down to his side. She didn't let go of his face and kept his gaze the whole time James grabbed Adam from the next room and pushed his wife out of the door. He looked back at Rachel at the very last minute; wondering if he would ever see her again. The first girl he had ever loved. She was still holding onto Sean and didn't see him.

"What are you doing?" Sean asked the question without really wanting to know the answer.

She didn't get it. Even after all the terrible things she had learnt, she couldn't switch it off. She didn't know where she had found the courage to do what she had just done. Something had taken over her. She couldn't let him hurt anybody else, yet being so close to him now she felt like she couldn't breathe.

"I'm addicted to you." She murmured. It was such a soft voice, an almost whimper. "It's like I can't think, without you interrupting me in my thoughts; in my dreams. You've taken over me. I should hate you right now. Why don't I hate you?"

Sean leant his head against hers. He could feel her whole body shaking. Her smell was overriding every sense he possessed. He was overcome, that she was so close after what she had just heard. The crushing urge he had to kiss her was becoming more irresistible with every passing second.

"I can close my eyes to things I don't wanna see, but I can't close my heart to things I don't wanna feel. I want to hate you Sean. You're evil or possessed or... I don't know."

"Sometimes good people make bad choices. It doesn't mean they're bad... it means they're human!"

She tried to push him away from her then.

"Human? Sean how can you be human? What you did to that poor girl, what you did to your own sister; and Greg... I can't even go there."

"Because of you. It's all because of you. I couldn't bear anyone getting in the way of us. I couldn't lose you again." He interrupted her, feeling the panic rise again; realising she hadn't stayed for him, she stayed so the others could go.

Rachel was mortified. She had bought all this about. She shook her head in disbelief. Opening her mouth to say something she suddenly changed her mind. Before Sean knew what had happened, she had taken the gun out of his hand. It had been such a complete and quick manoeuvre, even Rachel was surprised at her agility and speed. She pointed it up at Sean who impulsively stepped backwards.

"Rach?"

"This wasn't because of me. You chose to do all of this Sean. You chose." She screamed at him.

She knew she was beginning to lose it. She told herself she had to remain calm. She knew she should just run out of the house, but she couldn't, not yet.

"What did you expect? Getting yourself involved with omeone like him… eh?" Kenny's voice came out of what seemed like nowhere.

Both Sean and Rachel became aware of not being alone in the room. She spun round and pointed the gun at him. Kenny put his hands up in mock terror; laughing at her he moved towards her, stopping just a few feet from where she stood. He could see the fear and chaos in her eyes as she had Sean's.

"All of this was always going to happen sweetheart. There were never any choices. There is no such thing as free will. It's just an illusion. The universe is either determinate, where the future is set, or indeterminate, where thoughts and actions happen at random. Neither option works with free will."

Sean put his hand up to silence Kenny but he chose to ignore him. The drama was all getting too cliché for him. He adopted the self-educated, intelligent persona he liked to use when he intimidated somebody. Coupled with his coarse accent, it always served well to throw his opponent off balance.

"Now our actions have consequences and choices arise out of those consequences; But even if we can make choices that make a difference, does that make them anymore our own?"

Rachel knew this man was trying to play games with her head, but she couldn't figure out why. Kenny knew it too. He didn't see what Sean was so entranced with when it came to this woman. She was attractive, held a nice figure and all that, but she seemed to consist of nothingness.

There was nothing special about her that made her stand out. For Kenny, people had to stand out, make an impact, otherwise what was the point of their existence. Rachel he found was just plain annoying in every sense.

"I tried to stop it. I tried to make him see that you would be the catalyst to the end. Dozy sod wouldn't listen though; believed that you were the one that could change his destiny. But that's the things about fate. It's already set in stone." Kenny snapped at her.

He loathed the power she wielded over Sean. It was jealousy, although Kenny would never admit that. He despised the love he saw between them. It ate away at him, even more so since Rachel had come back into Sean's life; an act that was down to Kenny's own making, though he would never accept that either.

"If people have the ability to act differently from what anyone expects, then surely free will exists. Each action follows a conscious choice." Rachel retorted back.

She looked at him up and down. He spoke well but had that cockney, east end tone to his voice. She had heard Sean speak about him before, he held him in high esteem. All Rachel saw, was somebody that seemed to spur Sean on in his perverted demeanour.

"The problem with that idea my love, is that we may just be merely automatically reacting, to the incentives in our environment. Therefore, all of our actions are restricted by powers beyond ourselves, or by casual chance." Kenny begun to look bored.

He took out a pack of cigars from his jacket pocket and made a prolonged show of taking out a cigar and lighting it with a silver Zippo lighter.

"You still aint getting it; are you? Oh I aint making fun

of you, it took me a while too, to fully understand." Kenny said, still fiddling with his Zippo. "You see free will, is nothing more than a mere illusion; like I said. It's a velleity, an artificial feeling, which is falsely related with many of our actions when we perform them. On reflection, you realise that they were necessary and determined all along, by fate and destiny Rachel."

"This... this is fate and destiny?" She turned back to Sean. "You listen to this guy? Seriously, you actually listen to the utter crap that comes out of his mouth?"

"Rachel... baby I can't explain any of this... I don't know what you want me to say. I do these things but it's not me, well... it is... I know it's happening... but it's like something is telling me I have to... it needs to be done..."

"I don't know who you are." She wailed. It was like a child whining for something she had been told she couldn't have.

Both men could see she was faltering. Her hands were shaking with the gun. She looked back at Kenny with disgust.

"You were there! When he murdered Greg... Maisy's letter said you were there? You manipulative scheming bastard."

"This isn't about him Rach" Sean tried to reason with her. She knew this. It wasn't going to work; she was never going to be able to understand any of what had happened that day or this one.

"I have to get out of here. I can't listen to anymore." She backed away a little but Sean moved towards her. "Just let me go."

She retreated slowly towards the front door. Kenny, who was still standing in the middle of the room, smiled at her as she reached his line of vision. Rachel didn't return it. Instead she turned and ran as fast as she could to her car, for once being grateful she never locked it.

She yanked her keys out of her jacket pocket; how she managed to find the coordination to put them into the ignition and drive off she has no idea. Her whole body was shaking. She glanced at the gun that was sitting on the passenger seat next to her. What the hell had just happened? Who was he? What was he? Had she really spent ten years missing a monster?

She knew he had done the most despicable things. She thought about James' wife and what she must have been through, at the hands of the man she professed to love; that she did love ultimately. Then she saw it; the reason why she ran the first time.

At seventeen she never understood the voice that lived way back in the depths of her head; the one that screamed at her to get out as fast as she could. Things had been great between them. It was intense and commanding from both of them, but they had both wanted it that way.

They would hardly spend a minute apart. Then the voice started to get louder and she listened. She had always punished herself for listening; but she should have kept listening. Then she wouldn't be in this mess. Maybe none of them would.

She didn't know where she was going to, or that Sean was just a few minutes behind her. It had been a long day of motorways and she had no idea where she was heading. She had to get away, so she could think. It had only taken just over an hour to hit Leeds. It wasn't far enough; so she kept going.

There was the option of turning off the major busy roads and follow a more scenic route up to Harrogate and then across to York or to keep going. As strange as it seemed,

Rachel saw the decision as an indicator. Does she change the direction in which she is going?

She had been changing direction for as long as she could remember, so this time she wasn't going to look back or think. She put her foot down on the accelerator and sped off from the roundabout. If changing direction is bad, then she decided going forward had to be the way. Changing direction had made dreadful things happen.

Having no idea why or how this made sense humoured her for a while. It did though; make sense that is. In her muddled and confused head, there was a small glimpse of some clarity. She joined yet another motorway, this time the M621 that was going to take her to Hull.

The rain was coming down heavily now. The wipers on the windscreen were frantically trying to clear the water away. It was late and she was completely shattered from the day. She hadn't even let herself reflect on the fact she just let James take her baby; the one thing in her life that had been constant and pure.

She wouldn't allow herself to ponder on the colossal effect of that decision. She needed to have Adam safe; James was all she had left to ensure that would happen.

* * *

Sean had run out the flat almost immediately after Rachel had. He had just seen the back of her car turn out of James road. He was in his and right behind her within seconds, although when he had caught up to her, he made sure he kept a safe distance between them. He didn't know what he was doing yet. He couldn't let her disappear though; he knew that.

She was the only one that could stop all of this, stop him. She had stood in front of that gun and put her hand over it. She had touched him in a way nobody else had ever done. That simple action had reached deep into his soul; entirely blowing him away. Sean didn't even know he had one, although he was sure there was many a person who would argue against that revelation. Sean was almost certain, that if Rachel hadn't of done that when she did, he would have put a bullet straight into Ginnie's skull.

Kenny had tried to stop him, tried to reason with him to let her go.

"Every woman has a breaking point; even Rachel. Just because she didn't say "it's over" doesn't mean you haven't already lost her."

Sean wouldn't listen though. He had pushed Kenny so hard, the older man had flown across the room. Sean hadn't stayed to see if he was alright. Sean was adamant that Kenny was a major contributor to the downfall of everything around him.

Kenny should have known that Ginnie was still in Liverpool, he should have told Sean that that's where he had taken her. It was a loose end that had been waiting to unravel. Kenny was supposed to be the guardian of information. He had let him down and he made sure the old man knew it too.

Another hour had passed when he followed Rachel off the motorway and into the centre of Hull. It was the early hours of the morning by now.

Hull is situated on the northern bank of the Humber estuary. The city centre is west of the River Hull and adjacent to the estuary. The city was built upon alluvial and glacial deposits which overlay chalk rocks. It was these that were shinning from the dock lights; their vast and immense sharpness bordering the picturesque scene.

The Hull Tidal Surge Barrier is at the peninsula where the River Hull joins the Humber Estuary. As soon as the river reaches the outskirts of Hull, its course is marked by a series of bridges, most of which open to permit boats to pass. There are swing bridges, lift bridges and bascule bridges and the river becomes part of the Port of Hull.

The river, which is the dividing line between the East and West of Hull, bisects the city's industrial area. It rises from a series of springs to the west of Driffield and enters the Humber estuary at Hull

It was along one of the many bridges that cross the infinite watercourse, that Rachel's car begun to cough and splutter. She looked down at the dashboard to see the petrol light frenziedly flashing.

"No! No! No!" She groaned loudly, slamming her fists down onto the steering wheel.

As her car breathed its final rev and cut out she slumped down in her seat. The head lights that pulled up behind her were bright. She expected them to turn off once the car had stopped but they didn't.

Rachel looked into her mirror. She couldn't see anything with the lights blaring into her car. Nobody got out. If they had stopped to see if she was okay, they weren't doing a very good job she thought. Squinting at the light, she tried to make out the car but she couldn't really see anything.

Then the dread came over her. It started in the pit of her stomach and rose up to her chest. Sean, she realised, had not let her go quite so easily this time. The lights went out and she immediately recognized his car. A wave of anger and frustration swept over her; grabbing the gun from the seat next to her she leapt out of the car and walked towards his.

The aggravation and obstruction exasperated her. She couldn't do this anymore. The conflict between her head and her heart was too much for her to handle. How can you love something, you hate so much at the same time?

The rain was in the midst of a torrential down pour. It was the rain that got you from every direction. The wind blew it sideways and the ferocity with which it hit the ground made it appear to be raining upwards, as well as downwards. When Sean saw her walking towards him, he slowly got out the car.

"I can't let you go Rach." He shouted to be heard over the wind; the howling was deafening.

"You were the one that watched me walk away before and did nothing to stop me. Why did you come back Sean? Did you hate me that much? Was all this to punish me in some way; because I left you?"

She had stopped just a little in front of his car. It was so dark, now the lights were out, she could barely make out anything around her. She knew the bridge was quite narrow, only allowing one car to pass through at a time.

The edge was close; even if she couldn't make out exactly where. She could see him though; maybe his image was imprinted in her brain for the rest of her lifetime, she didn't know. But he was as clear as day. The rain was pounding down between them.

"I don't want to punish you. You are the only thing in my entire life I have ever genuinely cared about Rachel. Nothing has ever come close; don't you see that?"

"You have destroyed everything. Maisy was right. You annihilate and demolish at your own pleasure. You live in your own self-flagellation; a fantasy world that is governed by your rules."

He began to walk towards her. "Not with you, you make me someone else."

She backed away. If she let him near her it would be all over; she knew that. He still held the power to draw her in. Would he always have it?

"How do I do that? Huh… come on please tell me. Why am I the special one Sean?"

"You saw something no one else did. It's that simple. I don't know why. I don't have any answers for you Rach."

She couldn't see properly, the rain in her eyes made everything blurry. She tried to concentrate on her surroundings. Sean had reached her within a few paces. The force with which he grabbed hold of her made them twirl violently around each other like a pair of angry dancers.

"I get confused in what I should do, what is right… and what I can do, what I am allowed to get away with. Nobody stopped me. Nobody made me question my actions or motives. Most people see me for exactly what I am; a monster." He paused, searching her face.

"Oh I know exactly what I am." His eyes pleaded with her to understand. "You stopped me. You made me think there could be another way. That maybe I could be a normal person, regular like…" He urgently needed her to understand.

She felt the pull of him once more. The man she frenetically loved, with all her heart. He tugged her closer to him, she tried to push him away and they stumbled further towards the edge of the bridge.

"No wait, I have to tell you this, all of it."

Rachel stopped struggling against him and felt herself relax in his arms. There was something in his voice; an imperative need, that no matter how much she knew she should ignore, she couldn't. She knew she should be running as fast as she could, but something made her stay.

"I love the pain and destruction. I revelled in the control I had over Maisy. Ginnie or Jane or whatever she was called was just a prop, for me to pretend for a while I had you back; that I could touch and kiss you any time I wanted. Then, when I finally had you for real, Greg was in the way. He stayed too long, arrived to early. He had a vested interest in you and I couldn't stand it. It drove me mental. I had to remove him from our lives so we had a chance. In the end it all counted for nothing; didn't it?"

She leant forward and kissed him; her lips buzzed with exhilaration when they touched his. It was unpremeditated; astonishment and distress devoured her. The conflict between her head and her heart was overpowering.

Was he confessing? Did he want liberation from his sins? The physical ache inside her was too much too bear; all she wanted was to dissolve into his embrace but her head was fighting her at every step; both entities just as potent and dominant as each other. She pulled away from him, this time he allowed her to.

"I was wrong you know, when I said people get to start again. No-one can go back and make a brand new start. You can make a new ending though Sean. You could give yourself up. Pay for what you have done."

He laughed at her then; a sarcastic dry laugh.

"And spend the rest of my life in prison. 'Cause it will be the rest of my life Rachel; they won't ever let me out. You gonna wait forever are you? Making do with prison visits every couple of months? Never feeling me kiss or touch you again?"

Rachel shook her head again. He wasn't listening to her. She wasn't making him understand what she was trying to say.

"Life is not the way it's supposed to be. It's the way it is. The way you cope with it, is what makes the difference Sean. You can't just obliterate things when they don't go your way. Don't you see that?"

He took hold of her again. He wanted to believe, wanted to have faith in redemption for him. He needed peace so very much.

"It's because of now; this very second. What we are living right now; that's why I ran Sean. Because I knew, one day it would come down to me or you. So here we are. What's it going to be? Is it me or are you choosing you? Destiny doesn't exist. We make the decisions. It's not left to the fate of the gods. That's bollocks. It is down to you Sean; right now. My way, or your way?"

He stood and stared into her eyes. This must be what judgement day feels like. The end is nigh. He tried to force down the monster that had been eagerly trying to unleash itself within him. He saw it in his mind's eye; standing at an empty junction of life.

The two paths were the choices Rachel had just presented him. One would provide him with familiarity, the death and destruction he was born to be devoted to. On the other path stood Rachel, the only girl he ever truly loved.

"What happened to 'no matter what' eh Rach?"

She shook her head at him in disbelief. "My way or your way Sean. It is up to you."

The choice, as always, was never really a choice. Not for him. He held her face in his hands, inches away from her.

"I can't."

The words were so final and so abrupt that they forced Rachel to close her eyes, his answer providing her with the knowledge of what she had to do. The rain still pouring out of the sky was now accompanied with great lengths of white light, streaking across the black landscape. The thunder and lightning seemed to increase in strength with every passing second; drawing its energy from the enveloping ambience that was mounting between them.

The crashing and colliding of the clouds was so deafening and vociferous. The boom sounded like an explosion. He dropped her face and staggered back from her, unsteady and stumbling. It was the most tremendous impact; the equivalent of dynamite exploding. His whole lower abdomen felt like he had been kicked over and over again by a horse. Then it changed from a penetrating sensation to a complete numbness; beginning in the side of his stomach and slowly creeping down towards his legs.

As the initial shock begun to subside, Sean felt what he thought was his right hip shattering like a porcelain vase. The muscles supporting his stomach wall flexed, in an attempt to support his injury, adding to the numbness that was slowly encircling his whole body.

He was surprised that he wasn't in more pain. Apart from the crippling numbness, all he could feel was a slight burn from the bullet entry. Due to the flight or fight situation he was in, he could feel the surge of adrenaline as it surged through his system, helping to ease the pain

Everything then seemed to go into slow motion, causing his central nervous system synapses to fire faster, like a high speed camera; producing the slow motion effect. Every breath was a knife turning in his lung. Sean began to lose his vision, a bright light erasing his visual field as he began to go into hypovolemic shock. Rachel watched in half fascination, half terror; everything slowing right down for her as well. She watched in half fascination, half terror. Everything slowed right down.

The shock and revelation was evident on his face; she had pulled the trigger. He didn't make a sound. He tottered into the darkness. Instinctively she held her hand out to grab him but he wasn't there. The water crashed against the rocks underneath the bridge. She yelled out his name but there was no answer. He was gone.

Rachel let the gun fall from her hand. She wasn't sure if she had intentionally shot him or if something had taken over her body. The thought had been there, in her head. As soon as he told her he couldn't change, the thought had manifested itself deep into her cerebellum; a hushed and gentle reiteration that increased with each passing second to a piercing culmination.

Pull the trigger…pull the trigger…pull the trigger…you know you have to…just PULL THE TRIGGER!!!

Rachel slumped onto the tarmac and stones. She stayed there staring into the black night. Her body soaked through from the rain. He would never hurt her again. Sean Fergus would never hurt anybody ever again.

THE END

About the Author

Born in 1979, Matilda Wren was the child of a policeman and a teacher; born and raised in the home county of Essex. She is a mother, daughter, sister, auntie and a best friend. As a small child, she was always writing stories to be read. After her two children were born, Matilda returned to university to read Psychology, gaining a Bacholor of Science degree.

Why do bad people exist? A question she has asked herself again and again; having long held an interest in human behaviour, in particular abnormal or anti-social conduct. Whilst studying and practising Psychology for the past five years Matilda has been exposed to a variety of diverse forms of deviant behaviour which culminated in 'When Ravens Fall' being created. As an avid fan of Dark Romance and Psychological Thrillers, She draws upon the inspiration she has already gained through authors of these genres and the knowledge and experience she gained from observing life and her work experience within various criminal settings.

Lightning Source UK Ltd.
Milton Keynes UK
UKOW052253270712

196692UK00001B/4/P